# AN INVENTORY OF
# HEAVEN

Jane Feaver

corsair

Constable & Robinson Ltd
55–56 Russell Square
London WC1B 4HP
www.constablerobinson.com

First published in the UK by Corsair,
an imprint of Constable & Robinson Ltd, 2012

A copy of the British Library Cataloguing in Publication
Data is available from the British Library

ISBN 978-1-78033-875-0 (paperback)
ISBN 978-1-78033-023-5 (ebook)

Printed and bound in the UK

1 3 5 7 9 10 8 6 4 2

*in mem. Georgina Turton 1913–2005,*
*and for Vicki Feaver.*

Grateful thanks are due to the
Arts and Humanities Research Council (AHRC)
for their financial support during the writing of this novel,
and to Professor Philip Hensher, my supervisor at
Exeter University.

# CONTENTS

Who'll sing a psalm?
I, said the Thrush,
As she sat on a bush,
I'll sing a psalm.

From *An Elegy on the Death and Burial of Cock Robin*

# *Aubade*

*4 January 2007*

Last night I slept deeply and dreamlessly, the sleep of angels. When I woke, I woke like Sleeping Beauty, as if I'd been quietly relieved of all the empty years. Mavis, my name came to me quite easily, but for a while I had no sure idea of my age. I might have been no more than a child, or as old as Auntie, who lived in this cottage before I did. She was called Mavis too, incidentally, and a Gaunt by birth, as I am. Mavis Gaunt.

It was Auntie who first told me that Mavis — a name I'd hated — meant 'songthrush' and taught me how to distinguish its voice from the blackbird's.

'Listen,' she said, holding me stiffly under the birches. She used to put words into the birds' mouths to differentiate their songs: 'The thrush,' she said, 'Listen: "*Did he do it? Did he do it? He did, he did, he did.*"'

I knew what my song would be, I told her. Daddy and I used to sing it in his car: *Heaven, I'm in Heaven, and my heart beats so that I can hardly speak . . .*

1

There: my voice is no more than a croak. And that song alone is enough to bring it all back. Because I kept it quiet. I didn't speak, not a word of it, not for years. Decade after decade after decade — and the silence was good as snow, smoothing everything in its path, to sleep, amnesia and to death. *Finis.*

I am nearer the end than the beginning, but I am not dead yet. In the semi-dark, my hands crawl over my limbs, a stir of warmth. The words that I feared for so long have all gone, cleared out, and miraculously I am still here, the tick of a heart. It is winter again. The day begins to galvanize itself outside the window. And then I hear that voice, trilling and insistent — '*You did it, you did it, you did*' — like an arrow hitting its mark, so joyous and explicit that I know at once: nothing can be as important as this.

# PART I
## *The Quick and the Dead*

# 1
## January 2006

According to the several courier companies who get stuck in the lanes trying to locate it on their navigators, Shipleigh doesn't exist. Keen walkers too will sometimes discover the anomaly, referring with excitement to their Ordnance Surveys.

'Here,' they'll say, smoothing the sheet out over the bar for inspection, '*Shep*leigh.'

The staff at the Seven Stars are used to it. Yes, they'll say patiently, it means 'shepherd's meadow', of which Shipleigh, they believe, is a corruption, going back further than anyone cares to remember.

I knew the pub in its heyday, the fifties, and even now it is the thing for which the village is best known, with a long-standing reputation for its stillage and its steak and kidney pie.

'Ask for the Seven Stars,' visitors are told, should they get lost in the lanes.

Many of the cottages in the village still belong to the estate, tiny two up, two downs, inhabited by the last generation of Estate workers or widows of the same. All the old shops – the post office, the grocer, the forge, the cobbler – are private homes now, most lived in by members of the same few extended families. There is a converted stable, a holiday home that has been shut up for the last two years. The only other unclaimed residence is the flat attached to the pub, generally reserved for members of the staff on short-term let.

There was once a school – I was briefly *at* the school – but after the war, it closed for lack of numbers and was converted into an echoey village hall. These days, for every wedding at St John's there are a dozen or more funerals. Death comes with little fanfare or surprise. In fact, at the teas afterwards – where store is set by a decent spread of sandwiches – it is not unusual to hear sanguine discussion about who might be next.

How easy it is to bury and become buried! We are 'sleepy', 'hidden', an unremarkable valley somewhere between Exmoor and Dartmoor. I imagine it is quite possible to find – as I used to – pockets of unexplored land, forgotten-about copses and bogs, unchartered loops of the river. The lanes around here are as arbitrary: deep, meandering gullies to nowhere in particular, a cottage incidentally tucked – roof shot, crumbling walls, iron grate long ago wrested from its hearth. *Godforsaken, middle of nowhere*, is how the van drivers put it, ringing in (if they can get a signal) for help. So naturally, when the boy and his mother turned up in the village – she'd taken work at the pub – they were met with a degree of curiosity. It was nice, apart from anything else, to see fresh faces.

The boy started at Buckleigh school after the Christmas holidays. The bus had to make a special trip in order to pick him up and drop him off. I have a view of the bus stop from my window and was able to watch out for him. In the dark afternoons it was hard to see clearly, except to note that he was a scrawny little thing, all over the place with his bits and bobs.

Usually his mother waited for him at the shelter, hugged him as he stepped down from the bus. But once or twice I watched him walk home alone – no distance – trudging up, around the back of the war memorial, and along the side of the green to the pub, and the flat's private entrance.

A week or so later there was still an inch or two of snow on the ground. I was at the window, watching. The bus drew up, then pulled away. He was so quick, at first I thought I must have missed him; my eyes aren't so good now. But then I began to doubt myself. Although it was bitterly cold, I felt the need to be sure; I pulled on a coat, a hat, and set out with the torch to have a look. Just in case.

The path was treacherous and I took tiny steps. The torch made a feeble circle in the snow; the grass crunched and crackled underfoot. I shone the failing light towards the railings of the memorial, enough to recognize that the gate was ajar. And then I heard him, the juddery hiccups of his breathing. I ventured closer until I could just make out his shape, hunched up in a little mound, his head buried in his knees.

'Hello?' I said nervously, keeping the railings between us.

His shoulders stiffened; he repositioned himself, his face turning towards me, pale as the snow.

'Are you all right?' I asked him. My heart was thumping.

He drew his arm tighter around his knees.

7

'Are you waiting for your mother?'

He hid his face again.

'Have you got a name?' I asked.

I couldn't hear what he said — something muffled — but now I was there, I didn't feel I could walk away. I gave it another go. I said, 'Mine's Mavis.'

I could tell he was listening because the sniffling had stopped. He surfaced again very slowly, his face smeary. He wiped his nose against his school trousers.

'*Brrrr*,' I said, 'you must be frozen. It's much too cold to be sitting out here.'

He looked into the light with blinking, rubbed-in eyes.

'Lost my key,' he said.

'What?' I asked. 'Your house key?'

'They threw it out the bus,' he said.

'Who?'

He pressed his lips together.

'Didn't you tell the driver?' I asked.

He sucked at his lips, turning them down clownishly.

'Is your mother at work?'

He nodded.

'Well,' I said, 'never mind. Why don't you come and warm up, wash your face.' It was all I could think of. 'That's where I live,' I said, pointing to the cottage. 'No distance. Come on, careful you don't slip.'

He looked unsure.

'Come along, I won't bite. You can't stay out in this — you'll catch your death.'

Reluctantly he began to shuffle along behind me. As we reached the door and I put my shoulder to it, he stood close

8

enough for me to catch that mushroomy smell of his; I pushed hard.

'There,' I said as the door gave way, 'go through.' I turned the light on and steered him straight into the kitchen, towards the sink. I fetched a clean dishcloth from the drawer, and held it under the running tap until the water heated up. I wasn't sure quite how to get hold of him, but without any prompting he offered up his face, his eyes squeezed shut.

I dabbed at his nose; he didn't flinch. Then I opened the cloth against the flat of my hand and rubbed all around as if I were mopping up a spill from the table. When I removed the cloth he blinked; his face shone pink.

'That's better,' I said, 'I can see you now. What time does she finish?'

'Six,' he said, adjusting his clean face. 'It's *The Simpsons*.'

'Well, how about a nice hot drink?'


I sat him down in front of the fire. His name was Archie. And they'd been teasing him about it on the bus though he wouldn't tell me what they'd said.

He was eight. I'm no expert, but he seemed small for his age. His hair under the standard lamp was a beautiful reddish chestnut; it almost touched his shoulders.

'I never liked my name either,' I told him. 'It's such a terrible old ladies' name, don't you think?'

He was sitting very still; hadn't touched the Horlicks I'd brought him as if I might have put something in it. I felt his silence like a weight; it made me rattle on.

'If you left a key with someone, you'd not get caught out.

We'll find your mother, shall we, once you've finished? Give her a surprise?'

I didn't have experience with children; I spoke, I realized, as if he were a chicken or a mouse.

'Do you know what my name means?' I asked, trying to buck him up. 'I'll show you if you like – come over here. Come on.'

He got up warily and shuffled over to the sideboard where I was standing. I reached up for the glass dome, holding it high above my head for a moment like a crown, then carefully lowered it down. The top was furred with dust.

'There it is,' I said. 'What do you see?'

He pulled a dubious face. And then, grudgingly, as if it was a trick, 'A bird? With glasses on?'

'You're right, it's a bird.' I paused to give him another chance, but I could see already that he was losing interest.

'It's a songthrush,' I said hastily. 'And can you guess what the country name for a songthrush is?'

Again he shrugged.

'Mavis!' I announced. It was like pushing a rock uphill.

He peered into the glass, his face half-reflected back, and asked, 'How'd it get in there?'

'Taxidermy. Stuffing.'

'How'd they make the feathers?'

'They're real. It's a *real* bird.'

He put his fingers to the glass.

I went on, 'It has the most lovely song. It trills and whistles . . . Can you imagine how pleased I was to discover that?'

Archie looked up at me for the first time, with unguarded

10

eyes. Then we both stood for a while, staring at the bird, the freckles on its sandy brown chest, its sharp little beak.

'Why's it got glasses on?' he asked.

'Oh, a little joke,' I said.

'Is it supposed to be you?'

How quick he could be! A memory jolted like a tooth. 'Who knows?' I said. 'I shall have to give it a bit of a clean one day, won't I?' I nudged it back on to its high shelf and turned away from him towards the safety of the armchair. With the poker, I fiddled among the embers to revive the fire, while behind me, the boy didn't move, looking up at the case like a cat.

For eighty-six years Joyce has lived where her family always has, in one of the small row of cottages between the church and the pub. I hadn't got halfway up her garden path before she spotted me, opened the door and ushered me in. She'd taken to using a stick around the house; her breathing was bothering her: *old pipes*, she said.

Alf, her husband, was sitting in his waistcoat, nodding off in the heat from the Rayburn. He moved his head very slightly as if his neck, like a baby's, wasn't up to it. I sat myself in the rocking chair next to his while Joyce went to put the kettle on. It was impossible to have a conversation with him these days. We watched the long-haired cat, Pickles, who'd sprung sulkily into his lap and settled there.

Joyce had an extensive collection of old photographs on the sideboard: Joyce and her two sisters in their best coats; Joyce and Alf on their wedding day; Joyce with Victor, when he was little, in his spectacles . . .

The door shushed open across the carpet and Joyce followed, easing her way through with the tray. She never let me help. She set it down on the low coffee table, removed the teapot, the mugs, the jug of milk and three tiny mats; then, without straightening up, she craned across with the corner of a tissue to dab at Alf's mouth.

'Better?' she asked, dropping back into the armchair, her lumpy ankles lifting from the floor.

'I saw the new boy yesterday,' I said.

'Ready for your tea, Alfie?' she said. 'Oh?'

'He was out by the memorial. Crying,' I said. 'They'd thrown his key out of the bus.'

'Who'd've done that?' she asked, placing Alf's cup carefully for him on the flat wooden arm of his chair.

'He seems small, for his age, doesn't he?' I said.

'Needs feeding up,' Joyce said. 'Little scrap.'

'Have you seen that hair of his?' I said, accepting the Diana mug from her. We both smiled.

'You know who *she* is, don't you?' she asked now she could concentrate. 'The boy's mother?' She leaned forward, 'Remember Beatrice Manning? Well, she's Beatrice's — her daughter.'

Beatrice. I had only known one Beatrice in my life. 'Beatrice?' I asked, my stomach sinking. 'What became of her?'

'Oh, she got married. To that chap she met at the university, couple of children they've had.'

Joyce spoke as if it was yesterday. Beatrice Manning had been the vicar's daughter, years ago, remarkable in the village for her appearance, that beautiful dark hair.

'You never told me—' I said.

'Didn't I?' Joyce cleared her throat, banged her chest. Her eyes were watering. She put her arm out towards Alf, reassuring. 'Nothing,' she said. 'Just a tickle.' She thumped again. 'That's it.' She adjusted the cushions behind her.

Alf blinked and gave a sympathetic moan. Then he shut his eyes. In a little while his jaw hung slack.

'Eve, that's her name. Well,' Joyce said, 'Beatrice. She died.' She checked on Alf as she said it, then mouthed the words to me: *Breast Cancer*.

I didn't meet her eye but lifted my mug and breathed across the surface so that for a minute my spectacles steamed up.

'Did you know we were on the *hin-ter-net*?' Joyce asked, changing her tone. 'Eve says she looked us up. There were pictures and all sorts – the pump, the village hall. She found the number there, at the pub.' She took a sip of tea. 'She said they didn't visit, not when her mother was alive. "Manning?" I said to her, "As in the Reverend?" "Yes," she said, "my grandfather." Well, can you imagine! I told her I'd known them very well, of course.' Joyce stretched her neck to take another sip, rested her mug again on the shelf of her bosom.

I was barely listening. 'From London?' I asked her.

Joyce said, 'There's a similarity, don't you think? She's got the eyes, I'd say.'

When I got home, it was already dark and I considered going straight up to bed, which I often did – it saved lighting a fire. But I knew I wouldn't sleep. Without taking off my hat or coat, I went straight into the front room and sat in Auntie's old chair. I hadn't seen or heard anything of

13

Beatrice since she'd left the village; I'd had no reason nor any inclination to find out. She'd had a child, children; she had a grandchild even (all of which, incidentally, was more than I did). She'd been a teacher, Joyce said. I tried to distract myself by imagining the life she must have led elsewhere. I pictured her with her long stick and her blackboard, her apron strings. Grey hair. But it was no good. *Beatrice*: she sprang up just as youthful and alluring as she'd ever been.

It is remarkably easy in such a small place to avoid some-one if you put your mind to it. Although I steeled myself against seeing her in church, it turned out, to my relief, that Beatrice's daughter was not a church-goer. I rarely went up to the pub; I could quite easily refrain from going out at school bus times – though it didn't stop me from *looking*, stationed at the curtains. After a few days, I calmed down. Nothing had changed, I told myself. On Tuesday I took my usual bus into town: Oxfam, Co-op. On Thursday, it was the village hall committee meeting where, as we sat waiting for the others to turn up, Joyce told me what further information she had gleaned: Eve was sick of London, her marriage had failed, her mother had died and she felt, in coming down here, she'd had nothing to lose.

'You'd like her, I'm sure,' Joyce said. 'She's a nice girl. In a funny way, she's not unlike you – like you were when you came back to us.'

My curiosity got the better of me. Around four o'clock the next afternoon, just before the bus was due, I went for a walk. I had only just reached the shelter when I recognized Eve, approaching from the opposite direction, around the bend in the road. She was wearing a jumper and jeans, an old padded anorak, her dark hair scraped back. I sat down on one of the new slanty seats.

She smiled as she drew up. 'Are you waiting?' she asked, catching her breath. She looked to be in her mid-forties, one of those women who was never outstandingly pretty in her youth, but who ages well. There was no acknowledgement of the fact we'd already met.

'I've only been down as far as the cross,' she said. 'I shouldn't be so out of breath.'

'Mavis Gaunt,' I said, introducing myself again. 'I'm from London too, originally.'

'Whereabouts?' she asked, surprised.

'West Norwood,' I said, 'a long time ago.'

'Really?' Her face lit up. 'We were only down the road. Tulse Hill? We had a flat. So how did you end up here?'

I was knocked by her enthusiasm. 'It was the war, I suppose. I came to stay with my aunt.'

'Where was she?'

'Paradise Cottage, where I am now.' I nodded towards it.

'Paradise?' Eve repeated, hugging herself. 'And is it?' She smiled. I let the question pass.

'How's Archie getting on?' I asked. I used his name, deliberately to jog her memory of the other day when I'd delivered him back home.

'Of course, we've met,' she said, placing me. 'It was so kind of you to take him in, thanks. *Again*. I hate not being here to meet him,' she said, glancing over her shoulder at the pub. 'The shifts are awkward . . .'

What possessed me to offer to meet him and keep him with me — just till she finished work — I don't know, but there was a silence between us that I felt compelled to fill. It took me aback when Eve agreed so readily. 'Would you?' she asked earnestly.

'Of course,' I said, though my confidence drained.

In the distance we could hear the drone of an engine, a lugubrious change of gear.

'There he is,' she said, lifting on to the balls of her feet.

It was like holding on to the end of a rope; I didn't want to let go. She was no longer looking at me, straining her neck to catch the first possible glimpse of the bus.

Once Archie turned up, I left them to it. She was typical of an older mother, I thought, asking him too many questions, sorting his bag for him, holding him — I was clearly surplus to requirements. I made my excuses and wandered off, as I'd said I would, through the village, towards the churchyard. I had half a mind to visit Auntie's plot. But instead I took the steeper path, straight up through the lych gate towards the older part of the graveyard.

Although the bulk of the snow had melted up here, there were still scraps of it, littering the grass. Just visible, on the horizon, was the bright disc of the setting sun. I paused for a moment by the church porch, looking out across the valley, the corners and ditches picked out in rosy white chalk. I didn't intend to venture much further — perhaps just as far as the small water butt around the side of the building, where we filled the altar vases — but as I rounded the corner, how unexpected! Sheltering against the transept wall were swathes of snowdrops, dozens of them, bright as fairy lights. I stooped and picked a small bunch. And then, before I could think better of it, I moved on, upwards, towards the Eastwood tomb, skirting its bulk. I stopped for only a moment because it was a steep climb but it was just long enough; for something caught my eye, something I had never noticed before. Against the wall of that tomb there was a small figure in relief; it was a girl with a fine, girl's face. She was pressed, cheek and shoulder to the stone, as if she were hiding, and as I came level with her, I was struck by the eyes, which shone out dark and limpid. *I know you*, she seemed to be saying, staring right at me.

For half a moment, I felt ashamed to have been caught with the snowdrops in my hand. I turned away, stepping out of her line of vision, determined to finish quickly what I had set out to do. But even as the path began to peter out, I couldn't shake off the prickling feeling of being watched.

Finally I reached my spot. Backed against the north wall, the glossy granite of the tombstone I sought was water-repellent, the serifs as sharp and crisp as if they'd been newly cut.

### Frances Elizabeth Upcott

**Who departed this life**

**2 January 1963 aged 34 years**

*Hast thou entered into the treasures of the snow? Job 38: 22*

I laid the flowers down so carelessly it may have looked as if they'd been put in the wrong place.

# 2

## *Snow, 1936*

On the day that Tom was born, Frances was almost eight years old. The snow was thick and flaky as plaster and was never going to stop. The world was falling down. Her mother knew it too: the noise from the bedroom was full of despair, low and guttural, like a heifer held against its will. And the way their father swore, as if the snow had been sent like a plague of ash or a forest of briar. The doctor, if he ever got through, would be arriving on horseback. Robert – a year older – was sent out to clear the yard with the turnip spade.

Joyce from the village had only been working there for a year. She was sixteen and panicking because it had fallen to her to be in charge, up and down the stairs for water, for towels, praying each time the doctor would appear at the door. She told Frances again and again not to bother her, that the sooner she'd go and play somewhere else, the sooner it would all be over.

In the yard Robert was bashing a thick hide of ice from the drinking trough. Frances put her boots on and came out wrapped in a sheet — her angel costume — the wooden toy sword in her hand. She stood next to him and watched, waiting leadenly for him to look up or to speak. The cold only sharpened her resolve. She knew that he knew it too: the baby would be special because it was new, and because it was coming at Christmas. Robert was being beastly; he had more important things to do. The ice was splintering under his furious pick; it lay in crazy slabs of yellow where he'd flung it to the ground like glass from a church window.

It was Robert who made her run away, she said afterwards, though she wouldn't tell their father what he'd said.

She disappeared from the yard, along the boundary of the house to the orchard, where she made her way under the heavy cornicing of trees through clumps of sheltered undergrowth, to the gate at the far end. The upright struts were black and eaten from years of frost, the top hinge rusted and broken. She had never been through this gate before without Robert. She pushed it and stepped out into the open field.

The sky was pearly grey. After two solid days, the snow appeared to have stopped falling. She surveyed the whiteness spread before her. The only distinguishing mark was the grey, tin line of the river, stripped bare, curling at the bottom of the valley, halfway between where she stood and the distant blurry horizon. There was no sign, anywhere, of movement (the sound of the river was no more than the blood pumping in her ears); and because nothing moved, she was no longer afraid — there was nothing to be frightened of.

She waded out in her camouflage of sheeting as if she had

found her element. She was up to her knees already, the snow shelving steeply to either side of her, so comfortable and so accommodating that before long she gave herself up to it, lying lengthways like a princess in a carpet to let herself be wrapped and unrolled – the groundswell of curves turning her over and over as she made a circuit of the planet, four, five, half a dozen times – until the cup of a ditch took the wind from her sails and saved her from the full-stop of the hedge.

For a moment her several limbs appeared disconnected and scattered. One by one, she drew them back to her, the compact icy cast of her own body. She lay exactly where she was, until the light shrank around her, a crystal ball revealing everything it was important to know about snow: how close it is to dying and how close it is to heaven; how excruciating its pains and yet how abundant its rewards. She discovered the calibrations of its process: that if she could weather the piercing cramps, she would be relieved by numbness; that if she could only outstay the numbness she would be delivered by the flowering of warmth to the end of every finger and every toe.

# 3

## *Badgers and Foxes*

The first few times Archie came round, I found myself waiting on him like a young emperor: I took off his coat, his shoes, sat him down, brought him a biro, paper, a biscuit, a beaker of juice. If I left him for a moment, I'd call him from the kitchen halfway through whatever I was doing.

'Archie?'

If he didn't reply instantly, I would imagine that in the space of a few minutes he had burned himself to a crisp at the fireside.

'You mustn't ever play with fire,' I'd warn him when I came back into the room, my heart going like a ping-pong ball, knowing that I should have said so earlier. He'd look up from the sewing table, pen in hand, confused.

I hadn't bargained on the homework, let alone that he would need me to help him with it. Archie was astounded that I couldn't work a calculator, that I had no idea about kilograms or metres. I was born, he had to realize, in *the olden days*. We discovered certain compensations though. I was not so bad at history projects: 'Roman Helmets', 'Victorian Canals', 'The Wives of Henry VIII', Archie deferred to me in these matters as if he believed I had first-hand knowledge.

Before we lit the fire one night, I made him put his head up the chimney.

'Can you see the light at the top? They'd send a boy up there,' I said. 'You'd have been the perfect size.'

I leaned over to the bookcase and pulled out my copy of *The Water Babies*, clapping the pages together to loosen an earwig.

'This was my favourite,' I said. 'About a boy, a chimney sweep, who ends up in the river. He turns into a water baby.'

Archie looked at me, then he said, 'Mrs Dobbs has got a moustache.'

'Look at the pictures,' I said quickly. 'I used to love the pictures.'

I lifted the cover for him. There on the flypiece was the scrawled dedication − *from Great-Uncle Lucien* − and the date, *15 August 1941*.

'My fifth birthday,' I said. 'It was a present.'

'*My* birthday's in August,' he said. 'The thirteenth of August.' He let the book fall open and looked from it to me. Suddenly an idea dawned on him. 'Are we related?' he asked.

What a sweet face he had sometimes. *If only we were*, I thought, and I confess I didn't tell him otherwise. When Eve called for him later and when I finished helping him on with his coat, I gave him a little tap on the shoulder and handed him the book, wrapped up in a plastic bag.

'What have you got there?' Eve asked.

'We were talking about a book. I thought he might like to borrow it,' I said.

'Thank you,' she said. 'Say *thank you*, Archie.'

'No need,' I said.

'It's lovely he talks to you,' Eve said, gathering him to her. 'On a good day, all I get is what type of pudding there was for lunch.'

If it was raining, we agreed I'd wait for Archie indoors. I'd watch out for him from the velvet curtains, his shape familiar now, his skinny legs and his clunky black shoes as he backed out of the bus through the electric door. On the last day of term it was bucketing down and Archie appeared to be particularly laden; he was clutching the front of his jacket, stunned by pellets of rain, looking as if he'd quite forgotten our arrangement. The vehicle hauled away through a dirty puddle, spraying his legs. It was no use signalling as I did, knocking on the glass. I hurried to the front door and opened it a crack, called out to him. By now he had his book bag over his head, which finally he lowered towards me, swinging a plastic bag in his other hand to propel himself forward.

'What a lot of stuff,' I said when he arrived, lifting the carrier from him, his coat, telling him to go and sit by the fire.

When I came through with his biscuits and drink, he was still standing by the piano, shivering.

'Come where it's warm,' I urged.

He didn't move. 'Can I have a go?' he asked, then plonked his fingers along on the loose high notes.

23

It was a horrid noise. 'Another day,' I said, a little sharply perhaps. He drew back his hand, held it to him.

It had rained consecutively for five whole days and he was looking as if he'd never been out of it, his hair plastered to his scalp.

'Come and get dry,' I said.

He came and stood. I handed him a biscuit from the tin and he proceeded to take tiny bites from it.

'Sit down,' I said. He sat on the edge of the seat.

'Did you ever look at that book?' I asked him.

They'd done Victorians, he told me.

'That was quick,' I said. It seemed to me that our conversation was more stilted than usual and that it was my fault.

'You can have another one, if you'd like,' I said. I had learned how quickly biscuits could cheer him up. His face was beginning to get some colour back into it. They'd been given a project for the holidays: 'The Second World War,' he said deliberately, as if I might not have heard of it before. He began to fish inside the red school bag, bringing out a crumpled photocopied sheet which he held out to me, the ink smudged where rain had got to it. I took the paper from him and smoothed it on my lap. There were four printed objects in a grid, a line or two ruled below each, some of which he'd already attempted to fill in.

'Miss said to ask old people,' he said.

I was going to say something indignant about being old, but it would have been lost on him. Instead I said, 'Well, she's quite right. I was right here in the village for a bit, in the war, before I went back to London. I lived in this very cottage.

24

With my great aunt, Auntie Mavis. Let's have a look.' I fixed my attention on the sheet.

'Did you live in London?' he asked incredulously. 'That's where *I* lived.'

It was rare that I could surprise him. I smiled. 'I never liked it much, I'm afraid.'

'Why?'

'It was the war. And my parents weren't being very nice to each other.' I surprised myself by my readiness to tell him. 'It wasn't a very happy place,' I said.

'My dad's gone away,' he said. 'He's gone to Scotland.'

I didn't want to pry. 'That's a gas mask, isn't it?' I said, pointing to a crude outline that made the mask look like a skull.

'Do you have one?' he asked. 'We're having a table after the holidays, for showing.'

I shook my head, 'We didn't hang on to them. They were horrid things. You couldn't breathe.'

'Don't you have anything?' he asked forlornly.

'What's that, do you think, Archie?' I asked, pointing at another sketch. 'Have a guess.'

'A rabbit hutch?' He was twisting about, bored already.

'Bigger than a hutch,' I said. 'I think it must be an Anderson shelter. People dug them into the bottom of their gardens so they had a place to hide from the bombs . . . Write it in, go on.'

'That's a Spitfire,' Archie said not listening, pointing to the aeroplane he'd already begun to colour in at school. He dug into his bag again and brought out his pencil case, all set to finish it off. Whenever he wrote or drew anything, his elbow rose like a sail, his mouth gaped, he went deaf. He was drawing a tiny man in the cockpit, with heavy goggles. I let him get on with it, took up the square I was crocheting for the hospice.

'My dad,' he said matter-of-factly when he'd finished, holding it out for me to inspect.

I wasn't sure how to respond. 'And what's the other thing for?' I asked, indicating with my crochet hook, though I could see quite clearly what it was.

'A label,' he said. 'For your name and address. They tied it to you on the train.' He had already filled in his name: Archie Maretta.

'I never had a label,' I said, which started him off again.

'Have you got anything? Like a bullet? Or *shrapnel*?'

I set down my work. 'Wait a minute,' I said, 'I'm sure I can find you something.' I was determined not to disappoint him.


I kept Mother's case under the bed. It still had the important things in it – birth certificates, post office book. It was a lady's case, for travelling. Crocodile. It came from Great Uncle Lucien, from India or Africa, somewhere he'd been posted. There was a tray in the top, with two shallow jars that used to contain a pinkish powder and leather-covered lids where Mother kept odd buttons, pins and brooches. Underneath were all the papers. She was more sentimental than I was – there were souvenirs of outings to the theatre, menu cards showing who ate what. She always had it close to hand and sometimes we'd go right through it so she could show me the things that proved that she and Daddy had a life.

When I came downstairs Archie looked hopeful. He crouched down as I laid the case next to the fire, smoothing the silvery dust from its surface. I unclicked the catches and opened the lid, lifted out the tray with the jars, which I laid to one side. Underneath was the familiar muddle of papers, and I began to shuffle through; I knew exactly what I was looking for.

'Here! This is it. Goodness.'

It was a small envelope with Auntie's neat brown handwriting. I had never held Archie's attention so entirely. I savoured it. There were two pieces of paper inside, the first of which I drew out. It was a letter I'd written from Devon, folded neatly into four.

'More a map than a letter,' I said, opening it out.

Archie was up on his knees, peering into my lap. I was surprised at how vivid the colours were still, blue and orange and red. I'd drawn cottages, flat on their backs, arranged around the Green in irregular squares. Attached to each there was a chimney pot out of which, like wisps of smoke, Auntie had written the names for me: wistaria, sanctuary, Seven Stars, post office.

'Do you recognize the names?' I asked him. Only one cottage had windows – Paradise. And there I was, with round crayon-blue eyes, scribbled-in red shoes, and MAVIS, capital letters, written in my own hand underneath.

'What's that?' Archie pointed to the top corner, where I'd drawn several lozenges and, in faint pencil, printed the word UPKOT, and an X.

'Is it treasure?' Archie asked wildly.

There they were, the Upcotts, right from the beginning.

I held my breath. My eyes stung. There was something so poignant about my misspelling of the name — a time *before*.

'It's the graveyard,' I said hurriedly. 'We used to play a game up there. Badgers and Foxes. It's where I used to find slow-worms.'

'Worms?' he asked, eyes fixed to where I was poking the letter back in.

I heard my voice as if through water: '*Slow*-worms,' I said.

'What's a slow-worm?'

I put down the envelope, extended my hands vaguely.

'Do they bite?' he asked.

It was a great effort to concentrate. 'No. They eat grass,' I said, then pulling myself together, 'dandelion leaves, little boys.' He was wide-eyed. 'Yes, little boys.' And then I remembered the chocolate wrapper Mother had filed away into the same envelope.

'Here,' I said, fishing it out. It was fudge-coloured, grease-proof. I opened it up, its torn edges the size of a postcard. 'Read it,' I said.

He read slowly from across the middle, 'Cadbury's. Rat—'

'Ration,' I said.

'Ration. Chocolate.' He looked up at me. 'Chocolate?'

'I'm afraid I've eaten it all up,' I said.


There were two teams: Badgers and Foxes. Badgers were Londoners and Foxes were from the village and we were at war. Badgers smeared charcoal stripes across their cheeks and down their noses; Foxes used the red soil at the back of the churchyard. Auntie wasn't enough of a villager herself to grant me village status and I was relegated promptly to the Badgers – the only girl. I didn't like the boys from London, and they didn't want a girl joining them. Michael Knight, who was a Fox, Joyce's nephew and the oldest, said it was only fair because he and Ian were stuck with a girl, their sister Fay, who was useless at fighting. Also, they had to have Victor, his cousin, a liability he didn't feel the need to explain: it was an 'even handicap', he said.

We divided the graveyard according to the names of the families buried there. 'Home' for the village children was wherever a grandfather, an uncle or an aunt happened to be buried – Knight, Endicott, Fairley. For the rest of us, it was a matter of staking a claim. The London boys, three or four of them, bagsied the Eastwood tomb, because, they said, they were from the East End. It was certainly the grandest, with its own huge box for the bodies, and railings around to protect it from rabbits. But the Upcott graves were the ones I chose: they were the most numerous, ranged against the north wall. One had a pool of green quartz chippings, from which we'd all secretly filled our pockets; another had a real anchor laid on top, boy-sized; another, a stone dove. The Upcotts lived a mile or so out of the village and there was only one Upcott the same age as us: Tom, who was so rarely allowed out to play that I thought I could get away with it.

It was Michael who came up with the rules of the battle: kidnap. Only girls could be kidnapped and the first team to get the other's girl and 'turn her' from Fox to Badger or Badger to Fox, was the winner. Immediately Fay said she didn't want to play; it was a rotten game. Being older than she was, I knew we had no choice. When Michael's policeman's whistle went off, Fay sat right down where she was. She was the first to be kidnapped.

She was already snivelling when we led her behind the water barrel. One of the London boys held her down while I applied her badger stripes. I wasn't mean, I didn't press hard, but Fay was giving me the flaming eye. Once I had finished my job I drew off, imagining the others would let her get to her feet and run away. But the London boy was showing off, wouldn't let her go, and Fay was kicking so hard that we could all see her puffy yellow knickers. The others had gathered round, pointing and laughing; even Victor was making his silly hooting noise. It was then we noticed a boy in a green jumper, climbing towards us. 'Tom!'

Tom Upcott took charge as soon as he caught up to us. 'Hold her legs,' he commanded.

One boy either side had hold of a heel. I shrank back, hoping that whatever was going to happen to Fay would happen fast so that I wouldn't have to get involved. She was shrieking now, which made it more difficult. Tom's whole face was lit up, he was easing her knickers down over one foot, then the other. Michael was with them now, and even though Fay was his sister, he did nothing to stop them. As soon as the knickers were free, Tom leapt to his feet, twirling the yellow material high above his head. Fay lunged out and then rolled around to sit up, pulling her skirt round, sobbing in fury. The boys weren't interested in her any longer, they were running after Tom as he wove in and out of the gravestones, flashing his trophy.

'We won the war! We won the war!'

Fay got to her feet, she was hiccuping and streaming tears

and snot; she tottered off towards the gate. The others were so fired up – including the ones who were supposed to be on Fay's side – that they seemed to have lost sight of the original game. I pretended to be absorbed picking daisies, and before long the shouting and running around me settled down and stopped. When I eventually looked up, there was no one to be seen or heard – only the dead-and-buried and the chittering of birds. I wondered if they'd gone home. Perhaps they'd decided to go down to the river? I got up, brushed my skirt, intending to go and find Fay. But as I rounded the corner of the church, I was ambushed. Michael and Tom jumped out from behind the Eastwood tomb, whooping so wildly that instantly my knees caved in. The London boys fell in behind – all of them ate spiders, none of them remotely interested in rescuing me. It was boys against girl. I could only pray that Fay would be telling tales, crying inconsolably as only she knew how.

It was Tom's suggestion that they take me up to the back wall. There were hands all over me, dragging me, pushing from behind. Where the path ran out, I crumpled on to a heap of dirt. Someone grabbed my hair and brought me face to face with the red earth. There were woodlice in it, the purpley saddleback of a worm. The boys were yelping with excitement. The more I shook my head, the more it was pressed down, until the soil got into my mouth and up my nose.

'Pull 'em off, pull 'em off,' two of them were chanting. Victor clapped and hooted in my ear.

My hands flew behind my back, clamping my skirt and I clenched my legs tight.

'You liars, you … you *buggers!*' It was the worst word I could think of.

'Buggers!' Michael repeated, realizing he had ammunition. 'Did you hear what she said?'

'Bug, bug, bug,' Victor chanted.

I wondered how much soil you'd have to eat before it killed you. Michael was sitting on my back and there were multiple hands attempting to snatch off my shoes and my socks when, at last, a commotion beyond the lych gate made Michael unlatch himself from me. There was a woman's shout. Joyce with a frying pan in her hand and Mrs Knight running close behind, huffing and hot-faced.

'What on earth's going on here?'

As soon as Michael was off me, I turned on to my back, pulling my skirt straight.

'Thomas Upcott!' Joyce said. 'Does your father know you're up here?'

The London boys were sniggering.

'I don't see nothing to laugh about here, you boys. Have you no respect at all? How can you do such a thing?' She turned on Michael. 'Fay says it was you done her cheeks? Is that right? Your own sister? You ought to be ashamed of yourself.'

'Mavis used a bad word,' Michael said.

'Is that right, Mavis?'

I couldn't speak. There was grit in my mouth, which I spat out.

'I don't want to hear another squeak, do you hear? From any of you. Tom, you get off home, before I do for you. And the others of you – how could you dream of such a thing? Come with me this instant!'

We were rounded up and prodded out through the gate, along the cobbled path, past Wistaria Cottage, Sanctuary Cottage, the Seven Stars and down to the Green. Joyce, standing at the iron pump, reached for my arm.

'I'm surprised at you, Mavis, I am. Playing rough games. Trampling on graves. I thought you were a nice girl. Now then. Line up!' she said and moving her hand from my elbow to clamp the back of my neck, she pushed my head down.

Without instruction, Mrs Knight had taken the lever and was beginning to work it. I could hear the gurgle in its belly, higher and higher, a horrid donkey noise.

'You're next,' she said sharply to one of the boys, 'so you can wipe that smile off your face. Exactly what Father'd have done to us,' she said as the chopper of water cascaded down on my head, 'had we dared in a hundred years to behave so disrespectful.'

There was a pall over the village for days afterwards. Chicken sheds and pigsties were mucked out, vegetables hoed to within an inch of their lives, hearthstones, doorsteps, gleaming. The London boys were even made to empty the school buckets for Mr Bird, who was church warden and our school caretaker, spreading the stinking night soil underneath the brambles. It was a concerted campaign: our necks and ears were scrubbed more viciously than usual, finger- and toenails cut to the quick. Only Tom Upcott, it seemed, much to our indignation, had escaped scot-free.

Tom Upcott didn't have a mother: we had to remember that. Sometimes, when he didn't turn up for school, our teacher,

Mrs Stubbs, sent Mr Bird to go and fetch him. But after his father found out Tom had been hiding down at the river, or in the loft of one of the barns, he took matters into his own hands. From then on, Mr Upcott or his daughter Frances would escort Tom all the way up to the school door every morning. Once, after the holidays, we had just finished saying morning grace, our eyes were still closed, when the door rattled. We dropped our hands.

'No need to turn round,' Mrs Stubbs said. 'Sit down in your places.'

Then she walked to the back of the classroom and had words. We tried to look as far round as we could without turning our heads. When Frances left, Mrs Stubbs brought Tom Upcott round to stand in front of the class.

There was *no talking* after grace. There was *no laughing* in class, unless Mrs Stubbs laughed (which was rare) and then we were only allowed to let our laughter out in small puffs. Tom looked like he'd been bombed. His hair was sticking up at the top, his skin was flecked with black soot, his cheeks and his forehead were raw and weeping. He tucked his chin into his chest and stared at a knot of wood in the floorboard.

Mrs Stubbs couldn't help herself, she was beaming at us. She was sick to death of having to tell Tom off, of having to make him sit on his own, of putting him in the corner, all of which only appeared to elevate his status. 'Well,' she said, lifting the elbow of his jacket so that his wrist hung like a puppet's for us to see, charred and blistered, 'perhaps you'd like to tell the class what has happened?'

Tom folded his head further into his chest. We were

looking at him in lurid anticipation. Had he been in a fight? In an air raid? Sid put up his hand.

'Yes, Sid?'

'Please Mrs Stubbs, has he been *playing with fire*?'

'Well?' she said to Tom. 'Speak up else I shall have to tell it myself.'


Every six months, Tom's job at the farm was to black the range and the grates, upstairs and down. The tin of Zebo, black and yellow striped, was kept in the pantry on a high shelf. Joyce would fetch it down for him, provide him with a suitable rag. With all the other things he had to do, depending on the time of year, it could take him all day. First he had to empty and sweep out every one of the six grates, and carry the ashes out to the heap in the corner of the orchard. Then he had to spit and polish to get rid of the dust. Joyce or Frances would come and inspect. Only then, if they were happy, could he tip the pure treacly liquid on to his rag and rub the metal until it began to shine, black and hard as a stag beetle.

The previous day, he'd done the four fireplaces upstairs – his father's room, Frances and Robert's room, his own room and the brown room. His arms ached; he wanted a rest. Downstairs in the rarefied light of the parlour he was unlikely to be disturbed. He closed the door quietly behind him. There was only one drawback to the peace of that room: the huge, sepia portrait of his mother that hung over the piano. She was pictured sitting in the tall cane-backed chair, wearing a black lace headdress, water-silk jacket and skirts, flanked by

Robert and Frances. Although he had never known her, she had always been a presence to him, not only in this formal representation, but in the way he could trace the watermark of her features in the faces of his elder sister and brother. He liked to imagine there would be a day when he would be able to outstare her. But not that afternoon. There they were, deadly serious, glaring down at him as if he'd interrupted, as if, already, he'd done something wrong.

He turned his back and went to sit on the footstool by the fire. He took the rag and with no real thought, tipped out the dark molasses of the polish, began to dab it on to the backs of his hands. It made a shiny blue-black sheen over his knuckles. He painted each of his fingernails, and then the length of his fingers. He turned over the pink pads of his hands. *What if I blacked myself out?* he thought. Above the fireplace there was a speckled, gilt mirror. By standing on the stool he was able to see himself and use the mantelpiece as a shelf for his equipment. He tipped the tin bottle again and began to smear Zebo on to his face: between his hairline and his eyebrows, carefully in circles around his eyes and mouth, as far back as his ears. His eyes blinked out at him, framed by their white skin like two beacons, blinking morse. He jumped down and turned to see if the three of them would recognize him now.

'And look what it's done to his face!' Mrs Stubbs said; 'Look at his hands!' She lifted the elbow of his jacket again to expose his blackened paw.

Someone sniggered. Now that she had established the tale as a cautionary one, with nothing whatsoever to do with heroics or battles, the other boys were safe to nudge one another.

'No laughing, there. You all know very well that it's a sin to glory in another's misfortune.'

She may as well have tickled them with a feather. One boy was purple, his shoulders shaking at what was being passed around the room, behind hands, mouth to ear: '*Badger!*' Tom was hardened to it, he was impassive. This was nothing to what he'd had at home.

It was Joyce who saw him first. She was finishing off for the day in the kitchen, wiping down the table and the sink. He came creeping in and startled her: everything shot out – the dishcloth, its spray of dirty water. She shrieked. 'Good grief! You'll give me a heart attack! What in the Lord's name have you been doing?'

At that point Tom was grinning, the skin of his cheeks so tight he could feel them crack.

'Go and wash your face, this second, before anyone else sees you. Go on, out of my sight.'

But the Zebo had already set hard. Between them – she and Frances – they tried everything: spitting into their hankies, carbolic soap, oats and water, paraffin, nothing would shift it. When Mr Upcott came in, he sent Joyce home. Tom's skin was stiff as leather. It was the culmination of several years of delinquency. He got a tin of turpentine and laid Tom out across the kitchen table. 'Don't move a finger,' he hissed, and his quietness shook the room. It was a surgical operation. Frances had a hold of the tops of his legs and their father didn't stint as he rubbed away at the skin, asking what he'd done to deserve it. When Frances wrote to Robert, who by then was away at school, she recounted in order the names their father used: *Blackamoor, Nigger-boy, Blackman's spawn.*

I was careful not to repeat those names – you can't use words like that any more. Archie wanted to know if the Tom I was talking about was the same Tom that was in the water baby book. What a connection for him to have made! I told him just how much the Tom I'd known had loved the river. I said we ought to have an expedition there one day; perhaps we'd take a picnic when the weather got warmer? I began positively to look forward to our conversations, the way he would bring me out of myself.

Archie's curiosity was of a different brand to other people's – wide open; his questions were not the old questions, predicated on the knowledge of what had happened (which, sooner or later, always leaked out). Sometimes I couldn't tell if he was serious or teasing me: 'I'm an old bird,' I must have said, getting up out of the chair. 'Can you fly?' he asked.

I've said, I treated him like a prince. I began to wonder what I ever did before he came along. I was asleep, that's what. He woke me up. It may seem ridiculous, but he made me take more care over my appearance. What was the point at my age in keeping clothes for best? I even got out the blue shoes with the little heel, gave them a polish.

I became more sensitive, more aware. Little things no longer escaped my notice. Mrs Dobbs, Archie'd said, had a moustache, and it shocked me to realize how eagle-eyed children could be. As soon as I'd dropped him back home that evening, I'd gone to the bathroom to inspect my face. I

38

so rarely bothered with the mirror. My teeth! My graveyard of a mouth! I lifted the sag of skin under my chin and strained to see. Grizzled and wiry in three or four different places. My heart sank. I determined to be systematic. Between the Milk of Magnesia and the packet of Senokot, I reached for Mother's tweezers.

# PART II
*The Echoing Green*

# 4

## *A Case of Hearts*

Daddy used to tell people that he'd rescued Mother from the French Resistance, that she'd been resisting him ever since – Ha-ha. Neither, incidentally, was true.

People express surprise if I tell them my mother was French. I don't look French, they say, whatever that means. And it's true, I hardly speak the language. Mother's name was Francine. Francine Eluard. She grew up somewhere just north of Paris and had a bicycle she pretended was a horse. Her father, an accountant, turned out – as Daddy had always predicted – to be a collaborator. During the war, Daddy said, it was safer to assume that all non-English speakers, including the Irish and Catholics generally, were collaborators. It did for her mother, too. In the early hours of a French morning, both parents were shot in their sleep with bullets from four pistols.

Luckily, by that time, Mother was already married and in England. She'd left home at seventeen to go to Paris, where she'd harboured a vague ambition for the theatre. She was working as a secretary in a bank when Daddy met her, drinking kir in a bar in St Germain with a motley crew of artists, all of whom Daddy recalled smelling of kippers. By comparison, Mother was extremely well turned-out, her lack of English only adding to her charm. Daddy was intoxicated with her tiny pixie feet, her hand's span of a waist; and after an acquaintance of barely two weeks, he took her back to London with him, *un petit souvenir*. The uncles had sent him to Paris to sow his oats before they tied him down with 'managing director'. They rolled their eyes when they were introduced to Francine, but made him do the decent thing.

My parents had been married for a year. 12 November 1935. I was got, Mother liked to tell me, in a rather grand hotel, the 'Royal Hotel' of an undisclosed seaside resort. She wasn't a fan of the outdoors and neither, in her short experience, was Daddy. When he proposed an afternoon constitutional along the cliff path, she demurred – as surely he knew she would – and he left her in the Grosvenor Bar, tucked up in a leather armchair with a pink gin, listening to Chopin. If she hadn't been such a fool, she said, she'd have suspected something was up. By the time he returned, several hours later, she was moving in waltz time. He declined the help of the young waiter, propped her against his shoulder and led her – two steps forward, one back – up the sweep of the main stairway. Once they were safely inside the room he let her drop from his arms across the bed.

Afterwards she wept, determined that the name he had moaned, finally, wasn't hers: *Mavis, Mavis* – a name that she would hear repeated in the relentless hissing of the sea outside their bedroom window.

The next day, going through his things, she found a clutch of letters in what she took to be a cursive female hand, addressed from one of the big houses along the cliff: signed with love, from M. E. Courtier, author (as she well knew) of Daddy's latest acquisition, *A Case of Hearts*.

'Mavis!' she shrieked triumphantly.

'My darling,' Daddy had said. 'You have, as usual, got hold of the wrong end of the stick. I dropped by as a courtesy, no more, given that we were here.'

'*Pas si bête!*' Mother had a way of clamping her lips that in the old days would run to a smile.

'Darling heart,' he said, 'come and sit on my knee.'


I can only assume – for I was never party to it – that at some point there must have been a spark of what passes for *love* between them. He bought her the usual trinkets – a black enamel powder compact with a golden Venus rising, a matching cigarette case elaborately engraved with two swanlike F's, her name entwined with his – but neither one of them took any pains to acquaint themselves with the other's tongue. Daddy had a form of French he'd learned at school: he could acquit himself fairly well in a restaurant or hotel. Mother's English was never more than charmingly defunct and, from the moment she set foot in England, she looked upon improving it as the final surrender. My French was never more than rudimentary. From Mother, I had *Papa*, from Daddy, I had Mother, or, in an occasionally truculent mood, *Mère*, which he'd make a point of pronouncing, long-drawn-out, like a sheep.

Mavis Eugenie Gaunt. When Daddy returned from the register office brandishing the birth certificate with the one name Mother had categorically vetoed, her suspicions were reawakened with a start. She told him that as soon as she was able to walk, she would be leaving him. On the next boat. Meanwhile Daddy was tying himself in knots, claiming – if she was so determined to make a fuss – that he'd named me after a Devon aunt, for obvious family reasons. The glass in the wedding photograph by their bed was cracked with a 'K' where she'd hurled it across the room at him.

For a week at a time when I was little, Mother would take to her bed and Daddy would sleep in his dressing room on the other side of the corridor. Mother had powders for her nerves and liniment for her aches and pains. We went to visit her once with flowers and bonbons in the Chelsea Hospital, where eventually they'd removed her extraordinary double womb, kept, for many years after, in a large pickling jar for the enlightenment of medical students. I was big as a seal when I broke out, she told me, and she never disabused me of the idea that her downfall had been my doing, warning me with tales of bloody evisceration, never to have children of my own.

In the summer of 1939, Nanny Jennings announced that she would be leaving us. The call had gone out for volunteers and she was going to sign up. It was an excuse, Mother said; the woman was appalling at her job. But they found it almost impossible to replace her. Even Daddy who said that the threat of war was a long-running ruse to gee the country up, had to admit that things weren't looking good. It was his idea to take us down to Devon. He'd introduce us to his Aunt Mavis — scotching Mother's most stubborn suspicion — and settle us in for the duration: two birds with one stone.

We travelled down in the Wolseley. I had a nest of cushions and blankets on the back seat for sleeping, and I must have done so most of the way because I remember little of the journey, except the waking up — a flat tyre on the Hog's Back, boiled hake and Eton mess at the Avon Hotel, currant buns at Honiton. By teatime, Mother had started crying. She had no idea the journey would take so long, the place so far away from London. She didn't care to meet this aunt, she said, she didn't care for anything; she wasn't going to set foot back in that automobile. I was pleased when in the end she decided to sit in the back with me, though she kept her eyes shut and a handkerchief stuffed over her mouth.

I was properly awake by now. The roads were so narrow that, where the trees and bushes hung over, we almost scraped the sides.

'This is where the bunny rabbits live,' Daddy said, as we entered a village, turning his head in a gesture towards me. 'Can you see?'

I strained against the window. 'Mother, look!'

In every village there was a church, a spire and among the cluster of cottages, at least one or two tiny little white ones, with windows so small, so spick-and-span, that I had no reason not to believe him. It crossed my mind with trembling that Auntie might be a rabbit.

We seemed to have been driving for as long as I had been alive. It was miraculous when eventually Daddy gave a great

47

sigh, 'Here we are!' He turned off the engine with a flourish, heaved the brake. 'Shipleigh,' he announced. 'Hasn't changed one bit.'

He was being jolly for Mother. He got himself out of the car and flapped his arms. Then he opened the back door.

'Out you get,' he said. 'Come on, chop-chop.'

It was hard to believe that we had really arrived. When the car door opened to the side of me, the air whistled and cheeped like a musical box. And then, from a gateway, a small, yapping dog ran out to meet us, dancing and springing up along the running board so that it was hard to find a place to put my feet.

An old lady emerged from the porch.

'My favourite aunt,' Daddy said. 'Phew, what a journey we've had.'

Mother staggered a little on her shoes. She was ill from travelling; she had a headache from Daddy telling her that the city was too dangerous for a child.

'Is too dangerous for a child,' she said, automatically taking the old lady's hand.

Aunt Cleverdon was wearing a long skirt and she had very rosy cheeks and dark rabbity eyes. She produced a piece of cord from her pocket and tied the dog to the gatepost, assuring Daddy over and over, 'She'd not hurt a fly.'

Daddy took her by the elbow, '*London*, dear Aunt, she means London. You must forgive my wife's English – she didn't mean the little dog, not for a minute.' He boxed her tiny hands in his.

I wasn't scared, though the dog, Peggy, could reach my nose when she jumped. Next to her there was a little iron garden gate, with gaps in the railings just wide enough for my feet. I clung to it and swung backwards and forwards while they talked.

Although Daddy's plan had been to leave Mother and me for a few months, until the war was over ('They'll have it in the bag by Christmas,' he'd said) he had made no allowance for Mother's delicacy. As soon as she saw the cottage, she refused point blank. There were no facilities, no privacy. No. No. Her purple hat with its single feather shivered on her head. She marched to the far end of the Green, her pale fingers shaking as she took the cigarette from its case. When she turned her back to us, smoke rose up from behind her hat as if from a chimney pot.

'She's a bit shook up,' Daddy explained apologetically, hooking his arm through Auntie's and taking her the small length of the front garden. 'Quite forgot how heavenly Devon can be.'

Auntie remained formal throughout.

'We hate to have to ask,' Daddy said, 'but it really is no place for a child. Not until this mess is over with.'

It all happened in the bat of an eye. Mother pressed me to her hips so hard I could feel the buttons of her underwear.

'Come on, old girl, least said—' And Daddy knelt down, balancing so that his watch chain swung out, pulled at my cheek. 'You'll be a brave little soldier, won't you? Look after your aunt.'

Daddy didn't like kneeling down. He creaked when he got up, saying 'creak', straightening his jacket. When they'd gone Auntie untied Peg and unhitched me from the gate. Together we went to pick snails from the delphiniums. Later on she showed me the anchor cufflinks. They were tied on a ribbon around her neck and tucked inside her blouse. She was a widow. Her husband, Ernest, had been killed on a boat in the Great War; it was a shame I wasn't going to meet him. She asked me if I knew that our name means 'songbird'. It was exactly what Ernest used to call her, *my little songbird*. A name that tasted of the gooseberry jam, which she let me have – the only time – straight from the spoon.

There were rules to learn at Auntie's, like no crying over spilt milk, no fidgeting at mealtimes, no chickens in the house. She conceded that in naming me, my father had made some gesture of contrition on behalf of a family with whom, for the many years since her marriage, she'd had little dealing. She took pleasure in introducing me as 'Little Mavis', as if I were an identical but miniaturized version of herself; for a time, I found myself exceptionally popular with the village ladies.

There were three in particular, sisters: Mrs Knight, Joyce Fairley and Dorothy. Mrs Knight was the eldest of them and lived at Redlands farm, Dorothy was the youngest, unmarried, who stayed with their widowed mother next to Joyce. You could tell they were sisters: they dressed in the same heavy brown shoes and apron overalls, though Joyce's were distinctly more cheerful – dancing girls and posies or motorcars and flags. Joyce was the one who'd be first to throw out a picnic rug, to pass around the sandwiches, to make sure everyone had something hot to drink. She and Alf (who was a cousin of Ernest's) had been together since they were at school and married a couple of years ago, when Alf turned eighteen. They made such a handsome couple that, for a decade or more, their wedding photograph kept pride of place in the window of the photographic studios in Buckleigh.

Before I went to school, all I remember was looking after the three chickens in the back. They were sisters too, Auntie told me. Peggy, Bunty and Hops. They lived in a shed next to the privy, and I was responsible for letting them out in the morning, reaching in to check for eggs, and, if it wasn't too late, shutting them in at night. Hops was the oldest, a rusty colour with a rosette of feathers on her chest. I made them little packages of straw to sleep on, I fed them extra scraps from my hankie. It didn't take long before Hops would let me have her on my knee. I crocheted a bonnet for her and I would sit and cradle her all afternoon, the heavenly softness of her feathers.

As soon as I started school, my world opened up. Joyce came round to ask Auntie if I'd come and play with Victor. At that time, Joyce was still working for the Upcotts and had to leave Victor for long stretches alone with her mother. Although he was two years younger than I was, Victor was already bigger than me, and a handful for the old lady. Joyce said he'd enjoy the company of someone his own age. She'd given up asking the boys in the village, who'd proven they weren't grown-up enough to be left alone with him – but she was sure that he and I would play handsomely together.

Victor wore thick glasses, like an old man, and his mouth had a hitch in it as if a fishhook had been snagged there. But I took it as a compliment that I'd been asked for and he didn't fight with me; he followed me around, as Joyce pointed out, like a little lamb. If it wasn't pouring outside, we entertained ourselves in the vegetable gardens where Joyce's old mother could keep an eye on us through the back window. Victor already had a house underneath an old hawthorn, whose branches I helped him hang with proper duster and apron walls. We kept two tin mugs out there, a plate between us and a spoon for digging.

One time, the plan had been to dig a tunnel to the plum tree. I was surprised by how seriously Victor took my ideas. In a week or two, he had managed a trench long enough and deep enough for him to lie down in unseen. My job was to sort the rubble he excavated, eagle-eyed for buried jewels. There was promise everywhere – bits of bleached pipe, meat lids, jars, long, rusty nails. I left the live things for Victor. He had a zoo, which he kept under the bench in Alf's shed – a cake tin with eleven nail-holes hammered into the lid. Mostly it was for wood lice. But then he found the dead vole, and very quickly after that, he developed a knack for knowing where things would be hiding or buried. The slow-worm was teased from under a rotten log. He brought it to me on the palm of his hand, cooing. It sat so still it might not have been real, except for the shock – repeated – of seeing its beady eyes blink.

If it rained and Joyce was at home, she found things for us to do inside. We'd pat butter with her, taking turns to use the two paddles that made the butter balls (just like she did for the Upcotts). Or she'd show me how to sew a book of blue felt for darning needles, how to finish off a scarf. She had a cylindrical blue toffee tin filled with ribbons and lace and sometimes she would sit and do my hair for me. She couldn't wait to have a girl of her own, she said, put all these ribbons to good use.

Victor never spoke much and it wasn't easy to understand him when he did. When his sister finally arrived he was nearly six, but he wouldn't call her Sandy, which was her name; he called her Ba-ba. It had been pointed out to me by then how stupid Victor was. He couldn't even hold a pen to do his letters. At school I began to distance myself from him; he was kept down with the infants. I made it clear that the only reason I went to Joyce's was because I loved the baby. I loved to look after the baby. Sandy was kept outside in the bouncy pram and Victor was forbidden to fuss with her – he was too rough – but because I was a girl and knew how, I was allowed to take her for walks around the Green. When she was big enough, I was allowed to lift her out of her harness, jiggle her like you were supposed to, scoop the mash from the corners of her mouth. Sandy was responsive and good-natured and I loved her as much as any doll. I had a way with her, Joyce said.

Auntie had been the baby in Bideford. She warned me off brothers or sisters, telling me tales of how relentlessly Gilbert and Lucien used to torment her, how her elder sister Eleanor (my grandmother) persuaded her from an early age that she was too ugly to be married. When she ran away with Ernest, her father told her she had made her bed, she must lie in it. But when it was clear that she was never coming back, he relented and sent on some of her things. The piano from the nursery was delivered by tractor. The journey took six hours from start to finish; another two hours to shoehorn the instrument into the cottage.

At five o'clock on weekdays, Auntie gave lessons. If I wasn't already out of the house, I was banished at such times into the kitchen. I'd hear the wooden ruler on the top of the piano beating time, and sometimes, foot stamping or tears or both.

Auntie inherited Frances Upcott from the organist at Buckleigh; he'd had an apoplectic stroke one Sunday and could no longer move his arms or speak. A stroke of luck, Auntie might have said. Frances was Tom's older sister. She was fourteen and the top of our school, almost grown-up. I used to watch her secretly in church. The Upcotts sat in the pew at the very front, under the lectern. The year before, she had cut all her hair off. I watched it as it grew back, inch by inch, until the point where she was able to wear it, as she did now, in two small buns behind her ears – a style which for many years I copied.

Even I could tell that Frances was head and shoulders above the rest. Whatever else I was up to, I'd make a concerted effort to be back in the house on Friday afternoons when she had her lessons. As soon as she sat down to play, the thin partitions between the downstairs rooms buzzed. Auntie could not contain her pleasure. For the first time, she was able to bring out the music scores from the cabinet, albums that she herself had learned from as a girl. In a month or two Frances had worked through half a dozen of Bach's Preludes; over the summer, she mastered two of Schubert's Impromptus.

One Friday afternoon, as we sat together waiting for

her, there were unfamiliar footsteps at the door, an abrupt knocking. Auntie went to answer it herself. There was a brief exchange and then the front door was pressed shut. Silence. A moment or two later, Auntie came through into the kitchen, jittery, she was holding a letter. I could see the disappointment in her face. I thought by the way she was clutching the paper that someone must have died. She drew back a chair and sat down opposite me.

14th day of September 1942

To Mrs Cleverdon,

A note to inform you that unless more suitable material can be found in respect to my daughter's piano learning, then all such lessons shall cease forthwith.

I remain, yours faithfully,
John H. Upcott, Esq.
Passaford Farm

Auntie pursed her lips. 'Goodness knows where he learned to write like that,' she said. She sniffed, wiped her nose briskly.

'What does it mean?' I asked.

The skin on Auntie's neck was taut. 'That he has not an ounce of civilization in his bones, that he is ignorant enough to be proud of it . . .' I had never seen Auntie so enraged. Later that evening, when I went to say goodnight, I found her with a dozen albums ranged upon the floor. She appeared determined to make the best of it. 'Look at this,' she said. It had a deep purple-red cover with ornate embossing. 'It was a favourite of ours – Ernest and me – before the war. Grieg. He was a Norwegian. I can't see any objection in *that*.'

When Frances returned sheepishly the next week, I could hear the triumph in Auntie's voice through the wall. Over the next few weeks I listened as Frances stumbled through the notes and began to pick up pace. I got to know the intricacies of every repeated phrase so that quite soon I was able to follow her, tapping out notes with my fingers on the kitchen table.

One day, Auntie called for me. 'Mavis?' her voice rang out. Instinctively I hid my hands. The door to the front room opened and shut. 'Mavis?' She appeared in the kitchen doorway. 'Come and listen,' she said. 'Come along, don't just sit there. Not a peep, mind,' she said.

Frances didn't turn a hair as I came in. Her back was poised as a stem, the music before her crammed with impressive flocks of notes. Auntie put me in her chair by the fire and raised a finger to her lips.

'Now, dear,' she said to Frances, 'imagine little Mavis is a rather important person come to listen. Tell us what you're about to play.'

'"Wedding Day at Troldhaugen",' Frances pronounced carefully.

'And the composer, dear?'

'Edvard Grieg.'

'Good,' Auntie said. 'Now, ignore us. Off you go.'

The minute she struck the piano keys, my whole body, even the chair, quivered. I pinched my fingers into the armrests. Though I'd heard it before through the walls, the immediacy of sound was a shock. It was the difference between looking

56

at a picture of something – a waterfall, for instance – and standing under the real thing: a bombardment that sluiced through every fibre of my being.

As Auntie rose in her chair to turn a page of the music, she was whispering, 'Now the fairies are coming,' putting a hand on Frances's shoulder, 'shh.' One fluid movement and she took her seat again. 'Now the wedding guests are flooding in . . .'

I could see it myself: a band marching and people dancing.

'Listen to the bell!' Auntie turned to me, raising her eyebrows in delight as Frances began to cross one hand over the other, plucking a single, lucid note.

When the playing finally stopped, Frances sank slightly in her seat. Auntie was beside herself with delight. 'Bravo, my dear.' She clasped her hands. The room swarmed; long after Frances had packed up and gone home, we sat listening to the strings in the back of the piano as they continued to shiver and strum.

When I first started at the school a year ago, Frances was one of the big girls; she was relied upon by Mrs Stubbs to keep us in order. In those days she had a single plait down to her waist, golden as the girl in 'Rumpelstiltskin'. She ruled us effortlessly. At Easter, Mrs Stubbs decided that Frances was quite capable enough to have sole charge of the Easter tableau: an annual event to which the vicar, the parish councillors and the mothers were invited, and whose preparations involved, as far as Mrs Stubbs was concerned, a vexing amount of mess and noise. And so, for the past two weeks during playtimes,

Frances had been corralling us into rehearsals; on the last couple of Friday afternoons she had been free to organize the manufacture of costumes and percussive instruments.

On the appointed day, Frances had been up before daybreak and had dressed herself in the chainmail from the trunk (knitted the previous year for her brother Robert – still asleep in bed – when he'd been the Lionheart). She crept over to the window and knelt down, looking out at the brightening sky. She prayed that all would be well, firing herself with the spirit of her heroine, with whom she believed she shared an unmediated line to God.

When Robert woke, he wouldn't be hurried. He sat in his nightshirt with his back to her, feet trailing over his side of the bed.

'Please,' she said. 'I want us to be early.'

'I'm not doing it,' he said.

She'd borrowed one of the crimson cassocks from the trunk in the sacristy and had laid it out for him on the chair.

'Dressing up's for young'uns,' he said. 'I'm not going.'

'But you have to go; and you're the main part,' she pleaded, 'the most important part. You're the baddy. You wanted to be the baddy.'

Robert kicked at the iron leg of the bedstead with his heel.

'Please,' she said.

After Easter, Robert was being sent away to school in West Buckland. '*You're* not the one who's got to stay at home,' she said.

It wasn't the first time she'd thrown this at him. He was sullen. She said dramatically, 'You won't have to do anything else for me, ever again.'

He scoffed. 'I'm coming back, you know. It's not for ever.'

She shuffled over to him on her knees. 'I'll give you something, if you do,' she said, 'something precious.'

'What?'

'Only if you agree.'

'What have you got that's precious?'

She knew she had him, that he was almost ready to cave in. She got to her feet. 'Wait a minute,' she said, and left the room. When she came back, he hadn't moved. She handed him their mother's sewing shears, handles first like a sword.

'You'll have to do it,' she said, kneeling down again at his feet, turning her head to him, offering the nape of her neck. 'Cut it off,' she said.


It was customary, if the weather was fair, to conduct the extended assembly outdoors in the schoolyard. Duly, Mr Bird had fetched the maypole from the shed. He'd set it up in the middle of the dirt patch, anchoring it with sandbags disguised with bundles of lightings borrowed from the wood store. Against the yard wall, he was in the process of arranging two rows of a dozen or so small wooden chairs to accommodate the audience.

We were hopping around by the stove, flapping our costumes, our shakers, practising our parts. Frances and Robert had come to school in their costumes. He was boot-faced, his fiery cheeks reflecting the red of his cassock. She had a string balaclava over her head with an oval opening that just contained her eyes, her nose and her mouth. There was a tabard across her breast with a green cross stitched to it and she had a red wooden sword in her hand. Her presence made us quieten down. She didn't smile once. 'Remember who I am?' she said.

'Saint Joan, Joan of Arc,' we replied in whispers.

At five to nine, she needed to be in place and ready. She took one of the older boys outside with her and stood against the maypole with her arms wrapped around her back. 'Tight,' she said. She submitted to two rounds of the skipping rope and three complicated sailor's knots.

By nine, most of the chairs were filled; the peasants in sacks, the soldiers in their cardboard armour began to file out. They were grimacing at their mothers shyly, poking each other. Frances had not anticipated how difficult it would be to choreograph proceedings from such a constrained position. Mrs Stubbs, who had sat herself in the middle of the front row, flanked by two councillors and the Reverend Manning and his wife, stood up and clapped her hands.

'I'm not going to say any more than is necessary but to welcome you all to our little Easter pageant, and – children – I think it's time to take your places?' She smiled stiffly at Frances as she returned to her seat.

The peasants jostled into a semi-circle behind the stake. Frances nodded vigorously towards the school porch. All eyes were turned as the scarlet Bishop emerged with a long, parchment-coloured paper. Robert had no intention of reading the speech she had so carefully prepared. Instead he handed it to one of the soldiers – who was horrified: he couldn't read big words! – and then produced from his cassock a box of Swan Vestas. He brought out a match and with a flourish began to strike the side of the box. When the spark took, Robert cradled the tiny flame, bearing it towards the boy soldier. The boy was transfixed by the turn of events and his part in them: he knew exactly what to do, dangling the paper to the tiny flame at arm's length. First the corner began to shrivel, then a vivid lick of yellow unfurled like a sail. Frances's eyes, wide and fierce, drank in the flame. Mrs Stubbs didn't hesitate. She set down her hymn book and marched over, took the soldier by his arm and shook until the paper drifted from his fingers in a basket of its own flames. As soon as it reached the ground she put her heavy black shoes to it, stamping every last scrap to ash. Then, with the boy still clamped to her, she stood facing Robert. He was already as tall as she was. It was easy to forget that he was only thirteen years old: he had the bearing of a man, a fact that occurred to Mrs Stubbs now with renewed force. She didn't meet his eye, but with as much authority as she could muster, and holding the other boy to her like a hostage, she asked Robert please to hand her the matches, to go and get changed.

Robert remained exactly where he was, the box held tantalizingly in the flat palm of his hand. Mrs Stubbs darted forward and snatched it from him, retreating a step or two before depositing it into her coat pocket, out of sight. Without moving from his spot, and keeping his eyes fixed on her throughout, Robert stooped to undo the buttons of his cassock, working up from his shins to the neck. When he was upright again, he shrugged the garment off, and as it lay in a red pool at his feet, he stepped over it. He was wearing hob-nailed boots, a heavy old silk shirt and a pair of his father's trousers and braces. He blinked at her as if it were the final cutting of a cord, and then he turned, sauntered straight past the assembled company and out of the school gate, never once turning back.

Suddenly, before anyone had a chance to react, a terrible squawking sounded from the porch. The youngest of us were the fire fairies. We were led out by two recorder players, nodding their heads in time to the only tune they knew: *London's burning, London's burning, Fetch the engines, Fetch the engines, Fire, Fire! Fire, Fire!* We danced along behind, rattling our rice- and pea-filled tins, shaking our brightly coloured scarves and streamers – reds and oranges and yellows.

Tom Upcott, who never did what anyone said, set his bullet head firmly in the opposite direction to the rest of us and began to run. The girls started to squeal and scatter. Joyce, who thanked her stars that Victor with his chickenpox had been confined indoors, rose to her feet. The time had come, she decided, for a hymn. In an indeterminate key, but with great conviction, she began singing, *Onward Christian Soldiers . . .* The Reverend could not resist. He stood up and joined her, unleashing his deep baritone, *with the cross of Jesus, going on before,* which, in turn, raised his wife, the councillors, the mothers from their seats, one by one. Mrs Stubbs warbled anxiously, glancing sideways at the Reverend's face. *Forward into Baa-tle, See his banners go!* By the chorus, everyone but Frances was singing. It had turned out – as the Reverend would put it later in his sermon – to be 'an occasion both educational and colourful'.

But that was no comfort to Frances now. She hung her head. All she could hear – though he must be halfway home by now – was the steady diminuendo of Robert's boots.

After a hasty blessing, everyone dispersed; the children were ushered inside and told to sit in their places and wait in silence while Mrs Stubbs went out with the scissors to release Frances Upcott from her bonds.

'Whoever tied these knots?' she asked, using one of the blades as a saw.

'I'm sorry,' Frances said.

As soon as her hands were free, Frances pulled off the terrible, itching balaclava.

'Oh Frances,' Mrs Stubbs said, horrified, 'your hair!'

Frances had forgotten what she'd done. She reached and touched the back of her neck: feathery tufts. She drew herself up. No matter. The time for dressing up had passed. Robert was leaving. Nothing could disguise that. In her head she'd already begun to bundle up the other costumes from the bedroom – the Tudor gown, the purple slippers, the Bo-Peep cap, the angel's gown – and stuffed them into a haysack, chucked them down in the cellar to rot.

The plait that had been Joan of Arc's, though, and which she'd secured at either end, carefully, with two elastic bands, she would give as promised to Robert. She had the exact piece of linen in mind from which she'd make a small square pillow to hold it in, embroidered in a bright green thread with the words: *Abide Now at Home* Chronicles 25:1 – so that he would have something to take away to school with him, to remind him he had to come back.

# 5

## *Club Day, 2006*

'Do you think it'll rain?' I asked, indecisive, holding up my mac. It was May Day, and nine times out of ten, it would.

Eve was standing in the porch, framed against the grey sky. She shrugged. 'Who can tell?'

Out on the Green, stretching their legs, were various members of the Buckleigh Silver Band. They'd left their black instrument cases stashed under the archway next to Eve's. Outside the pub there were little gangs of men, incongruous in their best suits, standing in twos or threes, catching up over a smoke. Club Day brings them out of the woodwork. From the village itself, there were three generations of Knights; Alf was out in his wheelchair and next to him Mr Bird, the old church warden, hunched over his Zimmer frame, determined, at the grand age of ninety-eight, to complete the full circuit of the march unaided. It always struck me how handsomely dressed the old boys were compared to the young ones, their suits from an era when suits were decently made, the black flannel of their trousers immaculately pressed. I'm sure some of the youngsters didn't even own a proper suit. Some of them appeared to be wearing the same black nylon trousers Archie wore for school.

Half the WI were hard at work in the pub kitchen, making the three huge vats of mash, the two gallons of gravy. Me and Eve had been assigned to help set up in the village hall where, as we arrived, it was clear that preparations were fully underway. It was a well-rehearsed routine. The trestle tables had been pushed together into two long lines, the tablecloths laid out, and Joyce's daughter Sandy was busily folding a set of napkins — a little pink cocktail boat at the side of each plate. Half the cutlery was on loan from Buckleigh primary school and Joyce was in a panic over it, working down the line, prising off spots of dried food with a fingernail, polishing with a damp cloth.

Joyce put us with Dorothy at the back of the kitchen, cutting and arranging semi-circular slabs of ham, buttering rolls. The Shipleigh Friendly Society was almost a hundred and fifty years old, Dorothy told Eve. It was a subject in which she felt confident. Members of the Society had to be proposed and seconded for election, she said. They had to turn up once a year in their black and yellow ties. 'The Society was used for the farm workers originally,' she explained, 'to pay for their coffins. But there're all sorts in there now: electrics, bus drivers, thatchers . . .'

'My father was a member one time,' I said, to illustrate the point.

'What did he do?' Eve asked.

'He was in publishing,' I said.

Eve was being much too generous with the butter, which had softened in the heat. When she held up her knife, a glob fell to the counter.

'Was it always like this?' she asked. 'The women doing everything? No women in the club?'

'Did you hear her?' Dorothy said, delighted by the question.

'Don't you mind?' Eve said.

'Gives the impression they's in charge,' Joyce said briskly, catching the tail end of our conversation. 'Once a year – don't hurt.' Her breathing was laboured though she ignored it. She steadied herself against the counter and stuck out her lower lip, blew the hair back from her forehead, then she inspected her wristwatch.

'Why don't you go and watch the parade?' she said. 'We're pretty much done here. Shame to miss it. Go on, Mavis, you take her along. They'll be out dreckly.'


The Buckleigh Band had been playing for Club Day ever since the end of the war. They were always first out of the church, falling into formation, warming up their mouthpieces. There was a fine mizzle of moisture in the air when they finally struck up: the *thud, thud, thud* of the bass drum and then, with a communal intake of breath, the joyful release of 'When the Saints Go Marching In'.

'Doesn't it lift your spirits?' I asked Eve, but she wasn't paying attention. She'd begun to glance about anxiously.

'I wonder where Archie is?' she said.

It was impossible to move until the band had paraded past us. There was a silver lick across the peaks of their caps and

66

along the yokes of their shoulders, twenty-two synchronized pairs of bellows, followed in turn by the stately crocodile of the club members, led by Alf in his chair. Alf supported one end of a great banner that read – SHIPLEIGH FRIENDLY SOCIETY: *Bear Ye One Another's Burdens* – and Michael Knight, the other. Slowly but surely the procession advanced up the steep slope, banner aloft, towards the Seven Stars.

'I wonder where he's got to?' Eve said.

Two lads had broken ranks to run to the front and take photographs with their mobile phones. Bringing up the rear was a gaggle of the newly enrolled, hair stuck up like barbed wire. Some were wearing bashed-up white trainers. They passed by with the distinctive reek I associate with men and toilet blocks.

'Perhaps he's down in the field,' she said. 'Do you mind if I go and have a look?'

The damp had formed a dewy net over my hair. I raised my hand to it.

'Don't come. You'll catch your death,' Eve said.

'Nonsense,' I said, 'it isn't cold,' though, as soon as we were on our way, it began to rain more resolutely.

A man from chapel was set up with his maroon hatchback at the entrance to the playing field. He had sweets and fizzy drinks and a huddle of children were already gathered under the raised lid of his car boot.

'Do you know Archie?' Eve asked them. The rain had turned their hair the colour of dirty hay. One boy smirked behind his hand.

Eve's cheeks flushed. I touched her arm and pointed to where Owen Knight was grimly measuring out a strip of land for throwing wellies. Archie was tagging behind him in a T-shirt, shoulders hunched.

Eve half-ran towards them calling and waving. 'Archie!'

Resolutely, Archie ignored her.

I watched her catch up with them. Owen Knight must be forty-odd years himself now, though I couldn't help seeing him as a boy. He was as skinny as he ever was, and as shy. The three of them were walking back towards me. Eve had her arm around Archie though he twisted from under her.

'Not a brilliant day for it,' Owen said to me in greeting, looking with exaggerated glumness at the sky.

'Do you want to stay?' Eve asked Archie. 'Will you be all right?'

Archie glared.

Owen said, 'I'll drop him off when we've finished, if you like? Won't be long, by the looks of it.'

'Thanks,' Eve said. The other children had begun to straggle down, sucking and chewing disconsolately. 'Sure you'll be OK?' she asked Archie again.

As we walked back up to the hall, Eve said, 'It's *Owen*, is it?'

'Yes,' I said, 'Michael's boy.'

'He's very patient with Archie – letting him help out. I hope he's not a nuisance – Archie, I mean?'

As soon as we entered the hall again my glasses steamed up. The air was hot and claggy. The young lads who'd been put closest to the exit were revved up, flicking bits of bread at each other; one of them had bought an additional supply of home-brewed cider and was now openly doling it out. The contingent from chapel were seated at the furthest remove, nearest the kitchen. Although they weren't drinking, they were traditionally first to be offered seconds of puddings, which they accepted with gusto, piling their bowls with an indiscriminate mixture of whatever was left: trifle, meringue, lemon cheesecake, strawberry blancmange, chocolate custard with hundreds and thousands.

The women were busy at the back end of the kitchen; they had already started on the washing-up, elbow-deep in the two sinks. Joyce's daughter Sandy and Sandy's youngest, Linda, were standing in formation with dishcloths for drying.

'Shame about the weather,' Joyce said. 'Ferret man's rung and cancelled. Morris men'll not come out in this.'

I began making piles of plates ready for the crockery cupboard; Eve was given the job of sorting the cutlery, separating the school knives and forks from the set that belonged in the hall.

'Alf looks as if he's had a good time,' I said to cheer Joyce up. He was sitting rhubarb-faced, nodding off into space.


By four o'clock, most of the men had staggered off to the pub. The place was deserted.

'They made a good job of it,' Joyce said, sighing, contemplating the white dog-ends of rolls, the crazy tangles of napkin.

Dorothy had taken Eve's elbow and wandered off with her towards the fireplace. She was pointing up at the framed photograph above the mantelpiece. 'We're all of us in there,' she said, 'if you look.'

It was a picture of the whole village in 1962, the day the hall was formally handed over by the colonel whose family had owned it originally and established it as the school house. The few children left in the village were bussed down to the primary in Buckleigh, where Archie went now. Joyce, who had driven everything, was centre stage, wearing a splotchy dress and matching jacket, a hat that was cut into the white petals of a lily.

'Three hundred and eighteen pounds, the building cost us,' Joyce said. 'You'll never imagine the bric-a-brac, the sponsored what's-its went into that.'

In the photograph Alf was standing proudly next to her in high-waisted trousers, his moustache catching the light so that it looked as if someone had ripped a strip from under his nose.

Suddenly Joyce bustled over, struck by an idea. 'I daresay your mother'll be in there somewhere, Eve.' She wanted to be the first to point her out, screwing up her eyes along the rows of faces.

'There she is!' she said triumphantly. 'See her there? Dark hair – that's your mother. I'm sure it is.'

'That's her, it is,' Dorothy corroborated, 'next to Tom Upcott. Grin on him he had!'

'Lovely-looking girl,' Joyce said. 'She sang that evening, didn't she? We had a wonderful time, do you remember, Mavis?'

Although the face was smeary, the eyes downcast, you could see it was Beatrice. Her long neck, the way she held herself. And Tom, bold as brass, as if he wanted everyone else to vanish.

'I'd forgotten that photograph,' Joyce was saying, 'right under our noses. I'd plain forgot she'd have been in that.'

'And the Reverend,' Dorothy said, pointing to Reverend Manning, who was standing at a remove, with his RAF back-and-sides and his dog collar. 'See him?'

'Grandpa!' Eve said. Her cheeks were flushed, she was squeezing the thumb of her right hand. She turned to me. 'Are you there?' she asked.

'Somewhere, I suppose,' I said.

'There she is,' Joyce said.

I was two or three places away from Frances. I remember the dress, with its wide skirt and collar, the weight of two plaited buns around my ears.

'Pretty,' Eve said.

'Not in those glasses,' I said.

'Don't be silly,' Joyce said. 'Don't listen to her. And there's Sandy, look, bit of a sulky teenager in those days . . .'

'I was not, Mother! I was married by then!' Sandy said.

'Lovely dresses,' Eve said.

'Where does it all go? Seems like yesterday, don't it?' Joyce said, gathering the pile of sodden dishcloths ready to put through the machine at home.

# 6

## *Beatrice, 1943*

I never told Eve what Frances Upcott had told me about her mother. It was second-hand and it wasn't particularly nice.

Beatrice Manning was an only child; she arrived when the Reverend and his wife, Eunice, were into their late forties. It had been an embarrassment to Eunice when she was first married not to have had children, but now she'd reached an age where it seemed even more embarrassing to have been caught out. For the last month or so before she was delivered she rarely ventured from the house. She had never imagined the prolonged physicality of pregnancy, how ridiculous she would be made to appear in front of the whole congregation. The Reverend agreed to give her communion on Sunday evenings, alone in the drawing room.

Eunice hoped it would be easier once the baby arrived. She decided that the best way forward was to accept the consensus: that the child was a blessing sent from God. Once the clucking and the fuss had died down, it became a matter of amusement and then mild irritation to the other ladies in the WI the way Eunice managed to extol her own baby's virtues to the detriment of all others. What they failed to notice was how terrified Eunice was. Scared at first of breaking the child, scared of waking up to find her stretched out cold, scared most of all that she would be unmasked as the unworthy mother she believed in her bones she was. She had no instinct for it, which made her the opposite of neglectful: she slept hardly a wink for the first year, losing whatever looks had been hers to lose – her eyes sunk into their sockets, her hair almost totally white.

For the first three years Eunice didn't let Beatrice out of her sight. Joyce's sister, Margaret Knight, came up from the village to cook and clean and would mind the child if Eunice was about the house, but Eunice would never leave anyone in sole charge. It was becoming increasingly difficult to manage. Even the Reverend, who was a relatively doting father, was growing impatient. Certain duties were required of vicars' wives. If he were ever to have a chance of preferment, they'd need to show their faces together at least a couple of times a year in Exeter.

The invitation was to lunch at the Chapter House, with the Bishop. He was going to have to insist. It would only be a few hours.

Frances Upcott, for instance, he urged his wife: she sang in the choir, she had proven herself quite capable of leading the whole Sunday school. Eunice herself must have seen how well she managed her young brother? She could come up to the house – Beatrice would hardly notice; it could easily be arranged.

By the time Frances turned up, Eunice was already in a state. She was pale and shrill explaining about the macaroni cheese: to be sure to blow upon it spoon by spoon before serving it up.

'And you haven't a cold?' she asked sharply.

'We've discussed how capable Frances is,' the Reverend said, cloaking his wife from behind in her navy dress-coat, shepherding her to the front door.

'And you'll telephone, if you need to, won't you?' Eunice insisted over her shoulder. 'Don't be afraid to. The number's on the pad on the table. No one will mind. Be sure to ring the number.'

There was silence when they'd gone, relief. Frances turned to Beatrice, spick and span in a tartan dress with a blue velvet collar, who'd quite happily waved her parents off, in spite of her mother's feeble effort to hide her tears and the handkerchief thrust out of the window as the car took off.

'Well,' Frances asked, 'what shall we do?'

'Mummy says we can play outside,' Beatrice replied immediately.

Frances was used to children. 'We'll stay indoors for a bit, shall we? We don't want to get mucky. How about a story? Do you know about the loaves and the fishes? Did you know that Jesus was a fisherman?'

'Jesus is the son of God,' Beatrice corrected her.

Frances had brought with her a book she'd read avidly as a child, *One Hundred Bible Stories for Girls*.

'Shall I read you a story?'

'Can we have the shepherds and the three wise men?' Beatrice had spotted them on the cover.

74

Although it was the wrong time of year and went against her better instincts, Frances agreed to start with the Nativity. But after a while, she was aware, hearing the oddly clipped sound of her own voice, that Beatrice wasn't listening. She wasn't looking at the pictures any longer, but up, at Frances's face.

'Where's your tooth?' she asked.

Frances was self-conscious about the gap on the top side of her mouth, which, she'd gone to some lengths to establish in the parlour mirror, was only perceptible if she smiled broadly, not something she made a habit of.

'It was a bad one. It had to come out,' Frances said.

'Does it hurt?'

'No,' Frances said. 'Not any more.'

'I can bite heads off.' Beatrice demonstrated as if she were holding a carrot in her fist. 'Mouse's heads.'

'Mice,' Frances corrected her. 'I'm sure you don't eat mice.'

'I do.'

'I don't suppose they taste very nice.'

'They taste of sweeties.'

'Sugar mice?'

'No. *Mouse.*'

'Are you hungry?'

They headed downstairs to the kitchen and after they'd eaten – one for Frances, one for Beatrice, one on a saucer for her toy lamb – Frances washed their things up, put the dishes away as well as she could. She decided that they'd stay down there: it was warm by the Aga. She drew the armchair over and let Beatrice climb up on to her knee.

'Tell me a story,' she said.

'We've left the book upstairs,' Frances said, reluctant to go and get it.

'A story about when you were little.'

Frances tried to think. 'I'll tell you a story about my brother, if you like?'

She began to tell Beatrice about the time Tom had blacked his face. Beatrice had quietened down. It was a well-worn story, easy to tell. 'He looked like a chimney sweep,' Frances said.

'Did he go up the chimney?'

'No. He didn't. I told you, he painted his own face like that. He looked just like a golliwog.'

Beatrice was stroking Frances's bare forearm as she listened, which at first Frances took to be a sign that the child was getting sleepy; so she persevered. But instead of falling asleep, Beatrice only continued to stroke more insistently, almost ardently. It was the strangest feeling, making her shudder to recall it.

'Would you like something to drink?' Frances asked, withdrawing her arm.

Beatrice smiled, her tiny teeth perfect as Snow White's. With no urgency at all she said, 'I need a wee-wee.'

Frances shifted Beatrice aside. 'Where's the potty?' she asked, getting to her feet.

'Upstairs,' Beatrice said. She wriggled down from the chair. 'I know: I'll be the mummy, you be the little girl.'

Beatrice clambered up the narrow back stairs into the hall, then stood waiting at the foot of the main staircase, her arm hugged around the newel post. As Frances caught up with her, Beatrice was intent. She stood very still, then she lifted

76

her foot. A trickle of pale liquid ran down her plump shin towards her sock. She lifted her foot a little further, pointed it sideways like a ballet dancer. A drip fattened on her thigh and, in a succession of delicate droplets, splashed to the parquet floor. Frances scooped her into her arms. 'Quickly, where's the lavatory?' she said. 'Tell me, now, before we both get wet.'

Beatrice sank between her arms as if in a hammock; she was heavier than she looked and it was awkward carrying her upwards, negotiating the unfamiliar staircase. 'Is it up here?' Frances asked breathlessly. When they reached the landing, she set Beatrice down. 'Off you go, quickly. Show me.'

Beatrice refused to be rushed. As she wandered off Frances glanced down at her summer dress. There was a damp patch across her abdomen. She pulled the material away from her petticoat, holding it there as she followed Beatrice along the corridor. The child was walking a tightrope along the edge of the runner, taking her time. Then she tottered and stopped outside a door.

'This one?' Frances turned the handle and pushed the door open.

There were twin beds inside, as far apart as it was possible to be, thick maroon counterpanes, the damp incense-smell of church. Frances paused. The dressing table between the beds, with its large, heart-shaped bevelled mirror caught them in a trap. Beatrice was looking up at Frances's reflection in the same artful way she'd sometimes catch her mother, sitting there, her straggly hair around her shoulders, the monogrammed hairbrush in her hand, her wan, weak smile.

'This must be Mummy's room,' Frances said, 'but where's the lavatory?'

'*I'm* the mummy,' Beatrice reminded her.

'Is there a lavatory up here at all?' Frances asked, exasperated.

Beatrice had hopped on to one foot. She squealed delightedly, 'It's coming out, it's coming out,' as if it were a mouse.

'Mummy will be cross when I tell her. You're not a baby any more, are you?'

Frances didn't want to have to lift her up again. She didn't want to touch her.

'If you want to be wet,' she said impatiently, 'if you want to be dirty, you can stay like that. It doesn't matter to me.'

'I'm the mummy,' Beatrice said belligerently, and then she said it again, 'I'm the mummy,' but this time her chin was wobbling.

'You're not,' Frances said. '*I'm* looking after *you.*'

'Go away,' Beatrice said. She sat down on the spot with her knees and elbows pointing outwards. 'I don't want you. Go away from my house.'

Frances struggled to control herself. And then she panicked: she couldn't be found like this, at cross-purposes with the wet child . . . and there was something awkward about being upstairs: it was too quiet.

'Don't you want to find some nice, clean clothes?' she asked.

'Go away,' Beatrice said.

'I can't go away,' Frances said, 'can I? I'm looking after you until Mummy gets home.'

Beatrice was unresponsive.

'Come downstairs. We'll find some hot milk, shall we? Some honey maybe to put in it, if you're good. For a little bee. It's a special recipe for good girls, if you come now, with me. Come on.' Frances began backing away from the child towards the stairs, holding her hand out all the way.

Eventually, painfully slowly, Beatrice lifted herself to her feet; she began to tightrope back along the edge of the carpet, keeping a determined distance from Frances. It took them twenty minutes like this to get down the stairs.

'Come and warm up by the stove,' Frances said, her voice worn out, 'on your special stool. Let me fetch you some milk.'

When at last they heard the crunch of the car and Mrs Manning at the front door, calling out and then rushing down the stairs to find them in the kitchen, Beatrice leapt up from her stool and threw herself into her mother's arms. Eunice was taken aback by such a show of affection. Then she exclaimed, looking over Beatrice's shoulder, 'She's wet!' She couldn't disguise the accusation in her voice.

'I'm sorry,' Frances said, trying to explain, 'She wouldn't let me take them off her, and I wasn't sure where to find clean ones. I tried upstairs.'

'Upstairs?' Mrs Manning asked, surprised.

Mrs Manning couldn't trust anyone. She couldn't even trust herself. 'Has she been crying all this time?' she asked, on the verge of tears herself.

'No. Not at all. We've had a nice time, haven't we? We've been reading a book.' Frances held up the *Hundred Bible Stories*.

'She's young to be left. I knew she was. Bea, dear, don't be upset.'

Frances was exhausted.

'I'm not blaming you,' Eunice said and then, turning to Beatrice, 'Be a good girl, dear, and say thank you to Miss Upcott, to Frances. It was kind of her, wasn't it, to come and sit with you?'

Beatrice had shut her eyes. She took a deep stuttering breath and held it, until between them, hastily, her mother and Frances agreed that Frances would show herself out.

# 7

## *Tom, 1943*

I didn't see Eve all that often. Truthfully, I preferred it when Archie came on his own. We could be much freer in our conversation. I wonder if it was as simple as the fact that he reminded me of Tom at that age, or that he reminded me of myself, then? In any case, Archie actively encouraged me to dredge up those stories, particularly the ones about Tom, who was fearless, and did exactly the things that Archie – who appeared to be warming to the possibilities of the countryside – decided he might like to do himself.

Auntie, I'd told him, was content for me to spend whole days away from the house. I was happiest on my own, collecting bunches of flowers, paddling in ditches and streams, finding new ways in and out of the woods. I got to know the shapes of all the fields – the harp, the kite, the hind leg, the sheep's skull – and the names of all the farms: Redlands, Eastcott, Woodleigh, Passaford.

Passaford was where the Upcotts lived; generally it marked

the extremity of my expeditions from the village, about three miles away, off the road to Buckleigh. I never went into the farms, not on my own: I was scared of the dogs. But the buildings were useful landmarks and the knowledge that there would be people I could go to if the worst came to the worst.

It was the day I ventured beyond the entrance to Passaford that I discovered the cross, set above the lane on a mound, man-sized. The two stubby arms were tilted to where the track narrowed and dipped out of sight. I took it for a sign, as if they were urging me on, and obediently I followed the path, veering steeply, as far as it would go. At the bottom, I was in a dank grotto, overhung with foliage, the way ahead chained off. To the left there was a five-bar gate, overgrown with nettles. As it appeared to be the only way out, I braved the nettles, trod them down, and clambered over. On the other side, it felt like I was in a different country – a bright, flat meadow powdered with buttercups. I was so dazzled that at first I didn't notice the hulks of cows, sheltering under the trees at the far edge of the field. Nothing was ever straightforward: every foray into the countryside was a test of my mettle; and every little decision – like the way I'd negotiate a field of beasts – felt as if someone was always there, watching and assessing me. I kept close to the fence, hugging it until I reached a small picket gate, which, hastily, I let myself through.

I heard the water before I reached it, flowing and toppling as if a tap had been left on. The grass was a screen, tall as I was and it was only after I'd beaten a short corridor through that I found myself looking out across the wide brown ribbon of water. Under my feet, the stones rocked. The surface was smooth as a newsreel, reporting every flicker of life from above and below. I made my way along the bank, mesmerized, stopping only to unhook myself from twigs and brambles along the way. A pair of jittery dragonflies hovered, tying knots between them, in and out. As I followed their progress round, the surface of the water began to distort, the noise to intensify. The river appeared to divide into two like the prongs of a 'Y', and I found myself now, turning away from the main drag along a subsidiary stream. I kept going, idly, because there was no reason to turn back. But I hadn't gone much further when I glimpsed something khaki-coloured caught in a bush. I had been nervous before, but not frightened; now my scalp prickled all over. There was a button, an opening, a pocket, inside-out, like a tongue: it was a pair of shorts hanging. I caught a flash of movement and I fell to my knees, heart pounding. It took a while to focus my eyes, looking through my fingers towards a pebbly outcrop. I held my breath. Whoever it was had his back to me, a knobbled, skinny spine, the sharp hairline at the base of a neck. It was a boy, squatting, working systematically, examining a patch of ground before frog-jumping sideways to the next.

I don't know how long I sat there watching, locked-in, but at some point there was a violent movement just below me, a dash of water – a duck, struggling to separate itself. The boy twisted round. My mouth drained. *What if he saw me?* At that same instant, as if I'd willed it on myself, he rose to his feet, to his full height, and I dropped clumsily back on my heels. He lifted his head, squinting, listening. Then he put his hand to his forehead, shielding his eyes. He was naked as a water baby: I saw the outline handles of his pink ears, the bullet hole of his belly button, and what was below, a rag-end knot of skin.

'Oi,' he called.

There was no doubt who it was. Tom Upcott. I lifted my head very slowly. He didn't bother that he had no clothes on, jiggling a pebble from one hand to the other.

'Be *my* river, this,' he said. 'How long've you bin there?'

He had a confidence that outstripped his nakedness. It made me feel hot and overdressed. As I got to my feet, the blood rushed to my head. He'd already turned away, his arm sprung back. A full stop stamped spontaneously in rings on the water – once, twice, three times, four. He didn't seem to mind me watching, bending to consider another stone, drawing himself back again like a bow and imprinting another sequence across the surface, plip, plip, plip.

After a while he shouted, 'Bin't you hot?'

'No,' I said quickly, 'I'm not.' But my face was burning and my vest damp.

'You'm go for a swim,' he said, 'if 'ee take that lot off.'

'Can't,' I replied in a panic.

'Swim?'

'No,' I said.

He began to move jerkily, his wet toes making animal tracks, his pointy shoulder blades drawn up, heading straight for the brown, stony water. *Whoosh*. He shrieked as he bounded forwards, sucking in his stomach to a ledge. His body disappeared, his face lit against the tinfoil of water, hair spiky with light. Then he ducked completely like a stone, rings expanding where he'd gone.

I could just make out the dull stripes of his body, wobbly,

half-formed, then the fist of his head bursting out of a drum. He bared his teeth, two neat rows, as he whipped the water with his hands, scattering a shower of shale. Then he disappeared again, a necklace of bubbles.

When he got out, he bent his head and shook it so that the colours cascaded off him like glass beads.

'What you looking at?' he asked suddenly.

He began to cup his hands about himself as if he were melting. For a moment I thought my only option was to jump into the river and sink. He made a tiny movement towards me and I panicked, stumbling back through the scrub, with no thought now for the thorns scratching at my arms and legs. My throat was burning. When I got to the field, I ran before the cows had a chance to lift their heads, the thought of him pursuing me playing over and over like a cartoon, the daggers of his eyes, the scythes of his multiple legs.


I hadn't seen either of my parents properly for years. Mother wouldn't contemplate the journey down again; Daddy had dropped in once or twice, in passing, on his way down to a printer's in St Ives. Nevertheless, I kept a picture gallery for them in my head: Mother, in her three-way mirror, dabbing perfume on her wrists, lifting the sparkly sherry glass – '*Courage!*' – the beautiful pink caterpillar-print of her lips around the rim; Daddy and a game of elephant leg, me on the pedal of his foot, clinging as he dragged me over the Turkey carpet in a walk like Captain Hook, breathing the fusty smell of his trouser. If I imagined them together, it was in the cage of a lift: two pairs of eyes coming up or going down, hat rims emerging or shoe-leathers sinking behind an iron trellis.

This time, Daddy booked himself in at the Seven Stars, not wanting to put Auntie out, he said. He had decided to make a break of it and come down for several days. It had been a damned difficult journey, the trains half-cock, no suspension in the hearse that had picked him up from the station, so that by the time he arrived he felt, he said, half dead.

I was beside myself: all this, for me. I found him lying on the bed in the rose room, *The Times* spread over his face.

'Daddy!'

He bashed at the paper as if it were a great moth, sat up, his hair a little awry and said, 'Afternoon, old girl – long time, no see.'

He waited until we got to Auntie's to hand over the box set *Evening in Paris* for her and *First Term at Barton Heights* for me. After we'd put our presents aside, I sat next to him on the edge of the drop-arm sofa eating hash sandwiches, while Auntie jabbed the fire with the heraldic poker.

'She remembers you, doesn't she?' Auntie said fondly as Peggy snuffled at Daddy's trouser leg.

'Funny old thing,' he said, letting the dog jump up between us.

'She likes you, Fletcher – doesn't she, Mavis?'

Peggy had settled down, rough as a doormat. She was impossible to throw off, her eyelids flickering.

'You still play?' Daddy asked, looking uncomfortable, nodding to the piano.

Auntie held up her hands, her little fingers crooked with arthritis.

86

Daddy didn't like illness. 'Still teaching?' he asked a little more loudly.

When Daddy raised his voice, the strings inside the piano strummed sympathetically and Peg began to growl softly.

'Frances Upcott plays the piano,' I said. 'She's *splendid* at it.'

Frances Upcott was Auntie's only remaining pupil. The others had dropped off one by one, the lessons, a luxury that, at any price, few could afford. Frances was the only one of them whom Auntie would contemplate teaching for nothing.

'What about you, Mavis? Haven't you taken advantage of your Auntie's expertise?'

Auntie had tried to teach me once or twice, but got too impatient. I couldn't keep the notes in my head. It confused me, Every Good Boy Deserves Favour.

'Fletcher, dear, do turn her off! Have another sandwich. Don't let them go to waste.'

As Daddy leaned forward, Peg grumbled again then sluggishly got to her feet. She yawned, trembled, gingerly contemplated the edge of the sofa, then dived nose first to the hearthrug, and padded, tail half extended, to sniff Auntie's shoes.

I didn't want to draw attention to it, but there was a nasty smell of fish paste and where Peggy had got up, a slug of something not quite solid coiled on Daddy's knee.

I showed Daddy the part of the churchyard I still secretly regarded as my own, leading him up over the shoulder of rougher grass to the north wall. It was the highest spot in the village, the valley below sweeping out and around like a huge glazed bowl.

'Splendid view,' he agreed.

I took pleasure in reciting for him the names on the grave-stones. I knew exactly where Amelia, Henry, Robert, Herbert, Eleanor, John and Henrietta Elizabeth Upcott lay and in what order they'd been interred. I pointed out the anchor and the green chippings.

But already he was distracted. He was peering at an ancient stone that was half-toppled forwards. He called me over.

'Look at that,' he said. There were three distinct varieties of lichen – an acid yellow, a pea-like colour and a darker, scabby green – so prevalent that only the fat horseshoe of the 'U' was decipherable.

'They're all Upcotts,' I told him.

'Remarkable sort of family,' Daddy said, 'goes back as far as that.'

I was pleased at how readily Daddy took up my interest. 'It's Frances that Auntie gives lessons to,' I told him. 'Tom Upcott's her brother, he's at my school.' I took him into the church and showed him the pew at the front, under the lectern, the Upcott pew. Above it there was a marble plaque in memory of Amelia Grayling Upcott 1710–1773 and Henry Alfred Fisher Upcott 1704–1775. And to the right of it, the list of who'd died in the Great War, including Henry and his brother Thomas John Upcott.

'You're quite the expert,' Daddy said.

The London boys were rude about my father. They asked me what he was doing in the war. He wasn't a soldier and he wasn't a farmer. He was most probably a spy. Working for the

Krauts. Like Miss Blumstein, whose sheets, to stop her signalling, they'd robbed from the line, dragging them through the mud.

'It's secret,' I said unconvincingly.

They were more appreciative of Daddy at the Seven Stars. Mr and Mrs McManus had taken over the pub; they'd come down from London after the Blitz. Mr McManus had bad lungs. He had pink blistery skin with the beginnings of a beard and in those days I only ever saw him, like a bust, mounted on his side of the bar. Daddy called him 'the wretched Scot'; but Mrs McManus was a different kettle of fish, and the feeling appeared to be mutual.

'Diana,' she said, extending her hand.

'Ah,' Daddy said, 'the huntress.'

And then they discovered they had a friend in common. 'Never!' Diana shrieked, 'Vivien Rhys-Morgan? Epsom Downs?' – whose name was henceforth brandished like a key.

'*Such* a small world,' Diana kept saying. 'Can't wait to tell Viv.'

On Sunday, Auntie and I collected Daddy on our way to church. I tugged Daddy's sleeve to point out the Upcotts. At the end of the service, while Auntie set off home, we waited at the lych gate for everyone to file by, Daddy tipping his hat to all the ladies. When the Upcotts appeared, last out, Daddy sprang forward,

'We've not met,' he said, extending his hand. 'Gaunt. Fletcher Gaunt.' Daddy prided himself on his knack with all kinds of people. 'Hope the weather holds.'

Mr Upcott was a tight, wiry man with a face like hessian. He slowly raised his palm. His three children trailed along behind him, Robert, Frances and Tom. I didn't know where to look. Frances always made me shy, and the last time I'd seen Tom, he had been naked.

Daddy was saying, 'Been a while since I've been out on a farm. Smell of the hay, that sort of thing.'

Robert and his father shared the same hawkish nose, the same wary eyes. But where Robert's lips remained tight shut, Mr Upcott made noises, adjusted his brown trilby. Daddy lifted his hat in response, 'S'll be pleased to take you up on that, one day.'

Mr Upcott had already moved off, down towards the forge, where the horses and cart were tied up. As the others trouped after him, Daddy raised his stick. Then he turned to me, 'We shall *have* to visit, sometime,' he said. 'What? Mavis?'

'Where's Fletcher got to?' Auntie asked as I caught up with her. The cottage exhaled, as it always did, the scent of tea caddy and stale dog.

'He's going for a lie-down,' I said.

'Lie-down? This time of day? He must be getting old!'

Daddy was restless, his gout was playing up. *Crikey! What's a chap supposed to do round here for a bit of peace!* I didn't want to let him forget about our visit and pestered him the next morning and the next.

'I know the way,' I said, reassuring him.

'All right, all right.'

Joyce let him have a knapsack of Alf's, into which she'd packed us sandwiches and a map. We were going to make an expedition of it and set off energetically as if we might be out all day. I found it hard to contain myself, skipping downhill ahead of him.

'Steady on,' he said, catching me up, his top lip already sweating.

On the flat we established an easier pace. The air was honey, shimmering ahead of us. The hedgerows, the fields, everything brimming to show how beautiful the place was.

'It's the *Wizard of Oz*,' I said.

'What does that make me?' he asked. 'The lion? Or the scarecrow?'

'The wizard,' I said without hesitation.

'Are you buttering me up?' he asked. Then suddenly enthusiastic, he said, 'Ever thought about a little brother or a sister?'

'I love babies,' I said, thinking of Sandy and of the wooden doll Auntie let me play with.

Daddy was in an unusually good mood. 'Splendid,' he said, every now and again springing his cane on to the road. 'What d'you say, we get a little farm, eh? You can come along and milk the goats. How 'bout that, eh? Think you could manage?'

The sky was almost translucent, a pale turquoise. There was a flock of tiny birds rotating. I had taken his hand; I skipped as high as I could.

'Good strong hands, you've got,' he said, giving my hand a squeeze and then letting it drop.

At every gateway in the narrow lane, Daddy had a rest. I'd climb up on to the gate until I was taller than he was, balancing, opening my arms to the multiplying fields. It was like bursting out of a long drain into the open sea.

'Come on,' Daddy said, 'jump down.'

At the entrance to the farm there was a platform tucked back into the hedge and three or four tall milk churns. As

91

soon as we stepped beyond the gate, a furious barking set up. Daddy swished his stick and crooked it under his arm.

'Hope they're around,' Daddy said nervously. 'I'm parched.'

We followed the track, past the huge dun screen of a barn. Close up, you could see the holes under the eaves, spatters of white where birds were nesting. Around the corner, two shaggy tan and cream dogs came padding, tails half extended, lugs of mud dangling from their bellies. One and then the other lifted its chin and began to snarl. Daddy slowed to tiny steps, stopped and raised his stick.

We shuffled past the dogs and into a cobbled yard of purplish river stones. There was someone there, crouched behind a granite trough, the shape of him silhouetted against the sun. He was moving round on his knees, his eye squint to the end of a long rifle, the barrel aimed straight at us. My heart was pounding. Tom. I recognized his sticky-out ears, the way his hair stood up.

'Hello there, Sonny,' Daddy said uncertainly, raising his hands in surrender, his cane dangling at an angle that made the dogs frisk backwards.

Very deliberately, Tom lowered the weapon to his side and used it to lever himself to his feet. He made a salute.

Daddy put his fist to his mouth and coughed. 'All right, Sonny?'

Mr Upcott appeared in the doorway, his bow-legs, and his arms like two black wings flapping in the sleeves of a jacket he was in the process of putting on.

'Bruno! Hector!' he growled and the dogs lowered their heads, backed off. He turned to Tom. 'I'll not tell 'e again — inside. This minute.'

He was turning down the collar of his jacket. Father held his hand out mid-air. 'We were passing—'

Mr Upcott's jaw appeared stuck. He peered under his eyebrows. Eventually he nodded. 'You'll be comin' in?'

I had never been into the farmhouse before. It was like entering the Ark. In the hallway, there was an ancient, church-like coffer, on and above it a collection of oilskins, sacking, a coil of rope. I followed Daddy as he followed Mr Upcott around the base of the staircase and through a door into a kitchen, long and dimly lit.

Tom was in there already, he'd climbed up on to a low stool and was straining to fix the gun to hooks along a beam. He jumped down. 'Out and see to your brother,' Mr Upcott said. Then he turned to Daddy, motioning towards the end of the room. 'Take a seat.'

Although it had been hot outside, it was clammy indoors. Between the chairs Mr Upcott offered us, there was the glow and tick of a smouldering fire.

'Frances!' Mr Upcott called.

Daddy sat down on a tall, carved wooden seat with ivy balls at the ends of the arms. He sat forward, the knapsack still fixed to his back, and propped his cane between his knees. I pressed against his elbow.

Mr Upcott kept to the middle of the room, next to the huge long table, his head swivelling.

'Frances!' he called again.

Frances appeared silently through the scullery door. She had a face like a boiled sweet, pale and oval with the pink juice just showing through.

'Visitors,' Mr Upcott said to her, as if she hadn't seen us.

93

I watched in suspense as she moved wordlessly and without looking at us, methodically sorting the kettle from the fireplace beside us to the glass-fronted dresser where she brought down cups and saucers.

Mr Upcott chewed his bottom lip impatiently. Suddenly, Daddy started from the chair. 'I haven't taken your seat, have I?' He half stood up, folding himself at the waist.

'They'm all mine,' Mr Upcott replied. 'Makes no difference to me.'

Then Daddy said, nudging me forwards, 'I daresay you know my daughter, Mavis? Stays with Mrs Cleverdon, my aunt?'

Mr Upcott turned his dull eyes to me until I winced and bobbed as we did at school.

Daddy looked around. 'Lovely old place you've got here.'

Mr Upcott's head hardly lifted above the yoke of his shoulders. He continued to press against the table as if it were a pain for him to stand.

Frances handed Daddy a cup and saucer. Then she disappeared, re-emerging with a beaker of milk for me. I was aware of the privilege of witnessing such intimate acts; I was too shy to thank her.

'Lovely day for it,' Daddy said.

The dark, beamed ceiling bore down. It was Mr Upcott who eventually, irritably, turned to Frances and said, 'Perhaps the young maid here would like to see the piglets? Take 'em some meal?'

'She adores babies,' Daddy said, 'don't you, Mavis?'

Frances silently obeyed her father. She waited for me to follow her out, along the thin passageway of the scullery.

There was a bucket by the back door, brimful of milk and peelings, which clanked as she lifted it, and carried it with an effort at arm's length, out into the fierce daylight of the garden. I followed behind, not wanting to get in the way, taking tiny excited breaths to keep up with her. We took a path out through a tall gate and into an orchard. It was well-trodden, bordered by low-lying trees that stretched away to one side of us, downhill, into dense undergrowth. At the far end there was a rough wooden shack with a brick wall hemming it in, high as my waist. Frances stopped and heaved the bucket over the side, setting it down in the dirt. Then she doubled over the wall, picked the bucket up again, and began to slosh the contents into a low metal tray. As soon as the mixture made contact there was a squealing from inside the shack, and then a bundling of bodies in the slant of the doorway, piled two or three high. I was nervous and stood behind her.

'We'll keep the gate shut,' Frances said briskly.

The piglets had slits for eyes, their ears were raggedy, rolled like pastry.

'There's so many,' I said, half afraid that they'd spring over the wall.

'Ten of them. Poor Olive's flat out.'

'They're difficult to count,' I said lamely, resisting the urge to grab on to her skirt. After a while, the splotchy pink bodies appeared to sort themselves out, ranging more or less in line, snouts dilating between the wires of the tray, snuffling, sucking. Some had their ears swept back, a funnel of spotless pink enamel; each had the scrawny antenna of a tail. It was only as they quietened down that I noticed one, disengaged from the rest, lying just inside the doorway, the tiny bellows of its belly pumping. Frances let herself into the pen. She crouched down, prodded it, put her fingers under its back and lifted. She was totally unafraid.

'Mother's trodden on him,' she said.

'Will he get better?' I asked.

She balanced on her haunches, wiped her hand against her apron, then looked up at me. 'It happens. Can't be helped. Tom'll see to it.'

Her green eyes were determined and unruffled, not upset at all. And because she wasn't upset I knew I shouldn't be either. I wanted to come back another time, imagining that if I showed her how used I could be to the country, I might be her helper. I followed her back to the house, stepping as far as I was able in her footprints, swinging my arms in time with hers, pretending I, too, had an empty bucket.

Daddy was relieved to see us. He rubbed his hands. 'Well,' he said, making a slapping sound with his lips, 'thank you for your – hospitality.' He got to his feet. 'What do you say, Mavis?' he asked. 'Ready for the off?'

Mr Upcott led us to the front door and stood watching us go. The dogs patted after us as far as the milk churns and then turned back.

'Not half as high and mighty as they make out,' Daddy said, once we were out of earshot and on our way. 'Phew, it's hot.' He took off the knapsack in order to remove his jacket, which he hooked on a finger over his shoulder. Then he plunged his stick into the tall grasses of the hedgerow. 'Take that!' he said, uncharacteristically sporting.

'We fed the piglets,' I said.

'Good show,' said Daddy. 'Pretty girl. Buried away like that.'

'I wish you could have heard her play the piano,' I said, urging him to be as impressed by Frances as I was.


The next day, Daddy told me he had a surprise. He was going to pick someone up at the station, could I guess who?

'Mother?' I said, feeling my chest tighten.

'Try again,' he said.

I couldn't think. 'Uncle Lucien? Uncle Gilbert?'

'Ah-ha. You'll just have to wait and see.'

He was anxious as a hare. He was going into Buckleigh with the post van, and no, I couldn't go with him.

I was relying on Peg to announce their return. She habitually yapped at the slightest provocation and she sounded a dozen or so false alarms that afternoon. But it wasn't until the evening – a jigsaw puzzle, the beginnings of a sock, a brief, stumbling effort on the piano – when the burring in the distance finally resolved itself to the grinding of a car's engine. The vehicle swept past Auntie's cottage to deposit its load right outside the front door of the Seven Stars. They'd been given a lift in a jeep. I wanted to rush straight out but Auntie held me back. There was the sound of laughter – high-pitched like Laurel and Hardy.

'There'll be time enough in the morning,' she said.

I wasn't sure whether I slept or not. All night long through the thin partition between our rooms, I could hear Auntie's snoring like a whistle, as if a pea were stuck in the back of her throat. But I must have slept at some point because I had a dream.

A huge bird fell on to the Green from the top of the flagpole, flumpf. I watched Daddy rush out and lay his hand gently on its shoulder. When he lifted his fingers, they were black. The bird must have spent the night on a chimney pot. I watched Daddy as he rubbed his sooty fingers and then leaned over to stroke the soft ball of the bird's head. It was an eagle. Suddenly I realized I had to warn him: an eagle like that could take out an eye. Another second and I thought I saw the bird stir, its eagle-eye twitch. I knew it was too late to get to him. The wound across his face would scar, red and jagged as the edge of an open tin can.

I woke before I could see him. Alone. The tiny room was dusty grey; there was the first skitter of a creature somewhere above my head in the roof.

When I got downstairs for breakfast, Auntie was on her knees by the fire and she'd changed her tune since last night.

'I don't know what he's thinking. Work, that's what he said: work! Bringing her here as if we're all fools.'

'Can I go? Can I take the flowers?' I asked, full of foreboding.

'You eat your porridge first,' she said.

Mrs McManus was keen to expand business at the Seven Stars. She was renting out three rooms and had requisitioned the back bar as a dining room, offering evening meals throughout the week. It suited Joyce, living more or less next door, to give her a hand.

As I went through, I could hear clattering. There was steam pouring from the kitchen doorway. Joyce was up to her elbows at the sink, pushing hair from her face with the hub of a fist. A low iron pan was spitting on the stove, the concentrated sea-smell of bacon, which I realized I hadn't smelled since London. My mouth watered.

'Not this morning,' Joyce panted. 'I'm far too busy – shoo.'

I had a bunch of Auntie's snap-dragons tight in my hand, and I decided to go straight through to the dining room.

'Ah, Mavis, my dear. Look who's come to see us!' Daddy said.

It took me a minute to work out where I'd seen her before.

'You were tiny!' exclaimed the woman with inky hair. 'Do you remember, you sat on my chair, had a go at my typewriter?'

'You remember Miss Minchin, don't you? Patricia? From Daddy's office?'

The office had smelled of black. It was before the war. Miss Minchin. Daddy had taken me into work with him one day and I'd sat on the swivelly padded chair to watch her. Miss Minchin's desk was big enough to live under. She had pigeonholes and a place for everything: a drawer with paper clips and pencil sharpeners; a drawer for nibs, a drawer for the Quink, for the amber gum. She had a hole-punch and a stapler, an embosser for the headed paper, stamps in several denominations, envelopes in four different sizes.

'What do you say?' Daddy said.

'How do you do,' I said. 'Pleased to meet you.'

Daddy was red in the face from eating, his napkin tucked into the top of his waistcoat. Miss Minchin wasn't wearing spectacles any longer. She had livid red lips, pale cat's eyes. Like a flash she smiled at me, as if a switch had been flicked.

I handed Daddy the flowers.

'For me? Well, that's very kind. What do you say we give them to the lady?'

I couldn't tell what was different about her, but she seemed to have come in disguise. She waved the long black cigarette holder like a wand scattering ash, took the flowers from him in her free hand and laid them on the table, pushing their heads upright.

'You were such a sweet little girl,' she said.


Auntie was showing me her old things again. Daddy had sent me home and I was bored already. It seemed to me then that the cottage was cluttered with old lady things, dark as a pond behind its green velvet curtains.

Here was the photograph of Ernest Cleverdon on the deck of the *Lusitania*, in a striped blazer and a straw boater. *All the way to New York and back*, she said, *and he promised he would take me with him, it was always 'one of these days'* . . . She trailed off, staring into space.

She hadn't wound the clock on the mantelpiece and the hands were fixed at nearly half past nine. It made me itch. I could hear the tick stuck in my head. I sat on my hands.

Auntie made me sit close as we looked through the odds and ends in her sewing box.

'Can I go now, Auntie, please?'

In the compartment with her silver thimble, there was a tiny ebony mute. She didn't appear to have heard me.

'That was his,' she said. 'His spare one. He let me have it.' She laid it in the dead centre of her hand and poked it gently with a finger as if it might get up on its tiny legs.

'Can I go outside now, please?' I asked again, convinced that I was missing something.

Auntie lifted the mute and put it back. She folded a piece of lace collar, wound a thin strand of red ribbon around her finger as slowly as she could and deposited them too. Then she set the delicate square lids into their places, tapped the star-shaped mother of pearl buttons. She shut the lid, tight-lipped. At last she turned her eyes to me and blinked assent.

Outside the house everything throbbed, smuts of flies nuzzled into the walls. I was singing under my breath as I climbed the slope to the pub, embarrassed to find that Daddy and Miss Minchin were already sitting outside on the bench together, watching me. Daddy had his flecky jacket across his knees, his shirt sleeves rolled up and Miss Minchin, tucked in next to him, her mustard-coloured bag all ready, flapping her hand at her neck for a fan. They were packed up, waiting for Wilf to fetch the horse and trap around.

As I drew closer, Daddy sat up straight. 'Just caught us,' he said. 'Day for it, I thought. What d'you think? Might as well make the most of the weather.'

He wasn't looking at me; he had got to his feet and began rolling down his sleeves. As if to explain, he handed his wrists over to Miss Minchin who was fixing the studs on a pair of cufflinks.

'Little drive, nothing special. Show our guest some of the delights.'

I took it I would not be going with them. 'I'll go to the river, then,' I said, hoping to alarm him.

'Splendid idea!' he replied as he shrugged on his jacket.

The cloud of dust behind the cart swirled in a vanishing trick. I tried to hold on to the distant clopping of horse's hooves as they tripped out of the valley; from the pub's kitchen, it became the vague tapping sound of the dismal life in which I'd been left.

I crept upstairs. From his bedroom there was a door to a smaller dressing room. The door was open. Inside on a narrow bed, Miss Minchin had laid out her clothes. Two embroidered silk blouses, a sailboat dress, a satin all-in-one. I climbed on to the wide windowledge and drew up my knees to sit in lookout for them.

It sounded as if a wireless was on somewhere, the constant chatter of birds, scooping from the eaves, parading themselves. I already knew most of their names, the tiniest of them, blue tits, coal tits, housemartins, and then the swifts wheeling high over Mr Bird's vegetable garden – his hut, his beans, the cat's cradle measures of his string. They swooped over the roof of the school, over three rows of hedge. In the corner there were little gangs of sheep. I followed the scrubby outline of the lane, field by field, a pattern of diminishing tiles, layer upon layer of spongy trees, until, just before the leap into clear sky, everything stopped short – the ogre of the moor sleeping, spare and massive, the prehistoric mound of his backside.

I sat there, pins and needles coursing through my legs, until I could no longer feel anything. There was no sign in any case of Daddy and Miss Minchin. It was agony as I got to my feet, my legs crumpling under me. I made my way back down the stairs, supporting myself on the walls like a cripple. *What if I was ill?* It was an appealing thought: I would have to be looked after; they would have to find a cure. But by the time I'd got out of the front door, my legs had begun to work again and I decided I'd go down to the river, just like I'd said.

Only a day or so ago I would have shrunk from the very idea of facing Tom Upcott again, but being left behind had hardened me. Now the possibility was a dare and a thrill. I needed to be able to tell Daddy *something* in order to save face. I knew instinctively that stories with people in worked better, people more interesting than Miss Minchin.


Tom Upcott was thigh deep in water. He was flicking a fishing line under the shade of the bank. I was rewarded for my courage. When he saw me, he acted as if he'd been expecting me all along, raising his finger to his lips. After half a dozen castings forward and back, he gave up. He turned to me and beckoned for me to follow as he began to wade upstream. He was so sure that I would do as he said that I didn't hesitate; I sat down and took off my sandals and socks, then tucked my dress into my knickers, and paddled out towards him, up to my knees. He was the leader: when he asked me to, I froze, stock-still, following up to my thighs, the river water around my legs like two gelid stockings. Three times we saw a kingfisher, a dazzling blue streak zip up and down. It meant *Good luck*, he told me. *Good luck*, again and again.

Soon we reached the promontory where he'd set up camp.

We hauled ourselves out. I was shivering with pleasure at being so casually included. There was a ring of blackened stones and Tom was on his knees, crouching with a box of matches. He'd brought a bundle of sheep's wool from his pocket and he was busy making a doughnut shape out of it; set it down in the middle of the stones. Then he struck a match, fed tiny bits of twig and grass gently to the flame. It was like Cowboys and Indians. I wondered if we could stay all night. I helped him drag a rotten branch, collect together bits of dried-out grass and reed. Once the fire got going, Tom threw in the horse-hair fishing line, tangled and sodden, and we watched it recoil and hiss.

'No more fish,' he said. I hadn't thought to bring us anything to eat. How stupid of me. Next time, I thought, I'd come prepared . . . But Tom had already moved on. His eyes shone with the fire; his teeth slanted backwards and he smiled with gusto, easily. I couldn't help looking at him. It was as if another continent had been opened up to me, a continent with all the lights on.

I didn't want to be the first to break the spell. And Tom had a whole list of things to show me, pointing out a heron's nest snagged high up in a tree, a lizard disappearing against the rock, the spot where if we were patient enough, we might see an otter. There was a sense of urgency that kept me there, as if leaving, I might risk not coming back. But it was getting dusky and I had further to walk than he did.

'I'd better go,' I said, not for the first time. But as soon as I began to make a move, Tom found another distraction for me. He said, 'I'll show you, if you like.'

He leaned over and drew something out of his pocket.

If he let me see, he said, I had to swear not to tell. It was a secret.

I did swear. I knew that a secret more than anything would make us friends. He made me swear again and the way he was holding what he had made me think there might be something live wrapped up in it.

'Sure you want to see?' he asked.

He flattened the paper out against a big purple stone, keeping it hidden from me under the curve of his hand.

'Swear?' he said again.

'Promise.'

He lifted his fingers. It was the paper itself that he was showing me. It was printed.

'What is it?'

'See for yourself.'

The printing ink had eroded in fine white lines to make a cross where the paper had been folded and rubbed. There was a picture of a soldier, a Nazi armband. It was a black and white drawing, so fine it could have been a photograph. The soldier was sprawled headlong, fist over his head, helmet worked loose, a twisted mouth.

I sat down on my heels and held my hand out for it.

'Open 'im up,' Tom urged. He was on his haunches.

I held the paper with the very tips of my fingers as if there might be germs on it.

'Go on,' he said.

Slowly I prized apart the two halves. There was writing on one side, German — a thick, indecipherable script. On the other, a picture: a tiny room with curtains and a bed, on which a lady knelt. She had no clothes on, the swags of her bare chest, her hair swirled in a pile on her head. And underneath her, lying back like a rug, there was a man with dark skin, naked too, apart from socks. She was smiling just like Miss Minchin did. All her front bits showing. And his.

I dropped the paper. Tom grabbed at it to stop it blowing away.

'It's disgusting,' I said. 'Where'd you get it from?'

'Robert had it from a Yank. All the young farmers got one.'

'Why?'

'They drop 'em down on the Krauts. Get them all worked up.'

'What do you mean?'

'That's their maids,' he said, pointing, 'up to their tricks.'

'You should burn it,' I said. 'Put it on the fire.'

'You asked.'

'I didn't.'

'You swore,' he said, though it was hidden now, as if it had never existed.

I didn't want to cry, not in front of him, but he had ruined everything.

He smiled. 'Haven't you never heard of the birds and the bees? *That*,' he said, pointing to his pocket, ''s'like shaking up the hive.'

The water churned around my legs as I waded back, soaking the skirt of my dress, sucking the river through the soles of my feet to spin out of my eyes. *I hate boys*, I was thinking, but more than anything, I hated Miss Minchin — more than anything else on earth.

# 8

## *Ears*

It was a Sunday afternoon when Eve rang and asked if they could pop by. She wanted an excuse to get out of the house. I didn't think twice before agreeing, but it was a shock when I opened the door. She hadn't warned me. She was holding Archie by the shoulders, rolling her eyes.

'What a difference!' I said. He'd had his hair cut. Eve pushed him ahead of her and he dodged past into the front room.

'He's decided he's not talking to me,' she said. 'So I've brought him out for some fresh air.' Then she called into the room, 'Don't forget to give Mavis what you've brought.'

Archie came to the doorway, the spiky crown of his head, and lifted his arm rigidly, holding out a long packet of Kit Kats.

'No need,' I said. 'But, thank you.' The packet buckled in my hands.

'He's cross with me,' Eve said, stepping out of her boots and following me through to the kitchen, 'about his hair.

107

But it's getting warmer all the time. And I thought it might be why he was getting teased . . .'

'You can see his ears,' I said. I wasn't going to tell her what a shock that had been, as if Tom himself had been standing there, lowering his gun or shaking himself out of the river.

I rarely bothered at this time of year for myself, but for something to do, for a focus, I asked, 'Shall we have a fire?' It was a job Archie liked. He helped me scrunch up the newspaper, arranged the lightings into their wigwam.

I found I couldn't take my eyes off him. I handed over a couple of logs and then I let him take the matches from me.

'He doesn't ever do this on his own,' I assured Eve.

'No. It's good,' she said. 'I'm impressed, Archie. I didn't know you knew how to light a fire.'

When the flames had got going, Archie sat on the little footstool and unwrapped his biscuit. He took no notice of us but began to nibble systematically, biting off the chocolate from round the edges.

'Eat properly,' Eve said.

'What have you been up to?' I asked him.

Archie shrugged, concentrating.

'A proper answer.' Eve glared at him.

He posted half the biscuit into his mouth.

'Can I go now?' Archie asked, his mouth full.

'We've only just got here,' Eve said. She scrunched her red wrapper and threw it into the fire, where it stretched like a cat.

'It's *Doctor Who* now,' Archie said, the neck of his fleece zipped up over his chin. 'It's a *special*.'

'You've seen them all before,' Eve said. 'A hundred times.'

'I haven't.'

Eve ignored him.

'I haven't, Mum.'

'Would you like a drink?' I asked Eve. 'A proper drink. It's Sunday; I'm sure we've earned it.'

Eve had one face for Archie and another for me. She smiled.

'Would Archie like some juice?' I asked.

Archie shrugged again.

'For goodness sake, Archie,' Eve said.

'I'm sorry I don't have a television,' I said, though he'd never mentioned the lack of it before.

'He watches far too much of it,' Eve said.

Without his hair, Archie's face was bright and exposed. 'It's a proper haircut, isn't it?' I said. 'A proper boy.'

He turned on me, suddenly. 'I *am* a boy,' he said.

'Archie!' Eve said. 'What's got into you?'

I caught his eye. For a moment I saw him stripped naked, his small pigeon chest, his bony shoulders. 'What a silly thing for me to say,' I said. I turned from them, embarrassed. 'Don't take any notice of me.' I knelt down at the dresser cupboard and began fumbling around. 'Whisky?'

'Perfect,' Eve said. Then she looked again at Archie and caved in. 'Do you mind, Mavis, if we let him go?'

'Of course I don't.' I looked back over my shoulder as she handed him the keys. 'Go on,' she snapped, 'let yourself in. Keep your fleece on if it's cold.'

As soon as he'd pulled the front door shut, Eve sank back into her chair. 'Peace!' she said. 'I'm so sorry, I don't know what's wrong with him today. Do boys have hormones?'

We took a moment to adjust to his absence, watching the spit and catch of the fire. Although I'd become relatively easy in Eve's company, there were still moments when I felt we must have exhausted everything we had to say.

'He's homesick I think,' she said. 'Though I can't think why.'

'It was the opposite for me,' I said. 'I told Archie: I was taken *back* to London, about his age. I hated it.'

'I suppose it depends on what you're used to,' Eve said.

'He'll get used to it here.'

'Did you know my mother at all?' she asked suddenly.

I told her, honestly, that I didn't remember Beatrice from during the war. She can't have been born before 1942 or 1943?

'Forty-three,' Eve said, 'third of September.'

'It was 1943 when I went back to London,' I said. 'I didn't come back to the village after that, not until the sixties.'

'It was so weird seeing that photograph,' Eve said, 'to see my mother there, with you and Joyce and Dorothy. And for me to be standing in the same room . . .' She paused, 'The man, the one standing next to her,' she said. 'Upcott, I think Joyce said? Was he a friend of my mother's?'

I know I must have flushed. I could feel the whisky burning under my skin. For a moment I didn't respond.

'Joyce told me a bit about his family,' she went on.

'Did she?' I asked, surprised. I could feel myself catch fire. It had only been a matter of time. I took up the poker. A splinter shot out from one of the logs and landed by Eve's foot, singeing the hearthrug. I reached over for the little brass shovel and bashed the cloth where it had landed. The joints in her chair creaked as Eve shifted and raised her feet for me.

I returned the shovel to its place and took another swig from my glass. My jaw clicked. I determined that I wouldn't say anything. But then, I couldn't help myself. I said, 'I knew the family better than anyone.'

Eve was looking at me with a strangely blank expression. I wanted her to leave, but I couldn't find the words to do it pleasantly. I picked up the poker again and drove it into the embers. My innards were packed hard. My head hurt. Eve set her glass down precisely on the tabletop. 'I suppose I ought to get back. I should go and see what Archie's up to.'

I made no protest. She levered herself from her chair and into the hall to slip on her boots, stood there waiting apologetically. Every muscle in my body ached; I pulled myself together to see her out. She leaned quickly towards my ear, made the sound of a kiss.

The air outside had that peculiar brassy quality of light after a day's rain, the flowers bashed but radiant.

'Isn't it lovely now?' she said, turning and sniffing the air, pointlessly polite. I stood and watched her to the porch of the flat, the way she ducked inside.

# PART III
## *Underground*

# Carole

It was the second time I'd been up to the top of the graveyard this year, the second time in perhaps as many decades. I had come out specifically to look for her and yet it surprised me how easy she was to find. Her arms were smooth as marble. She had beckoned me in her white robes up to the top of the graveyard and made me stand with her on the platform of the flattened grave of her great-grandfather. She was reciting something in a low murmur: *Apple orchards, fields of wheat, the river bristling with things to eat, copses of oak and ash and beech.* The sound was like an approaching train, chugging from deep in the tunnel. 'The quivering doe, the red-faced fox, the milking herd, the shearling sheep . . . everything,' she extended her arm extravagantly, 'literally, everything,' she said, 'as far as the eye can see.'

My eyes followed the sweep of her arm out across the valley, but there was nothing there but a blanket of snow; no colour, no distinguishing marks, nothing. I turned to her with my mouth open to speak, but it didn't stop her chanting. 'Stitchwort, periwinkle, spotted orchid, lady's smock, the cheese factory, the abattoir, TB, foot and mouth . . .'

'But there's nothing there,' I said. 'Nothing but snow.'

'Where do the words go, then?' she asked, glaring. 'And why do they mean something to you?'

I had to think. 'Because somewhere they exist,' I said, 'under all that.'

She folded her arms, looking at me, waiting.

'What do you want me to say?' I pleaded.

'Tell me who you are?' she said, changing tack.

'I'm nobody,' I said, my answer quick as a reflex.

She sniffed. 'Then you might as well be buried, too,' turning away, surveying the graveyard.

'I mean I haven't done anything worth mentioning,' I said, trying to placate her.

'"*What have I achieved?*"' she mocked me scornfully. 'Don't you think that's what everyone says? Isn't it enough that you are alive, and in the world?'

'I don't have any children,' I said.

'You have a life, don't you?' she said coldly. 'You *had* a life.' Then she took a deep breath. 'Think of it as an inventory, if you like, a record of account.'

'Think of what?'

In her eyes I saw the two black moons of her pupils contract. 'It's not over yet. Dig yourself out,' she urged, 'before it is too late. Before you are dug in for good.'

'From what?' I asked, feeling more and more confused.

'I need you to exist,' she said, barely disguising her frustration. She was close to tears. 'Don't you see that? I need you to remember who you are – who you were – before you could no longer distinguish yourself. I had no children. Without you . . . I am lost.' Her mouth wobbled in disappointment as she backed away from me, into the snow.

# 9

## *Victoria, 1943–45*

I hardly knew your mother, I was able to tell Eve: I was seven before Beatrice was even born. I was seven when Daddy visited that last time and decided to take me back with him on the train. It was the summer of 1943 and who knew how long the war would drag on.

I remember Dorothy weeping in her black lambswool coat, saying she couldn't bear goodbyes. 'Make sure he brings you back,' she said, pips of tears bouncing from her cheeks. I was wearing a beret she had knitted, and the last thing I remember was wondering how soon I could pull it off. Auntie came with us to the station and at the last minute, held my hand through the half-open window of the train. She didn't usually kiss or fuss but I thought she might never let me go. 'Violets are for remembering,' she'd said in a strange voice, poking a present of handkerchiefs through the window just as the world outside shunted sideways and the train shook and trembled into life like a bag of spanners, the *huff, huff, huff,*

*huff, huff* like a man standing with an umbrella – open shut, open shut, open shut.

'Home,' Daddy announced, pushing open the heavy green door. It was the middle of the night. I had slept and I had woken up, slept and woken, so that now I had no idea where I was. Daddy led us inside, switched on the light to a patterned hallway, then up a staircase to the outline of a door. He put his ear to the panel, knocked and took the handle, opening it into a room with high ceilings, which pulsed from one corner with a soft artificial light.

The small squat woman had risen to her feet. She was standing by a little round table in a belted lilac suit. Her face was sallow in the light. She stepped forwards and held out her hands, hugged me stiffly, then put me at arm's length.

'Such a *big* girl!'

I smiled hard. Auntie used to speak of Mother as if she were different from us, like a fancy breed of hen. In the studio portrait I'd taken away with me, she had hair like jet, a perfectly drawn bow of a mouth. In the meantime, she had fattened up. Her clothes were tight. She smoothed a place on the one-armed sofa for me to sit next to her, looking at Daddy to supply the words.

'We're whacked,' he said, fetching himself a heavy glass from a sideboard. 'Darling heart,' he said irritably, 'why don't you show Mavis to her bed? Goodnight, Mavis. Good to have you back, old girl,' he said, lifting his glass to his lips.

Mother moved with small, deliberate steps. The stairs were dimly lit; there was a huge piece of blackout the long length of a window tacked between the two landings. I followed her

119

up, along another corridor, where she pointed out the bathroom, and into a room at the far end. Mother leaned over to click on a bedside lamp. There was a wooden bed, a cupboard in the corner, a rug on the floor, as if someone already lived there. Then I saw lying at the end of the bed a doll with a beautiful white dress, a flat, circular straw hat, her eyes shut.

'*Alors*,' Mother said and she went over and turned back the embroidered counterpane, tugged at the sheets.

I stood in my shoes and then I reached out and picked up the doll, and as I did, her thick eyelashes tipped open, a pair of speckled conker eyes.

'*Is* a present,' Mother said and she trembled as I tipped the doll backwards and forwards.

She was beautiful. Her face shone in the lamplight, heart-shaped and rosy. She had tiny ruby lips and the blackest hair curled down to her shoulders. Her two brown eyebrows were painted high and in crescents just like Mother's.

Mother watched me as I touched the gauzy material of the skirt, its tiny green polka-dots, the matching satin bow across her chest. Underneath, she had frilly petticoats and knickerbockers, lacy white ankle socks and white leather boots. I had never held anything so precious.

'Sleep. Yes?' Mother said. She leaned towards me, her breath smelling of ash. 'You can turn out the light?'

I didn't want her to go. As soon as she left, the room hollowed out. I fumbled at my shoes, undid the buckles and slipped them off, then climbed into the bed in all my clothes, posting myself between icy sheets, pulling the doll towards me carefully by her crooked arms. The tag on her dress said Scarlett. But I was going to call her *Frances*, I decided, because I wanted to name her myself. I reached out and clicked off the lamp and then lay there hardly daring to breathe. 'Frances,' I whispered to her. My voice blew a hole in the blackness. Both of us lay stiff and rigid. All I could remember from the lamp-light was the pattern on the curtains: parasols, upside down and floating now like dandelion seed all around the room.

I'm not sure at what point it began to dawn on me that I wouldn't be going back to Devon. If I ever dared ask the question, Daddy would say vaguely, 'after the war'. He main-tained that, in general, things were looking up; but neither Mother nor Mrs Connor, our housekeeper, would be told. It didn't do to get complacent, Mrs Connor said. Because that Hitler was only like any other little boy: he'd get more vicious the more he thought he was losing. And she was right: some nights she'd have to bring me and Frances down with her to the kitchen to hide under the table. The drone might be as far off as a bumblebee, or so near it shook the legs of the table.

It was one of those nights she told me about Mr Connor. How, when she got home from the butcher's one day, she hardly recognized the street where she used to live. There were fire engines and cordons and at first they wouldn't let her past. But she watched as they brought Mr Connor out in his chair, like Henry VIII. She elbowed past the warden and went to grab his hand. Only then did she see that his legs had been blown off, there was a startled look on his face, *as if he'd been kissed by the Holy Mother*, she said.

At school all the boys played 'buzz bombs'. Everyone had seen one. They were daggers with flaming tails, they had eyes

121

and a moustache, they sounded just like a blowtorch. *There is a green hill far away*, we continued to sing, and I would be back in the village. Devon was always popping up in stories or in songs, *One man went to mow, went to mow a meadow*. London was cramped and hooded and smelled of ironing; there were whole houses with their fronts ripped off, beds and even lavatories, sticking out; someone's grandmama at school had been found floating in her bath.

Mrs Connor tried her best. On Sundays after church, if the weather was fine, she took me to the park. She saved up scraps from the week to feed to the pelicans; we watched them guzzle out of the water with their clapper wings. One Sunday it was particularly busy, people out in summer dresses and shirts, a boy going round in circles on a scooter. The air was greenish-grey and still, the lake a slate. It was almost funny when the man came running, cowering as if he didn't want to be seen. As he came closer, we could hear him shouting, the same thing, over and over, 'Duck, duck, duck,' flapping his arms, leering either side of him as people spun away and began to look up at the sky.

By then, we could hear the whine of an engine. It drew nearer, louder like a motorcycle, until we could see it, the dark tin underbelly, the stubby wings. Frances fell from my hand. Mrs Connor grabbed me and pulled me towards a bench where we crouched like tigers. People had begun running from over the blue bridge, towards the bandstand. I put my arms like Mrs Connor's over my head, around my ears. Still we could hear the sound of an engine running. When suddenly, in the distance, it stopped, everything froze. Mrs Connor pinched me so hard that it hurt. And just as it seemed to be over – motes of sunlight drifting in the air – the sky cracked in two: there was a shattering, ear-splitting explosion. I threw myself at Mrs Connor.

And then it was over. There was a child, dazed, wailing the all clear. Mrs Connor lifted her head and extracted herself from me, pulled herself to her feet, brushed down her skirt. We had to go back for Frances, who was lying with her eyes shut as if nothing had happened. I picked her up and shook crumbs of soil from her hair. I hugged her to me. Mrs Connor didn't say a word about it, but took my free hand high against her chest to lift me up and then began to walk as fast as she could, half dragging me along. The bomb had landed on the other side of the lake, in Birdcage Walk, where grey dust was falling like snow from the raggedy plane trees. Although we took a different route home, we had to cross the end of the walk to get out of the park. The sandbags there had been burst open and already the sparrows and one-legged pigeons had come, pecking for food.

On Monday, I didn't have to go to school. Mrs Connor was off for the day to work in the tea van for the men who were digging out the chapel where the bomb had hit. They'd be at it for days, she told Mother, the rubble was so deep. One warden came out and told her how alive he thought the bodies looked, like at Madame Tussaud's, the bandsmen caught with their instruments still held to their lips. Morning service had been packed. Mrs Connor told Mother how everyone who'd been in the blast had died or been injured, apart from the Bishop – there wasn't a mark on him, not a scratch – and the altar candles had carried on burning even after the roof had come down.

123

After that I made an altar in my bedroom. The cupboard had been Daddy's toy cupboard once. It came from the nursery in Bideford, constructed to fit into a corner, like a segment of cake. If I loaded everything on to the top shelf – my nursery books, the box of lead soldiers, a slate and chalks – there was enough room in the bottom half for me. It was my own slice of Devon. Every afternoon after school I took Frances in there and drew pictures for her on the walls of lining paper – foxgloves, owls, a horse, a cow, a long, long slow-worm. Every evening I repacked our bags. The few clothes I would need were folded in the suitcase under my bed; baby Frances's outfits, which were slowly accruing, were kept ready in the gas mask box: the party dress she'd arrived in, two crocheted hats, mittens on a string and a pair of overalls that Mrs Connor had helped me cut out and sew for when she joined the WAAFs.

On the day that Daddy was proved right, he couldn't contain himself. Mother was worried that there'd not been anything official, just a bubbling up from people who weren't necessarily in the know. But Daddy'd already begun ripping the black tape from the big windows in the drawing room. Out in the square there was a ladder propped against the lamp post; someone was hanging up flags, there was a roar in the air. Mother came and stood behind the curtain. She had powdered her face like a ghost, her mouth drawn thin and tight, worried that people would get out of control, the noise they were making; some of them were already collecting a pile of cartons and old furniture to make a bonfire.

'It's a party out there,' Daddy said as if he couldn't wait to be at it.

In the evening the uncles, Lucien and Gilbert, had been invited round with a military friend of theirs and a man who made films about factories.

'Hellfire,' Daddy said, as Mother sat under the aspidistra, with another glass of brandy. 'Buck up! Take a leaf out of Mavis's book.' All I could think about was Devon. Daddy put his hands under my arms and raised me on to my toes. 'Come and give your old father a kiss.' His squint eyes were on Mother as he delivered a fiery kiss.

In the end, an hour late, only the uncles managed to get through the crowd.

'Better parties, no doubt,' Daddy said, grumbling, taking their coats.

The uncles were bald, with very bushy moustaches. Lucien had a ruff of white hair around the back of his head from ear to ear, which was the only way I could distinguish him from Gilbert. Otherwise, they were almost identical, their suits even made from the same variant of Donegal tweed by the same tailor. Although Auntie had told me enough stories to make me wary of them, their visits were generally accompanied with an offering, which I had learned politely to anticipate.

Gilbert took my wrist in his huge soft hand; he shook it. Then he produced from inside his jacket a great flag made of red and white, big as an apron.

'Bravo,' they both declared at once, as I held it up against my dress. They turned me into the centre of the room and drew in Daddy and Mother, all of them clinking solemnly around me. 'To King, to country and Saint George,' they said, the several discs of their upturned glasses circling above me like a planetary system.

I was allowed to stay up late, sitting at Daddy's foot, feeling the vibrations of his conversation in the bones of his legs. He was in full flow, taking pot shots at religion (which he only did to annoy Mother); the uncles sat back together on the sofa indulgently, swilling their drinks so that he could lean forwards and top them up.

Uncle Gilbert, who was semi-prone, lifted his glass and said, 'It's all the same to us, dear boy. We're in the back seat. You're in charge now.'

'It's *quantity* we're after,' Daddy said, his face burning. 'The Yanks have been on the game for years: right jacket, right price – they'll read anything you can throw at them.'

He stood up to propose another toast, wafting his glass to the tall windows where floodlights were criss-crossing the sky, and a gentle and continuous roll of linking arms, of 'Auld Lang Syne', of conga dancers.

'To *Bulldogs,* to *Walruses,* and to *Peanuts for Monkeys.*'

It was impossible to get hold of a taxi. So in the end the brothers stayed where they were, snoring together on the sofa like bookends.

'Bedtime,' Mother said, wrinkling her nose.

'Nonsense,' Daddy said, flinging out his arm. 'Night like this! How about a dance?' He opened the curtains wide and stood as if he were on the sea front, breathing in the sea air. Then he moved over to the gramophone and shuffled through his records. He brought one out, balancing it on his fingertips and smiled at me.

Even before the needle hit the surface, I knew that he had chosen my song.

*Heaven, I'm in Heaven, and my heart beats so that I can hardly speak . . .*

Daddy began to totter about the room, his arm bent across his stomach as if he already had a dancing partner, a glass high in his other hand.

Mother sat upright in her chair, balanced on the edge. I thought any minute she might rise to her feet and let him take her in his arms. But he continued to wheel out of her orbit, around the sofa and the uncles, around the two armchairs.

*'Dance with me! I want my arm about you. That charm about you. Will carry me through to—'*

'Devon!' I pronounced elatedly, and I began skipping around the room after him.

Even when Fred Astaire stopped singing, the strings were energetic and the words wrote themselves around the tune like sparklers. Daddy picked up his cane. He could make it spring into the air as if it were an antelope, then snatch it back. *Oh I love to climb a mountain and to reach the highest peak . . .* We played one of our old games, me scurrying about the furniture for him to hunt me down, raising the tip of his cane to his eye just like Tom had done, looking along its length, following me round as I moved this way and that, trembling with the thrill of it. *Oh I love to go out fishing, in a river or a creek . . .*

'Puckhh.' He made a shooting noise, his thumb cocked as a trigger, which signalled that I should clutch my heart and fall on the floor, curled up, cheek to cheek with the carpet.

Daddy stepped over me elaborately. Once. Twice.

And as the record turned and turned on its own wheel of silence, the names came flooding like an incantation, *bluebell, stitchwort, campion, vetch . . .*

'What is wrong?' Mother asked eventually, irritably.

127

'Wake up, old girl. Joke's over.' Daddy prodded me with the side of his foot.

I could play dead for ever. *Buttercup, forget-me-not, pennywort, dock . . .*

'Mavis! Wakey-wakey.'

# 10

## *St Cuthbert's*

Mrs Connor helped me pack the long list of things I'd need:

2 pleated pinafore dresses
3 white shirts with collars
2 royal blue cardigans
1 striped St Cuthbert's tie
7 pairs white ankle socks
7 pairs blue knee socks
8 pairs blue knickers
4 liberty bodices
2 hockey skirts
3 Aertex shirts
1 greatcoat
1 felt hat with blue ribbon
1 boater with orange ribbon
1 pair stout winter shoes
1 pair summer sandals
1 pair gym shoes
6 handkerchiefs

It took us two solid days to sew a nametape into the collar or edge of every item, M. E. Gaunt.

By that time, Mother and I and Mrs Connor were living in West Norwood. Daddy had brought me his old school trunk, lined in stripy linen, with a shelf that lifted off. We had an early luncheon. Daddy had bought some glazed ham for Mrs Connor and she boiled up some potatoes and carrots to accompany it. She made her special rice pudding, which Daddy said he'd missed. Mrs Connor came to the door to see us off, but Mother was too upset and refused to come out of her room to say goodbye. Mrs Connor gave me an apple for the journey and a whole bar of ration chocolate for my pocket, which she said was from Mother. 'Look it doesn't melt,' she said.

As Daddy and I climbed into the taxi, Mother appeared at the gatepost. She was crying, *making an absolute idiot of herself*, Daddy said. If she was so against the damn idea in the first place, then she ought to have said. It was too late to tell him now. I didn't look back around, my eyes fixed to the back of the driver's seat. My stomach was churning along with the engine of the car. As we turned the corner, Daddy peered round furtively.

'That's right, Mrs Connor – in she goes,' he said, straightening himself up. He dropped his shoulders.

'You're a big girl now,' he said.


It rained almost constantly in Weston-super-Mare. St Cuthbert's was right up on the cliffs and battered so hard by the wind some nights, we thought the roof would blow

130

off. The corridors smelled of seaweed. Although we were nowhere near the beach, deposits of greyish sand found their way into our hairbrushes and our flannels, into the raw cracks between our toes.

Sunday nights were bath nights, down in the basement where there were no windows. Electric bulbs swung under green metal shades; water leaked down the walls, seeped up through the concrete floor. Ten showerheads were mounted uniformly along the ceiling of an open, white-tiled corridor. We were made to run naked from one end to the other. I had to take off my specs. I ran awkwardly, with my elbows over my head and my legs flailing to hide the rude bits, to where Lucinda Hicks-Mason, House Monitor, dispensed and withheld strips of towelling. *Tragic Mary*, she'd pronounce, or, *Hairy Ape*. She made me dance for mine, lunging hopelessly at what she held above her head. Even when I managed to clamp the narrow strip tightly over my front, I couldn't hide the dark tufts of hair sprouting from my armpits.

Through the winters it was impossible to get completely dry or warm. In the first year we used to climb into each other's beds. There were eight of us in Langlands. Four iron bedsteads, heel-to-heel. The lights went out at half past eight.

'What?'

There was often giggling, this time artificially prolonged by Lucinda, who, as Dorm Senior, was a couple of years older than the rest of us.

'Lucinda's got a boyfriend,' someone said dutifully.

'Have not,' Lucinda drawled.

'Tell!'

'Oh, do tell!'

Because of the showers, I hated Lucinda Hicks-Mason so much my bones ached. I said, very deliberately, 'I've seen a boy naked.'

'Liar,' Lucinda said.

But the attention like a beam had already passed from her bed to mine.

'Naked? What, full naked?' Dulcie asked.

Neither Dulcie nor I were dreadfully popular, but we had other things in common too. When I was asked in my first week about Mother, I decided that it would be simpler all round if I told people she was dead. She'd said it so often herself – *I might as well be dead* – it didn't seem such an untruth. Dulcie was a complete orphan and naturally, for a bit, we were best pals. She liked my stories of Devon, particularly details of the cakes, and my exploits with the Badger Gang, which I was happy to elaborate.

'Was he a Badger,' she asked now reverently, 'or a Fox?'

'Mavis? Boys? I don't think so,' Lucinda said witheringly.

The green blind at the end of the room didn't shut properly, was stuck halfway like a guillotine, letting in the peculiar bluish light of the moon.

'Tell, tell, tell!'

'There's no way she can prove it,' Lucinda said.

There were hiccups of suppressed laughter.

'If you really want to know,' I tucked my chin to my chest, waiting for quiet, 'it's like a worm.'

'A worm?' Dulcie repeated in a trance.

'What?' Lucinda snorted.

Dulcie reared out of her bedclothes to my rescue, releasing

132

a stench that made her neighbour clap her mouth. She held her hand high into the room and began to wriggle her little finger.

'You dirty beast,' Lucinda said slowly.

'You asked me,' I said.

'You dirty, dirty cow.'

The silence was deep as a pool.

But then Lucinda was out of bed, and two others either side of her. They were moving in a semi-circle towards me.

I attempted to get up on to my elbows.

'Get her,' Lucinda said. 'Grab her arms.'

I was pulled out of my bedclothes by my wrists. In the space between the end of my bed and the foot of the one opposite, a grey blanket had already been laid out for the bumps. They dragged me on to it.

'Help us!' Lucinda urged the girls at the far end of the room who were kneeling up on their beds like rabbits, watching. 'Let's teach her a lesson. Dirty girl.'

I had given up the struggle. The coarse blanket smelled of river.

'It won't hold,' Dulcie said feebly.

'Yes it will.' Lucinda's voice. 'Heave. Come on. One, two, three – heave!'

My legs were in the air, my left shoulder pivoting against the floorboards. I tried to move my arms to protect my head.

'Come on, weaklings! Heave!'

My back sagged and then with a thud, the base of my spine struck the floor. There was a lightning bolt of pain and then my limbs were released. A scurrying. The blanket relaxed around me like petals opening. I had shut my eyes, but could

133

tell by the film of bright orange that the electric light had been switched on.

To cover her tracks, Lucinda said that they'd been at their wits' end. And they didn't want to tell anyone because they couldn't because it was too filthy to repeat. Every night, she said, for two weeks, I'd been telling them foul things, which they couldn't get out of their heads. I'd given Dulcie Hemmings nightmares.

Three or four days later, as soon as I was discharged from the infirmary, I was taken by Matron to see the headmistress. Miss Stevenson's office was on the third floor, the largest room in the school. It was difficult for me to climb stairs; I had to take them one at a time, pulling myself up by the banister. Matron left me in the middle of the room, sitting uncomfortably in a chair that was angled so that I couldn't look out of the tall windows. Each polished floorboard was a plank that led inexorably to the desk. I was told to wait, to keep absolutely still.

Two sides of the room were lined with books, volumes ranged as evenly as the school's perimeter fence. On the wall behind the desk there were rectangular photographs, groups of all the good students, on prize days and sports days, in long skirts and boaters, or immaculate games strip, the pale racks of their legs. I waited; the bulb at the base of my spine throbbed. By the time Miss Stevenson entered the room behind me, I was beginning to feel faint. As she lowered herself into the leather-studded chair, her spectacles, in the dim light, presented two dull coins. She took her time, smoothing her skirts, adjusting her cuffs.

'Well?' she asked eventually. Then she smiled, brought out a little key from around her neck and unlocked a drawer near her lap. 'I wonder if you'll recognize the handwriting?' she asked. 'Bring up your chair.'

I shunted forwards painfully, clasping the seat, moving as if it were a shell and attached to me. She drew out an envelope and placed it on the tooled maroon surface.

'Take it. Open it, please,' Miss Stevenson said. 'Read it out. I'm not terribly good at deciphering handwriting.'

Mother never wrote to me; she didn't send me parcels — my birthday was conveniently in the summer holidays. But I recognized the colour of the ink, Waterman's green. I reluctantly took the envelope from Miss Stevenson and pulled out a sheet of writing paper.

'I haven't got all morning,' she said.

'Dear Madame Stevenson,' I mumbled.

'No, no. Begin with the address, if you please.'

'39 Acacia Grove, West Norwood, London, SE.'

'Does it sound familiar to you — that address?'

*Dear Mme Stevenson,*

*I write to ask if my daughter, Mavis Eugenie Gaunt, might be excused from the following:*

*1. Tennis*

*2. Lacrosse*

*3. Religious Instruction*

*Please accept my cordial sentiments.*

*Mme Gaunt*

For a moment, I was overcome. It was proof, quite unexpected, of Mother's attention to detail. I didn't think she ever listened. Conversely, it showed her to be very much alive . . .

'I confess, I am not quite sure where to begin,' Miss Stevenson resumed after what she considered to be a significant pause. 'It is one thing to hear that you have been treating your dormitory to unsavoury bedtime stories. Quite another to discover that we have, all of us, been victims of quite spectacular deceit. *This*,' she said, leaning forwards to retrieve the paper from my hands, 'is addressed, I take it, from the grave?' She took her time, tucking the letter back into its envelope, savouring the irony like a square of chocolate held under her tongue.

'I had no option,' Miss Stevenson said, 'but to telephone your father. I think you might imagine how he took it? He has given me certain assurances, and pleaded – shall we say – extenuating circumstances.'

*Amabo, amabis, amabit, amabims, ama . . . ama . . .* There wasn't a word left in my head.

'I wonder what you have to say?' she asked, lifting her spectacles from her face and revealing the shrunken nail-heads of her eyes. At first, I thought there must be an insect somewhere in the room doing the rounds, a winter fly awoken from its doze on the fifteen-volume encyclopedia. It was a distraction that made it impossible to speak even if I'd wanted to, a high-pitched whistling that circled and then homed in, making a beeline straight for my ear. And then from the end of a tunnel, far, far away.

'Miss Gaunt? Miss Gaunt. I'm waiting. Miss Gaunt?'

# 11

## *Mathematics*

My heart hit the roof when I heard the knocking. Although it stopped for a moment, I knew that whoever it was hadn't gone away. There was a squeak on the glass at the window in the front room – a hand, polishing. It was Eve, I could tell immediately by the height and the long oval outline of her face.

I had rung her to say that I wasn't well, that I hoped Archie, now that he was more used to the place, would be all right to let himself into the flat after school. I wasn't up to visitors. And yet it was Archie I missed, no one else. I'd put on an extra cardigan, one on top of the other, wrapped round with a belt; two pairs of thick socks too, the green poking through the blue at the toe – I had no intention of being seen.

I heard her again just outside the front door, the gentle thud and rustle of something being set down. She paused and then knocked again, three loud knocks as close and as loud as if they'd been blows to my chest. All this attention! I didn't want Mr Bird upset, or Joyce coming round, wondering what the matter was. If she knocked again, I resolved, I'd have to answer it. Then I heard the xylophone collapse of the two or three empty milk bottles, a cry of exasperation.

I reached for the latch and drew the door open a short way. Eve was poised on her haunches, with a bottle in either hand.

'Hello,' she said, embarrassed. I could tell already by the way she looked at me that someone must have told her the bones of it. 'I wasn't sure if you were in. I'm sorry. I came to see how you are. I thought you'd want this back?' She set the bottles down and stretched towards the plastic bag, handed it up to me and then rose to her feet saying, 'I think he's been careful with it. I hope so.'

I took the bag from her, realizing from the weight of it what it was. 'I expect it was a bit old-fashioned for him,' I said.

'He enjoyed it, I'm sure. You'll have to ask him about it.'

'It's just a bug,' I said. 'I hope I haven't passed it on.'

'We've been fine,' Eve said. 'In fact, since you've been unwell, Archie's been going after school up to the farm, to help. I don't know whether it was you, but he seems to have decided the countryside's not such a bad thing.'

'To help?'

She smiled. 'I'm not sure how much help he actually is. But he comes home stinking and pleased with himself.' She showed no sign of going. 'I'm sorry about last time,' she said.

'Would you like to come in?' I asked, in spite of myself. 'The house is a bit of a mess.'

She said, 'Yes, thank you. I will, just quickly. That would be nice.'

While she went through to the front room I strung out the tea-making next door, trying to compose myself. I got half a ginger cake from the bread bin. When I returned with the tray, Eve was standing just like Archie did, in the middle of the room, waiting for me to sit her down. Then she perched on the edge of the seat, and looked across at me with a nervous smile.

'It's only from the shop,' I said, offering her a plate. I'd cut some pieces for her to choose. She took one and broke it in two in her fingers.

'I'm so pleased he's settling down,' she said. 'I was beginning to think I'd made a terrible mistake, coming here.' Her fingers made a marble out of the crumbs. 'My Granny – Mum's mum – used to show us photographs of the house and the garden. I never understood why Mum wouldn't bring us. She looked perfectly happy in the photographs. There was one of her playing tennis.'

'She was keen on the garden, your grandmother, I remember,' I said. 'Won half the prizes at the Summer Show.'

'We used to come to Cornwall for holidays,' Eve said. 'Stop off on the way sometimes in Okehampton; but never here. I didn't realize until I looked at a map how close it was. Mum used to tell us there was nothing there. She died last year,' she said, looking up as if to excuse her.

'I'm sorry,' I said automatically.

'Mum told me before she died. She was surprised it took me so long to start asking questions. She was always funny about dates: when she and my dad met and when they got married. But children aren't interested, are they?' She looked at me again. 'Not unless it's *their* birthday or it's Christmas.

139

Dates are boring, anniversaries or other people's birthdays – I've never been any good at remembering them.'

She popped the marble of cake into her mouth and chewed. Then she said, 'I did used to ask her when I was young why there were no pictures of their wedding. But even if I'd worked out she'd been pregnant, I was far too stupid to work out that she wouldn't have known my dad for long enough to be pregnant by him.'

I was staring at her blankly.

'My dad,' she said. 'Chris, he's not my real dad.'

I had no idea how to respond.

'Mum thought I'd more or less worked it out. She told me when she got ill again. She didn't want me to find out afterwards and be left with that anger. But it didn't matter *who* – that's what she said. *It was one of those things*, she said. And probably a lot more common than people think. Before the Pill . . .'

She looked at me as if I would understand exactly what she meant.

'She said it had been a mistake – it could have been any-one. The last thing she wanted was to hurt Chris, who was there right from the start. He was at the birth, he cut the cord – everything . . . I was thirty by then. Chris was my dad.' Eve put her plate to one side, pulled up a leg and curled it under her.

'That was why I asked about the man in the photo-graph the other day. Seeing him there, standing next to my mother . . . Joyce explained. She told me about the family. I had no idea. I'm really sorry.'

She was hugging her leg. 'I never pressed Mum. It didn't

140

seem that important. All that mattered at the time was her getting better.' She smiled and bit her lip. 'Then everything came at once. It went like dominoes: she died. I'd lost her. It wasn't long after that I chucked in my marriage; I even distanced myself from Chris – he wasn't my dad any more, he was my stepfather. Everything had changed. There was no *connection* to anything. I was sick of London, work, all of it. I thought it would be a new start, somewhere different, away from all the mess . . .' She made herself take a breath. 'It surprised me, really, how easy it was. Once I said I was going, that was that. I had no idea! I heard myself saying, I was going back to where I was from. I didn't believe it. I had no idea about this place, how tiny it is . . . It was only when I got here I began thinking, *this is where it must have happened*. This is where she lived. She'd grown up here right up until she went off to university. My real dad must have been from round here.' She looked me directly in the eye, as if she expected something from me.

'I didn't know your mother very well,' I said quickly, heading her off. Then I said, 'She sang, didn't she? She had a lovely voice.' I could hear myself as if I were performing someone else's lines.

Eve snorted. 'We used to hate it, my brother and me; we were horrid to her, especially when she tried to sing pop songs . . .'

I turned my cup and slipped my thumb in and out of the fine bone handle; Eve was staring at the bald knees of her jeans and all the time I was quietly adding up the years, pressing my fingers into my side to mark the decades, 1972, 82, 92, 2002, three, four, five, six.

141

'Mum was right about lots of things,' Eve said. 'She was right about Marco. It must have killed her coming to the wedding. I thought she was being so miserable about it because she was ill and more neurotic than she needed to be about the future.'

'So Marco was your husband. Archie's dad?' I asked, trying to keep up a semblance of conversation.

'Yes. I was pregnant. I was all over the place: marriage seemed to be the only thing.'

'Does Archie see his father?'

Eve bit her lip. 'He's in Scotland,' she said. 'I know it's hard for him. I thought it might make it better, coming here, where everything would be different. But I think he feels it even more. It's so old-fashioned: he comes home from school sometimes and tells me everyone else has got a dad.'

'I doubt that's true.'

She sniffed. 'Marco hates Devon. He says it's *bourgeois*: cream teas. Yachts, *Midsomer Murders*.'

'Perhaps Archie could go and stay with him?' I said.

Immediately she looked anxious. 'In Scotland? He's never stayed the night away from me,' she said.

'He's old enough, isn't he? If he wanted to?' I didn't have to persist – but I felt if I didn't, I'd have to mention Tom and then I'd not be able to stop myself; I'd unravel. Suddenly Eve's leg slipped and she cried out, lifting her cup high in the air as tea slopped from the saucer over her jeans. It gave me a start. She fell back against the chair, held the empty cup and saucer at arm's length as if they were some terrible portent of her life. And though I'd had difficulty seeing it before, in that moment, sitting where she was, those welling eyes, she reminded me exactly of her mother.

It was raining quite hard when I took her to the door.

'Thank you,' she said, looking contrite.

'You haven't a coat.' I said. 'Have one of mine.'

'It's no distance,' Eve said. 'I don't mind getting wet.'

'If you hang on . . .' I turned to the cupboard under the stairs, and rummaged behind the hoover, the hoover bags, the paraffin can. Daddy's umbrella. I drew it out, brushed it off.

'Go on,' I said, 'it's a bit of an antique, but it'll get you home.'

I opened it up for her. The joints were stiff and, around them, the material spotted with tiny rust holes.

'Thank you for listening to me,' she said. 'I'm sorry I went on.'

She took the bamboo handle from me and held it like a shield against the pattering arrows of the rain.

# 12

## *Acacia Avenue*

There was no question but that when I finished school I would stay with Mother. *Where else would I go?* I asked her. We were quite capable of looking after ourselves. It was just before I went away to St Cuthbert's that Daddy'd moved us into the house in West Norwood. It was an investment, he'd explained to her, and only a hop and a skip from Victoria. He would keep a flat on in town for work, but it would be so much quieter for her and better for her nerves. All mod cons, he said, and she could, of course, take Mrs Connor.

I was excited to be in such a new house. In the tops of the bay window there were little *fleur de lys*, which cast their colours into the room like kites. There were matching kitchen cupboards, with red handles, two sliding drawers under the sink, a pantry with its own built-in meat safe. Upstairs my room was long and thin with flights of blue swallows in the wallpaper all the way to the window. The view out was of the cemetery, lavish with yew trees and angels. Across the landing was a lavatory and a bathroom with chequered tiles and crinkly glass. Their bedroom – it was always 'their' room – was at the far end of the landing, empty and square, overlooking the street, the pink clouds of the cherry blossom in the treetops.

A year or two after we'd first moved in, Daddy's visits began to slacken off. It was perhaps my fifteenth or sixteenth birthday that he misplaced his umbrella, an item he treasured. The handle was made from a single piece of varnished bamboo, finished with a tiny silver cap and his initials, F.L.G. It had been engraved for him, before he went to Paris, by one of the uncles. Mother remembered it exactly: him sheltering her against a downpour outside the Gare du Nord.

Usually he had the sense to make his exits brusque. But this time he was fussing. 'I'm certain I brought it with me,' he said, puzzled.

We both denied knowledge. 'Look in the hat stand, *by all means*,' Mother said, a phrase of his she had picked up.

He went out into the hall and began pulling out walking sticks, checking under the jackets, lifting up my beret where it hung, briefly catching sight of his own exasperated face, framed in the oak-leaf mirror, the coat brushes dangling at either side like two long ears.

'I went to the club. I took a taxi. I came over here.' He rehearsed his movements, ticking them off.

'Taxi?' I asked.

'What?'

'Maybe you left it in the taxi?' I said. 'People are always losing umbrellas.'

'What's this?' he asked crossly, pointing at the back door key on its hook. 'Silly place to leave a key.'

The line between Mother and me was a spider thread. She caught my eye as I followed him back into the living room. We both knew the umbrella was safely tucked in the pit of her wardrobe.

'Never mind,' he was saying, pulling on his gloves, affecting a brave face.

The success in this instance of our sustained *sangfroid* injected an unusual spirit of celebration to his going. As soon as the door closed and he was along the path, out through the gate, I ran upstairs to fetch it. For the first and last time, we threw caution to the wind, opened it up and balanced it on the floor between us, where he ought to be. It was more than a trophy, it was an incarnation, an avatar upon which we invested our highest hopes. Eventually he'd come back to us. He'd come home and he'd be what every husband and father ought to be – our deliverer from the storm.

The summer I finished at St Cuthbert's was the summer of my seventeenth birthday. Daddy was good about birthdays. He enjoyed the charade of present giving. He began, with much humming and hawing, by handing over a slim package, which he'd been commissioned to give me. Mother seethed. It had been a point of honour that he never mentioned Miss Minchin in the house. We could pretend for the scant time that he was with us, that he was ours. I was worried to open it in front of her.

'Go on,' he said, 'won't bite.'

Mother watched sourly from her chair as I undid the ribbon, pulled open the mauve tissue paper.

It was a sky blue copy of *Pitman's Commercial Typewriting*. Inside was an inscription: To set you on your way, with fond regards, etc.

'*Someone* remembered,' Daddy said, 'how keen you were on typing.'

Daddy liked a bit of drama. He tipped his nose and went out to the hall, returning with a case that, barring the handle, had been wrapped securely in brown paper. He set it down on the floor in front of the fire. I could hardly wait.

I tore great triangular strips. Underneath was a hard black case. There were two metal latches either side of the handle, which I unclicked, lifted the lid. That boot polish smell. The machine gleamed. It was a portable, a Royal, perfect in every detail.

The spools shone like hubs on a car; the keyboard with its serried ranks of letters, like a theatre waiting for the curtains to open. I couldn't wait to try it out.

Mother took a long sip of her drink, rolled it around her mouth.

I prodded the 'A' and immediately a leg flicked and dropped. 'It works,' I said.

'Should think so,' Daddy said.

'Is noisy,' Mother said, 'too noisy for the house.'

As soon as Daddy had gone, I took it off to my room. I had never been more determined to succeed at anything. Over the next month, I spent hours at a time upstairs, rigorously adhering to the diktats of the manual, until my fingers were numb with the effort. Soon, I was able to practise with my eyes closed.

*The thing, thing, thing, thing. Is in the tree tree tree. The great green tree*

147

*is in the grove. The great green tree is in the green green grove. Dear Sir, Since I last wrote to you I have decided, etc. etc. I have decided that I would prefer I would rather take my business elsewhere. Dear Sir, Dear Sir, Dear Sir. Then they gave her a beautiful dress. Then they gave her a beautiful necklace and a three piece suite. Poke poke poke poke. Queen Queen. Zoo Zoo. Ape ape ape.*

I timed myself with an alarm clock. On a good run, I could get up to forty words a minute.

'Bravo,' Daddy said, when I told him. 'I think we can forget secretarial college.'

When I told Mother what he'd said, she screamed, 'You go to him. You be like him. *Allez – Va t'en!* Live with him. Be like him.'

'Start at the bottom and before you know it,' he'd said, 'you'll be running the show.'

'*Laisses-moi,*' she said. '*Je mourrai seule.*' The more Mother drank, the more French she became, a snail pulling in her horns.

I didn't want to disappoint Daddy but told him that perhaps it might be better for me to gain experience under my own steam, closer to home. He appeared relieved. Later he told me how impressed Patricia – as we were now obliged to call her – had been. It showed a bit of spunk, she'd said. Daddy presented it as if Patricia were on my side, a familiar ploy of his. 'You girls,' he'd say and from across the room she would flash her eyes at him; 'You and your secrets.'

One night, in my dream I was helping Mother off the lavatory. There was hardly space for us to move. We turned as one to inspect the bowl and watched a translucent cloud of crimson bloom like a spot of ink in the water. Mother was

148

dismissive, as if she'd seen it all before. *What did I expect?* I had never before considered there might be consequences to her being ill. I was outraged. I stormed round to Daddy and heard myself say that he should never have left; that it was a crime to leave someone who was so unwell. Daddy was calm as pie; he stood up, arranged his hand like a pitchfork around my throat and pinned me to the wall. My neck! From the corner of my eye I saw Miss Minchin, dusting lackadaisically in a maid's outfit of black satin, little white apron. I couldn't move. I watched her as she drew closer, swish, swish, and came to stand behind him, with her brown ostrich feathers, dusting behind his ears, the dandruff from his shoulders . . .

When I told Mother how I'd turned down his offer, I hadn't anticipated the extent of her gratitude. Her eyes were fervent. She leaned over to the table and poured us both a drink; she made me sit down next to her. We clinked our glasses for the first time. *Santé*, she said and then impulsively she stretched her hand, stapling us together.

We had the house, we had the wireless; Daddy — although he seldom visited — continued to pay the bills; and Mrs Connor came round every morning to light a fire if necessary, to sort out the larder and something hot for dinner. I was determined to find myself a job and began practising my typing with renewed enthusiasm. Of my three original letters of application, I received only one response, from the solicitors on Norwood High Street, Stapleton and Dwyer. It took me a while to find the door, 67A: past Radio Repair, wedged between Posner Furs and Black's, the undertakers.

It was Mr Stapleton himself who saw me to his office on the top floor. In those days he liked to conduct the interviews. The room was hazy with tobacco smoke, the view down on the street, sepia-tinted. A square clockface behind his desk ticked out the seconds with a concerted tock, tock, tock, as if every one of them was being ticked off on account. Even sitting down, Mr Stapleton looked short. His glabrous head was dominated by dark tortoise-shell spectacles.

'You were sent away to school?' he said approvingly. 'Weston-super-Mare? Seaside? Good stuff. And what are your living arrangements now, Miss Gaunt?' he asked.

'I live with my mother, in Acacia Avenue,' I told him.

'Ah. Yes, so I see.' He was holding out my letter of application. 'And you typed this out yourself?'

'Yes, I did.'

'Shorthand?'

'I—'

'Not essential, I wouldn't say. I expect you can take notes?' He peered at me over the tops of his spectacles, amphibian eyes.

'Yes, I can.' I added, thinking that it might help, 'My father was in books.'

'I see,' (and I gathered by his uncomfortable expression that he took it Daddy was dead). 'Good. Excellent,' he said. 'Well, if your references measure up, I see no reason why you shouldn't start with us forthwith. What do you say? Monday week? How does that sound?'

Mr Stapleton seemed to be a nice man. At St Cuthbert's there were no male teachers at all, no men apart from the chaplain and the groundsman, who was supposed to make himself scarce when we came out for games. As he led me down the stairs, we could hear the racket of typewriters. Mr Stapleton explained that I'd be one of a dozen typists working in the large room at the back. We made a detour down the corridor so that he could show me, leaning in at an open door as a dozen heads perked up to acknowledge him, though continued to rattle away without breaking stride. He closed the door and smiled. 'Well-oiled machine,' he said. 'You'll fit in like a flash.'

*Two carbon copies: one for the 'day file' under your desk. Ruler, pencils, notebook, stapler, ribbons, to be signed out. Desk: yours for the duration, but don't leave anything personal on it: nail varnish'll be whipped, compact, lipstick, that sort of thing – anything that has legs – I'm not saying nothing against no one here, but don't put temptation in the way. My advice.*

'Have you got a boyfriend?' It was the first thing the girls asked me when they got me on my own. We'd gone out to Merton's for a proper debrief.

'You should get out more,' they said.

'Take your specs off a minute,' they said.

I didn't like to remove my spectacles. But I didn't want to make a fuss.

'Nice eyes you've got. Sort of bluey-grey. Shame to hide them. I suppose you can't see without?'

'No. Not much,' I said, trying to focus on a sugar shaker.

'How many fingers am I holding up?' one of them asked, stretching out a hand.

'Five,' I replied, poking the frames back on.

'Not as bad as all that, then,' they said. 'You should give it a go. Boys don't make passes – haven't you heard?'

151

There was the girl from *Strangers on a Train*: Alfred Hitchcock's daughter played the part. With her short dark hair and her spectacles and her very slightly protruding teeth . . . It was Patricia and Daddy who'd pointed out the resemblance.

'You should come dancing with us,' they said. 'We'll soon sort you out.'

Instantly I told them about Mother, how she wasn't well, how she couldn't be left for long stretches on her own, not in the evening.

'Bring her along,' they said, laughing. We all laughed at that.

It was only a week or two later that they persuaded me to go round to Mimi's. Mimi was married to Mr Black, the undertaker; they had three sons, two of whom were at home and helped in the business, the youngest, Jimmy, away at sea. Mimi did the embalming, and her own face was testament to her skill – skin, smooth as Pyrex. When Mr Black shut up shop, on the few occasions that the back room was clear of bodies, Mimi would push back the long trestle tables, bring down the standard lamp, an extra couple of chairs, and turn the room over to her boys and any friends of theirs they cared to entertain.

She'd argued it out with her husband, 'No disrespect, but doing what they do, they need a chance to let off steam. Wouldn't be healthy, else.'

There was particular excitement among the secretaries when Mimi's youngest son, Jimmy, came home on leave. Mimi would be so determined to celebrate that one time she'd resorted to carrying a cadaver down into the cellar for the evening. She was more generous than usual, providing quantities of cider, with liver paté sandwiches and jars of pickled gherkins.

'We'll have such fun,' they said, 'you'll see.'

Jimmy's arms were like pistons, the skin stretched to a drum, the green veins the same colour as the ink in which he'd written MOTHER and drawn himself a mermaid.

Jimmy always came prepared. Under his arm he'd bring the latest record.

'You've seen the film?' he asked, holding the plate of vinyl on the candelabra of his fingers.

'*The Girl Can't Help It?*' squeaked the girls. 'Best movie of all time!' They'd paid the extra for the back row at the Electric.

The second the music started, Jimmy sprang into the air. *A wop bop a lu bop, a lop bam boom.* I'd heard nothing like it before – it was an assault, like being forced to ride the Looper at the fair. My heart began to race, the blood drained from my ears. There were almost a dozen of us in the room. The brothers, each with a small queue of eager girls who were prepared to dance with each other while they waited their turn. I had already bowed out and pretended to be engrossed in the record sleeve, which I'd retrieved from the floor. *Specialty records. Sunset Boulevard. Hollywood.* By the time he was fourteen Little Richard had got himself a job with a medicine show, drawing in the crowds. He'd sell them herb tonic. Little Richard was one of fourteen. He wasn't little at all: he was nearly six feet tall.

Jimmy stood before me, legs apart, arms akimbo. I was shaking my head, which he only took to be a challenge. He stretched out a hand, the muscle tautening under the bridge

153

of his short shirt-sleeves. The others were in fits, clasping their waists, urging me to my feet.

'You have to try,' they said lewdly. 'You never know – you might just enjoy it.'

'It's a bit loud for me,' I said, refusing to let go of my handbag.

There were scoffs of laughter. 'Oh, Mavis. You're such an old priss!'

There was nothing for it but to subject myself to Jimmy's attention. The song had begun. I stood with my bag on my arm as he prodded and led. *Good Golly Miss Molly.* Bam, bam, bam, as if I were a lump of clay that he could twist and turn and spin into a shapely urn. He took both of my hands so that my bag hung from my wrist like a padlock, pushed me away, brought me close, pushed me away. The others had given up dancing to spectate, clapping their hands in a line along the sofa, wiggling their shoulders forwards and back in time, bursting with the novelty of Mavis, dancing.

The more he pushed and the more the others goaded him on, the more wooden I became. I don't know what it was that made me think of Frances that moment: Frances Upcott, poised and composed, dressed for church, a neat tailored coat and a hat. She wouldn't have believed her eyes. The thought was a needle under my skin. It felt as if she really *was* watching, and the very idea left me mortified, to be caught in such an undignified position. Jimmy was building up to something: he took me firmly by the forearms, lowered his knees and with a great thrust, threw me back, right off my feet, swung me up and then down under the archway of his legs. I came down hard, grounded like a canoe, a splinter from the floorboards entering the back of my thigh, laddering my stocking. I hung my head as he clambered over me, waiting only for the song to end. As soon as it did, I picked myself off the floor, collected my coat, my bag and without a word, stepped out through the corridor to the front of the shop, left them to it.

I had thought my days of humiliation were over: the showers at school, the blanket 'bumps' that had left me with a permanent weakness in my coccyx – 'cuckoo bone' as Mrs Connor called it: I could feel it now, the old wound, hobbling home as if I'd been set upon by thieves.

My only card was Mother, and I had no qualms in playing it – she was a demanding invalid, whose fragile mental state had been exacerbated by the war and by my father dying in it. It was just too risky to leave her on her own.

After a year at the firm I was up to sixty-five words a minute, my stamina second to none. I enjoyed the bravado of it: the ratchet as the paper came out, the turning of the roll, the definitive clunk of an indent or return. After three solid years – by which time every other girl I'd started with had moved on – I was made Senior Typist, sat at the front of the typing pool on a raised platform and given a modest rise in salary. Another couple of years and I had risen as high as it was possible to rise. I became Personal Secretary to Mr Stapleton. By now, there was no question that I would fraternize with the other typists and I had long since developed an imperviousness to the chatter and the carryings-on. My reputation as a cold fish was confirmed by any casual visitor next door: Mimi, apparently, would still ask after me, and then go on to tell the tale of my astonishing indifference to popular music and to her devilishly handsome son.

I was appreciated by the partners, I'm sure. I was the only member of secretarial staff allowed a key to the stationery cupboard. Summoned once by Mr Stapleton to fetch an elderly client a cup of tea, I caught him referring to me as 'a treasure'. It took me by surprise. Until that time, Mr Stapleton had appeared to take little personal interest in me, other than to observe that the clock could be set by my punctuality.

'Take a letter,' he would say. Now, instead of confining himself to the chair opposite, he'd pace the room, generally coming to a halt behind me, to peer over my shoulder when he had a word to spell.

'L-a-m-b-e-r-t-o-n. Lamberton and Son, formerly, Lamberton – ampersand and – Co. That's it. There.' He put a gentle hand on my shoulder, a pressure that continued as I drew my ampersand and produced a clot of ink to my final stop

'There,' he said again, as the ink smudged, giving my shoulder another squeeze. There was a detectable skip in his step. It was 1960, the end of a decade that had been a good one for the firm, slow but steady. Mr Stapleton asked me specifically what I thought to the idea of a Christmas party, 'push out the boat'. As Chairman of the local Conservative club, he imagined he'd be able to hire out the building on favourable terms. He didn't have a wife to ask. He knew he could rely on me, he said. I was a reliable sort.

'I—' I had sworn never to go to another party or a dance again.

'We'll invite other halves, of course,' he said, 'and I've suggested we join forces with Black's, beef up the ratio of boys to girls. I'm not such an old dinosaur, you know.'

I had to admit, the girls had done a lovely job on the inside of the hall. There were half a dozen Union Jacks and a criss-cross the length and breadth of the room of bunting, red, white and blue. Two of the juniors had spent the whole afternoon blowing up balloons, which they'd tied in bunches to various of the plaques and pictures. There was a signed photograph of Mr Macmillan; a seventieth birthday portrait of Winston Churchill, sitting at his desk ducking a trio of balloons; there was a colour photograph of the Queen at the coronation, that Hartnell dress, her red lips matching the red velvet of the throne, her black eyes, white gloves.

'God bless her,' Mr Stapleton said, moving over to me. 'Pretty as a picture.'

He seemed to have thought of everything; there was a generous supply behind the bar: beer and cider for the boys, Advocaat and lemonade for the girls (a cocktail, he informed me – with undisguised pleasure at the seasonableness of it – that was commonly known as a snowball).

A shallow glass of the yellow liquid was handed by him to each of us as we arrived. *God bless!* It tasted eggy and sweet with a grainy texture, not unpleasant. Against the far wall, next to a wooden lectern, a man in blue uniform was kneeling down beside a record player. I looked again: Jimmy Black.

Mr Stapleton was watching my face.

'Black's idea. Son's on leave, home for Christmas and only too pleased to help us out. Does this sort of thing for the boys in the mess apparently – *recreation*.'

Mr Stapleton hadn't the slightest idea about Mimi's parties.

'I made sure to say we were after something *classic* – Christmas carols, what-not. Bearing in mind where we are . . .' He looked around with pride, raised his glass.

I sipped my drink. 'You're not convinced?' he asked. 'No, I can see it in your face. Don't fret. Taken precautions.'

With that he produced from behind the bar a large brown paper bag, and drew from it a shiny record album he'd bought only that morning, expressly: *A Jolly Christmas from Frank Sinatra*. He tapped his nose, 'Wait till I hand *this* over.'

As he beavered off towards Jimmy I decided to find myself somewhere to sit, somewhere relatively inaccessible. There was a row of round tables and chairs lined against the right side of the room. I made my way over to the top corner and squeezed in, with my back to the wall. At that moment, the doors opened and one of the old girls sailed in, Violet, heavily pregnant. She had married the eldest Black son and he led her now by the elbow towards the bar, where each collected a drink. As soon as Violet turned and began to search the room, her eyes lighted on me. She freed herself from her husband and, collecting another glass from the counter, swayed towards me, moving from side to side as if she were walking up the aisle of a bus.

'What a treat! I'd quite forgotten you'd be here,' she said, sliding one of the glasses in my direction. 'Lovely to see you – cheers.'

She took one sip and turned down her mouth. 'Second thoughts, I think you'd better have it.' She cast her eyes over her huge belly. 'Shame for it to go to waste.' I drained my glass and swapped the empty for her full.

'Thanks,' I said, 'feeling's mutual,' which was something I remembered she used to say about everything.

I needn't have worried about the music. There was a gentle crooning in the background. One of the partners led his wife gamely around the dance floor in a waltz. A couple of girls were in each other's arms, waiting for the apprentices from Black's to turn up.

Mr Stapleton was working his way round the room, devoting a little comment and a pat to each of his staff as if it were prize day. The girls had nothing to say back to him. They were tongue-tied out of the office, done up in their best party dresses. 'I'll be keeping an eye on you,' he said, cheerfully, warning the boys. I had never seen him in such a chipper mood.

'May I join you?' he asked as he reached our table, pulling over a chair.

My third snowball tasted of thick baby milk.

'Would you care to?' he was asking and before I had a chance, he'd got to his feet, extended his chubby hand.

'Oh goodness,' I said, 'really, I can't.'

'Off you go,' Violet said, helping to ease me out from the table. 'About time you was winkled out.'

'This one's a bit of a favourite of mine,' he said, as he collected me, leaning into my ear. His breath smelled of onions. A bell sounded, voices humming, a steady strummed guitar. Mr Stapleton placed a hand in the small of my back. We juggled with our right hands and he settled for my wrist. 'You're looking rather lovely tonight, if I might add,' he said.

My spectacles were slipping down my nose, but I didn't dare loosen either one of my hands to set them right. I stared down at his black pin-head brogues, my orange satin pumps. There was custard in my mouth. I could feel the weight of the liquid I carried, like one of those tribeswomen with a pitcher on her head. I scrunched my fingers in the arm of his jacket to get a purchase.

'Steady,' he said at one point.

He set his hand more firmly against my flank. I hung my head still further to keep up with the declining angle of my spectacle frames. I wrong-footed myself, we came undone. For a moment I spun away from him into thin air. I might have keeled over altogether, had he not grabbed my hand tightly and pulled me back towards him.

'Let's sit you down, Mavis,' he said, 'nice and steady.'

By now his voice – particularly as he pronounced my name – was thick and cloying.

'Feeling a bit faint?' He was peering into my face.

There was an egg-shaped object in my mouth, my lips pursed around it. I shook my head dumbly as I got to my feet, held the delicate egg all the way across the dance floor, lunging towards the back of the hall and the door that led through to the lavatories, banging through a second swinging door and into a cubicle where I delivered into the open mouth of the lavatory the entire scrambled contents of my stomach. I reached out for the wall to balance myself, a string of albumen dangling from my lips, my eyes inexplicably wet with tears.

After a while there was a shuffle outside and a voice through the door. 'Mavis! Are you all right? I can't come in. I'll heave. It's the smell . . . Shall I fetch someone? Are you all right?' It was Violet.

I didn't dare speak.

'Mavis, are you all right? Answer me!'

'Yes,' I said weakly, 'I'll be fine.' Which made my eyes weep again.

'You sure?'

'Yes.' It was quiet in there and blissfully contained. I didn't want to leave. As Violet lumbered off to report back – the swing of the hall door augured a complete change in tempo. There were yips of delight. *One two three o'clock four o'clock, rock.* Spontaneous clapping and pattering of feet. I set down the lid of the lavatory seat and sat on it with my head in my hands. My stomach was an empty dance hall, creaking and gaping.

Suddenly the door to the Ladies was open again. 'Phwar, pongs of steak and onions in here,' a voice said. 'Pwoof.'

'They've gone barmy, those boys,' another one said.

'They've got a bottle of fortified wine out the back, didn't you know?'

'Staples'll call it a night, if they carry on like that.'

'He's one to talk. Look at the way he was groping little Gaunty. Urgh. Dirty old man.'

They laughed. 'Look at us,' they said, 'look like we've been dragged backwards.' They were standing together at the sink. One of them got out her lipstick. ''E's 'ot a 'ovely 'ouff,' she said.

'You what?'

161

She popped her lips, made a kissing noise. 'Will Black: his chops.'

'Hang on a second,' the other one said.

The door to the cubicle rattled.

'Who's in there?'

There was a nervous silence. I wiped my mouth with the back of my wrist, coughed and rustled. Then I pulled the chain – the obliterating clank and whoosh – and bundled myself out. I went straight for the sink, without looking at either of them. They backed away to give me room, their eyes in the mirror circling above my head as I filled my hand with a cupful of water.

By the time I had walked the long length of Acacia Avenue and reached the front door even my hands were steady. It must have been after eleven I was thinking, turning the key as gently and quietly as I could.

'*Mayviss*,' Mother called as the staircase creaked under me, '*tu es là?*'

'I'm fine, Mother. Sorry it's late.'

'*Viens ici.*'

I clutched my coat around me, walked along the landing to her door, which was ajar.

'*Ici*,' she said.

I walked to the end of the bed. 'Sorry I'm so late. I couldn't get away. Hope I didn't wake you?'

She scrunched up her nose and put the back of her hand to her mouth. '*Oph*,' turning her head away.

It was only because I was home the week over Christmas that

I noticed, even by her own meagre standards, that Mother wasn't eating. She'd had flu from Mrs Connor earlier in the month, which had left her more tearful than usual. On Christmas Day I tried my best. I took up a pair of crackers to her room, but she was disinclined to pull them with me. She didn't like the bang. In fact, she didn't touch anything I brought up – not Mrs Connor's miniature plum pudding, not even her usual whisky and milk.

'Christmas is always a gloomy time of year,' we said. Between us, Mrs Connor and I tried to jolly her along. But by New Year's Eve, a Saturday, each of us was dreading going up there. All morning, Mother had been crying quietly and relentlessly, so much so, we discovered, that she'd quite forgotten to take herself to the lavatory. I felt impelled to call out the doctor. I didn't know what to do with her. When he arrived and laid his hands on her, he pursed his lips and said I should have called him sooner.

'But it was Christmas,' I said feebly. 'She wouldn't let me.'

He pinned me with a glare over the top of his spectacles, ticking me off. That afternoon he had the ambulance pick her up and take her to the Dulwich Infirmary.

'Double pneumonia,' the second doctor confirmed. 'Severe dehydration.'

'*Ma poupée*,' she whispered when I arrived to see her on New Year's Day. She had stopped speaking English entirely. It made her more affectionate. '*Ma petite fille*.' She was delirious. The nurse came with a silver syringe in a dish; Mother's pupils darkened to ink. When she quietened down, I stroked her forehead. It was dry and soft as an opera glove.

'How long has she been like this?' the second doctor asked at lunchtime.

'I didn't realize she was so ill,' I said, feeling foolish. 'She has always been like this.'

'She hasn't always had pneumonia,' the doctor said a little impatiently.

'I mean. She's always been a bit ill.'

'You didn't believe it was serious?'

'We have Mrs Connor. Mrs Connor looks after her.'

'There,' the nursing sister said, 'I'm sure you've done your best.'

'I'm not going anywhere,' I said to Mother firmly, though she wasn't listening. I insisted I would stay the night; I'd sit in the tweedy chair. The Sister brought me a patchwork blanket, a second cup of sweet tea. Every now and then Mother stirred, her huge eyes shiny as sea anemones. I hadn't noticed without her clothes how shrunken she'd become. She was dressed in a pale hospital gown, her arms like twigs.

'If she wakes, make sure she has a drink,' the nurse said. 'It's the best thing you can do for her.'

I woke with a start at half past three: the lights were dimmed, I'd drifted off. Mother's head was raised from the pillow, as if she'd had a shock, but I couldn't tell what she was looking at.

'Mother? Are you awake?'

I reached for the glass. There was an urgency about her expression. Recalling a list. *Du beurre, du pain, du médecine* . . .

The water, when I tipped the glass for her, ran out of her mouth and over the sheets.

'Mother? Please don't,' I said.

# 13

## *Ladybird, Ladybird*

It hit Mrs Connor hard that there was no one but us in the yellow-brick memorial chapel to send Mother off. If only I'd asked Father Allen, she was sure he would have helped provide a creditable congregation. Didn't Mother have relatives abroad? Daddy had signed a card (written out, I noticed, by Patricia) and rung to say, although he couldn't be there, he'd ordered a wreath of carnations, professing surprise later that I hadn't noticed them there.

Mimi had laid her out as I'd requested, in her silver fox fur. Mrs Connor had pointed out how the white nimbus of hair, which Mother had neglected to dye over the last few weeks, gave the impression of a halo. So when Mimi suggested we might colour it, I declined. But I let her paint Mother's lips the deep red that she favoured, her skin as powder pale as she'd have wanted it. Mimi worked her wonders: somehow, the cheeks, which had looked so drawn in the hospital, had regained their youthful plumpness. But there was nothing she could do about the eyebrows: that final aspect of reproach.

'Looks like a queen,' Mimi said to make it better.

I told her that Mother had wanted once to be an actress.

'Well that makes sense,' she said. 'Something out of Shakespeare — something regal, washed up in a barque?'

Outside the sunlight was unforgiving and jubilant, the group of birches in the designated place sparkling a confetti of light and shade. Francine Eluard, 3 August 1910 – 2 January 1961. The plot had been staked out. There was a sac of liquid like a drop of dew at Mrs Connor's nostril. Mother was only two years older than herself, she said. Hard to believe it.

We walked back to the house in our black skirts and sat in the kitchen with a bottle of Mother's favourite sherry.

'Free as a bird,' Mrs Connor sighed, lifting her glass. But having said it, looked towards me, dismayed. Her eyes were glazed. She pulled off her squashy hat.

'Do you mind?' she asked, jiggling a packet of cigarettes. I shook my head. Although Mother enjoyed the occasional cigarette, she didn't allow Mrs Connor to smoke in the house. 'It's just so sudden, isn't it?'

'What will you do?' I asked her.

'Sure there's plenty out there,' she said stoically.

'You've been very patient. Thank you.'

'No trouble at all. She had her cross.' She shuddered. There was a rose-coloured kiss of lipstick around the end of her cigarette. I got up to fetch her a saucer.

'It's going to be a big change, sure it is,' she said. Then, her voice so light that it almost cracked, 'Will you be staying on?'

The shoulders of her suit were browning under the electric

166

light; her hair was sticky where it had been flattened beneath her hat.

'I had an idea I might go back to Devon,' I said. It was as easy as tapping a knee-cap with a spoon; I'd been mulling it over ever since the Christmas party.

She sat very upright, clutching her handbag so that the fine workings of her hands showed through. For a moment we were both flummoxed. Then she said, in that same high register, 'Well, I'm sure it's lovely down there. Seaside and all. Oh, I'd be envious of you. Sure, if you've the chance – why not?'

It was as if I had only been waiting to hear myself say the words out loud – they set like concrete.

'We'd keep in touch,' I said, 'whatever happens?'

She sucked down to the pink filter of the cigarette. Then she went to the sink very deliberately and rinsed the stub under the tap. She came back to the table, unclipped her bag, and began poking about inside. 'I don't think it's sunk in, I'm sorry.'

She brought out a handkerchief and wrapped the wet stub in its folds, held it there like a precious thing. Then she began to chant under her breath, '*Ladybird, ladybird, fly away home, your house is on fire, your children have flown.* Do you remember that one?' she asked, her charcoal breath, but I was miles away, watching the tears plink freely from her face as she finished it off in a whisper, '*All but a little one, under a stone.*'

# PART IV
*Paradise*

# 14

## *Amorphophallus Titanum, June 1961*

I rang Daddy from a telephone box. I had something to tell
him, I said. He had news for me too, he said. I said I wanted to
see him on his own, I didn't want to come to the house. It was
the only time I stipulated anything, the only time I stipulated
anything that had any effect.

'Kew Gardens,' I said. I wanted it to be outdoors and I
wanted it to be an effort for him.

'What's all this about, then?' he asked irritably, turning
up at Kew Bridge five minutes late. 'Funny sort of a place to
want to meet.'

He used to tell me how the uncles brought him here when
he was a boy and lived across the river in Chiswick. How they
used to encourage him to sweat it out in the hothouses, wanting to make an explorer of him. I didn't forget those things.

It was pure accident that we had turned up on such a
busy day. There was a knot of visitors waiting to get in, the
attendant gesturing and explaining to anyone who'd listen

where they could find the rare flower that had been in all the papers: titan arum. Daddy perked up. 'Bit of luck,' he said, with the boyish enthusiasm he generally reserved for Patricia. 'Before you start . . .' he said, raising his hand, 'now we're here, let's go and take a look.' I couldn't tell whether he was prevaricating on my behalf or on his own.

The Palm House glittered like an icy hull. Inside, the air was spongy, lime-coloured; we followed the general direction of the other visitors, on clanking serrated planks. Daddy behaved as he always did, as if he were a policeman with a right of way, so forthright that no one questioned him, parting to let us through until we reached the foot of an ornate spiral staircase.

'Phew,' he said. It was the obnoxious stench of rotten meat, as if we had indeed arrived at the scene of some foul crime. He lifted his elbow to his face and I held my hands to mine. At our feet, like a large gramophone, the plant was visibly in motion. A deep trumpet of raggedy-edged taffeta unfurling around a bony yellow pistil.

'Now we know,' Daddy said, his eyes watering, 'why they call it a corpse.'

Outside, gulping in the fresh air, we found ourselves seats at a table at the edge of the tea pavilion. I was twenty-five, but Daddy treated me as if I were still a child, pushing me in on my chair. 'Well?' he asked. 'I suppose you're wondering why I didn't turn up for your mother?' He had perfected two expressions for me: harried or off-the-hook.

'I'm thinking of leaving London,' I said.

'What?'

'Leaving,' I said.

'What's brought this on?'

'I don't know . . . Mother. Work.'

'Thought you enjoyed that job of yours?' He pursed his lips, glancing about in case anyone could overhear us. 'Is this because I didn't come? You know——'

'No. It isn't that.'

'Well, as long as it's nothing I've done . . . No harm in a visit, I suppose,' he said, looking dubious. 'Anyway, I've——'

'I've given in my notice,' I said, 'I'm tidying the house. I'll leave the furniture.'

'Bit sudden, all of this?' He was distracted, glancing off to find a waitress. 'Actually,' he said, still peering in the opposite direction, 'as I said, I've a bit of news of my own.' He turned to face me boldly. 'Not to beat about the bush,' he said, holding on to the bottom edge of his waistcoat, 'but I've asked Pat to marry me. Make an honest woman of her – what do you say?'

The train from Waterloo took several hours, and in all that time, I never once relaxed enough to read the book I had bought for the journey or to eat my sandwiches. I was in a state of permanent suspension, as if we weren't travelling on a grounded, horizontal line, but were ascending, vertically, from the depths. When eventually I emerged from the station, my legs would hardly support me. I kept to the tag-end of a small gaggle of other passengers who'd left the train at Buckleigh, tottering out into the golden-green sunlight. As they dispersed, I was left, squinting around, wondering (though we'd swapped affectionate letters) if Joyce Fairley had forgotten about me after all. The only vehicle remaining in the yard was a rambling black Austin, big as a bus. As I put my hand up to shield my eyes, a skinny goat-ish man got out and nodded in my direction. I set out tentatively towards him, lop-sided with my three cases.

By the time I reached him, it dawned on me who he was: Wilf McManus. 'Joyce sent me over,' he said. I was too effusive. He shrank from me as he took my cases. He was wearing an old black suit — it might have been the *same* black suit. My heart clattered as I watched him load the back seat, setting my two cases, my typewriter, one on top of the other. There was a crate next to them with hens in it, fussing and prattling. Wilf nodded for me to let myself in at the passenger door. 'Pull,' he said, 'it's stiff.' In spite of his brusqueness, there was a musical lilt to his voice.

I sat waiting for him to get in, trying to control my breathing. I watched someone drag a bicycle out from the shed and set its nose into the main road.

'It's very kind of you,' I said as he climbed in, took the wheel. 'I hope it isn't putting you out?'

He didn't contradict me. 'Market day,' he said as we swung out of the yard, passing the bicycle, and back across the railway line. He smelled sweet and bitter and smokey all at once.

'It's been years,' I said, wondering if he remembered me. 'Eighteen years. It feels like a lifetime.'

He grunted. 'Don't expect much has changed.'

*You've changed*, I could have said. He had shrivelled. There were flecks of white in his beard. His eyes were pale as harebells.

'You didn't have a car before,' I said. He shrugged.

Already the lane had narrowed and was closing about

us, two undulating walls of foliage. Pairs of swifts darted ahead, skimming the gills of the engine; the blues, yellows and whites of the hedgerows fluttering like bunting. I told him that I felt like royalty. He snorted; then he changed gear violently. The car lurched as we rounded a tight bend and then began the tortuous ascent of the hill. At the crest, for a moment or two, you could see for miles, the infinitesimal curving away of the earth, and then as we dipped over the other side, we were in free-fall, we might have been flying.

Ever since I'd announced myself – to Mrs Connor, to Mr Stapleton, to Daddy – I had been going through the motions of a leap. I had kept some version of Devon vacuum-packed. Now that I was here again, the seal had been broken. Everything exhaled. Every muscle of every blade of grass seemed to be flexing itself. Every leaf. It was too much to take in. The oily animal smell of the car, the rush of air, the juddering and jolting. As if it had been possible after all to turn back the hands of the clock.

There was a new metal sign at the approach of the village, SHIPLEIGH, which we passed before I had a chance to point it out. Mr McManus veered round the hairpin bend and up the narrow incline of the Green, right to the door of the Seven Stars, where, just short of the bench outside, he braked hard. I didn't have a minute to get my bearings. I was aware of the open doorway and then of someone filling it. On my side of the car, there was a fumbling, a blast of new-mown grass in the air as the door was prised open, and then there was Joyce reaching, almost dragging me out. Joyce, her fine hair fluffier than I remembered it, but I knew her at once. She was more demonstrative than I'd dreamed, blossoming, clutching me to her middle-aged bosom.

'You were a maid before,' she said, muffling me in her lily of the valley scent. 'Look how you've grown.'

Joyce must have been about forty. She held me from her, taking a proper look. I was taller than she was. 'I shall show you straight up,' she said briskly, 'then we shall find you a bite to eat.'

There was hardly room for her on the twisting stairwell. She'd put on weight, the petticoat under her skirt hissed. She ducked her head under a lintel. 'There,' she said.

The room was at the opposite end to where Daddy had stayed. It was more or less box shaped, with a bed, a chest of drawers, a square window and a jar of honeysuckle and rose.

'Not a deal of space, I know,' Joyce said, moving towards the head of the bed, bashing the pillows. 'Through there,' she indicated a green chenille curtain, 'you'll find a rail for your things.'

I set my cases and typewriter by the bed.

'How's your father?' she asked. Her eyes were all over me. Then she said, 'A typewriter?' nodding to the black box.

'I was a secretary in London. At a solicitor's,' I reminded her.

'Well of course, you're all grown-up. Of course.' She fussed with the curtains for me, pulling them back.

How efficient I had been at leaving. I'd even gone back to sand the ink blots from inside my desk, removed every last paper clip, every trace. Joyce pulled out the top drawer of the chest of drawers to demonstrate. My weightlifter's smile showed how I was longing to be on my own.

'Well,' she said, 'I expect you'll need time to sort yourself out. There's water in the jug.'

She backed out of the door, her bright strawberry face.

I sat on the bed and pushed open the window, clipping the iron bar to hold it in place. There were flurries of tiny birds. For a while I watched them squabbling, pulling the air in a hundred different directions. I was eager for a sign – some hint of recognition: the whitewashed walls of the cottages glared, the bright new telephone box on the Green; the horizon, distancing itself, hazy and smudged. I couldn't expect it to be immediate, I told myself, not after such a long time away. I turned back into the room and brought the suitcase up on to the bed, flicked the catches. The clothes at least were familiar – my flowery silk frock, my green and blue cardigans, my suit, my underwear. When I got to the suit jacket, folded at the bottom, I remembered the slim cardboard box that I'd wrapped in it for safe-keeping.

Mr Stapleton hadn't wanted to 'rattle the hens'. In case I changed my mind, he said, he'd decided that he wouldn't tell any of the other typists I was leaving until my very last day, when, duly, he called a meeting. 'Miss Gaunt has given the matter a great deal of thought,' he told them, 'and has decided to quit London entirely.' He'd let a ripple of curiosity sweep the gathering before handing me the package, 'a small token of the partners' appreciation,' making a shovelling gesture of his hand.

It was an oval frame, silver-plated, with two little ball feet to stand upon. At home, in the process of rationalizing my few possessions, I found the photograph of Mother and Daddy: him in his monkey suit, grinning on the steps of

St Olaf's, Mother gazing up at him, wearing a lilac dress-coat – her favourite colour. It had always needed a new frame – the glass in the old one was cracked – so I got the nail scissors out and trimmed the corners to fit. Now I propped it, facing me, on the chest of drawers.

It was a picture from before I was born, from the fairy tale that was my mother's marriage. *Fairy tale!* How quickly I betrayed her. As if I had never spun gold from straw.

# 15

## *Take a Letter (any letter)*

I hadn't specified to anyone the length of my stay and tactfully no one asked, making the assumption perhaps, as I did, that it was as long as it was long.

'Tsk, tsk,' was Auntie's habitual greeting as I let myself in, Daddy's failure of duty towards me only another in the roll of failures that she felt extended from her side of the family. She hardly moved from her chair these days, yet she was curiously up-to-date. Father had treated my mother abominably, she said. Only bounders and ruffians behaved like that. She considered my decision to *return* to Devon to be a moral repudiation of him, the whole family, and therefore – *Hallelujah* – a good thing. She leapt to Ernest's anchor cuff links, grasped them in her fist. And it was disgraceful, she said, when she discovered for the fifteenth time of asking, that I was still living at the pub. Surely his allowance would stretch to more than that?

I divided my time almost equally between the kitchen at the Seven Stars and Auntie's front room. Through Joyce, I was soon abreast with developments in the village. After her daughter Sandy got married, she'd moved to Buckleigh, where she was working in the post office, as if waiting for a parcel of babies to arrive. Victor, on the other hand, with no qualifications to speak of, was still living at home. But he wasn't doing badly for himself. Old Mr Upcott had taken him on at harvest times, and after he passed on, there was work enough to keep Victor down there permanently.

'Turns out he's a perfectly good herdsman,' Joyce said. 'So there's no favours there.'

'When did he die?' I asked. 'Mr Upcott.'

'Oh, a couple of years ago, now. Heart attack it was.'

'How are the rest of them?' I asked, giving the question hardly any weight.

'Oh, much the same,' Joyce replied. 'Airs and graces. Nothing's changed there.'

'Joyce!' It was Mrs McManus, who followed her voice through into the kitchen. 'Ah,' she said, 'there you are.' She tipped her head in my direction, and said, over-politely, 'If you'll excuse us? Joyce: can we look at the menus?'

I got to my feet, ready to go back up to my room.

'Mavis was telling me about her office,' Joyce said, as if she needed to explain, 'in London. I was hoping I could pick up a few tips.'

Mrs McManus had a smile like an elastic band. 'Of course, I'd quite forgotten that you'd *worked*. You must find it dull with us, I'm sure you do.'

It was true that after nearly eight years at Stapleton's I had become accustomed to a routine and used to being kept busy. After a week or two, twiddling my thumbs, I knew that if I was going to stay on in Shipleigh in any permanent way, I would have to find myself something to do. It was hopeless trying to get Auntie to let me help her with the house. She was too habituated to its various trails, she said: she knew the pitfalls, tapping her way around the furniture with an old riding whip. At the Seven Stars, I did what I could by way of running errands or helping out in the kitchen. But there was no disguising that I loitered a good deal. It struck me, hiding up in my room, that having nothing to do was a sort of sickness. There were days when I even contemplated the humiliation of going back to London; Mr Stapleton after all had said I might.

It must have been one such afternoon, in a spirit of dejection that I turned to my typewriter, sitting unopened all this time on top of the chest of drawers. As soon as I lifted the lid, my fingers sought their places, pressed themselves automatically against the familiar circles of their keys. My nostrils filled with the reviving smell of ink, my shoulders dropped. I had quite forgotten how much, in spite of everything else, I'd enjoyed typing.

*Dear Mrs Connor . . .* Who else was there to write to? *Dear Daddy . . .* ? Buoyed up and in a frivolous mood, because there was strictly no necessity to type anything, another idea suggested itself to me. I'd once staggered Daddy by completing *The Times* crossword in under thirty minutes (only when he came to examine the newspaper properly, hours later, did he discover that my ladders of words bore no resemblance to any of the clues). I fed a fresh sheet of paper between the rollers and, with similar abandon, began to type whatever came into my head.

> *After a particularly trying day, Verity returned to the cottage.*
> *She was neat and she was trim. She had lost her betrothed to*
> *the war — shot down over enemy lines like a pheasant — and*
> *although she had determined to make the best of things, there*
> *were times — times like these — that she could not shake him*
> *from her mind.*

At last, the applause of the keys, the regular ping and zip of the return. In no time at all I had completed a page and held it at arm's length to inspect. From a distance, it looked perfectly rendered; it might have been *War and Peace*.

Joyce and Diana McManus were as impressed by the professionalism of the noise as they'd have been by anything I might have produced. After a week or two, my reputation was such that every now and again, shyly, I'd be asked by one of the frequenters of the bar if I'd kindly type up a letter of sale or of recommendation, to which, more than happily, I'd oblige. It was Diana herself who approached me about Wilf.

When she'd known him first, she told me, Wilf was working in a bookshop on the Charing Cross Road, frequenting the pubs of Soho, and — she said it in a lowered but excited voice — quite a bohemian. He had ambition then, she said. 'They'd shout their poems out to each other across the tables; sometimes there'd be a fiddle there, sawing away behind them ... Dancing, singing. We had good times,' she said pensively. Then, as if she'd confided quite enough, she said, 'I wonder if you'd type them up for him? He's so many of them. I'm sure if we typed them and put them into some decent order, it might buck his spirits – don't you think?'

I was more than happy to have the commission and Diana did everything she could to facilitate the process, providing me with an old schooldesk, which we managed to slot alongside the chest of drawers, a little chair, and supplying all the paper I was likely to need. It had been a job in itself to prise the notebooks out of Wilf, but she brought them up to me triumphantly one afternoon, four of them, bound with elastic bands.

'I've told him how well qualified you are,' she said. 'He remembers your father, of course . . .'

I was meticulous. If I'd misread a word, or misplaced a comma, I insisted on typing out the whole page again, urging Wilf, through Diana, to circle my mistakes. By the thirteenth or fourteenth poem, I had become accustomed to his handwriting, the peculiar squeeze-box of his letters. Even Wilf had begun to admit, the poems looked quite decent typed up. He started keeping a notebook again under the counter, a pencil behind his ear. The farmers began to call him Milton. Which he liked.

'You remind me of my older sister,' he told me unprompted one evening. 'Jean. She was very proper. No nonsense. She never married, of course. Taught in the primary school.'

His voice was so soft – disconcertingly, quite the opposite in tone to the verses I was typing up for him and puzzling over as I went to sleep:

> *O the oak and the ash and the rowan and the birch*
> *The only way to heaven is a hop and a lurch*
> *O the bishop and the nun and the drunk and the tart*
> *The only way to say it is to stop before you start*

'I wish I were less ignorant,' I said, handing him back a typescript, having failed to pin down his meaning.

Wilf so rarely laughed that when he did, it was like the flash of a bulb. 'I'm sure you're not half as ignorant as you say. You're a waif, aren't you?' he said, not unfondly. 'A blow-in, like me.'

'I came here when I was a child,' I said, a little defensively. 'It feels like home to me.'

'Doesn't it seem quiet?'

'I like the quiet,' I said.

'*The grave's a fine and private place,*' he said, touching his nose. That eye-to-eye contact: I was so unused to it that it rocked me. I blushed, too confused to place his reference and said the first thing that came into my head: 'I thought nature was supposed to be good for poets?'

He snorted. 'If you say so.'

It was only when I got back to my room that I remembered exactly where that grave was from. His coy *mistress*! Now I detonated like a soft summer fruit.

After a while, Wilf started coming to me, rather than me always going to him, with minor alterations, with new poems even. We never shut the door to my room entirely. I took the chair and he sat on the end of the bed. It made my back burn to think of him there, his eyes upon me as I typed.

184

'I'll bring it down, when I've done,' I said and as the two of us got to our feet we were so close, our limbs so involved in the tiny space, that without even knowing it, we might easily have embraced. I looked down to the buckle of my dress, the top of my head glancing his chin.

'Thank you for that,' he said.

'Wilf!' Diana would shout. 'Where've you got to? Wilf!'

'His master's voice,' he said.

There was something of a *Brave New World* about my infatuation with Wilf. Perhaps it was only that he'd happened to be the first person I clapped eyes upon. Perhaps if the countryside itself had been more receptive, less indifferent to me? If I had found my way to the Upcotts sooner?

And there was no question but that I knew it was wrong — he was a married man — but there were some nights — I know there were — I lay in bed and swooned, clasping myself under the blankets, imagining Wilf's sinewy arms about me, his tough, skinny face next to mine.

Before Christmas, things were particularly lively. The stairs to my room ran up beside the giant chimney breast in the main bar, which meant that, although I rarely went down in the evenings, I was party to the rumble of whatever was going on. I'd hear loud claps of laughter; the air, warm and fuggy from all those mouths thrown wide, and caps and pipes and little Scottie dogs doing tricks. Joyce had a huge brass pot of glühwein on the go. There were always one or two women who'd venture into the bar that time of year, any of whom could be persuaded by a sweet, warming drink.

185

'He won't show me,' I heard Diana complaining to the man she played tennis with. Diana's voice was always icily distinct. 'He's been writing *love* poems, I can tell,' she said mockingly, 'the way he's mooching about.'

This particular man enjoyed getting Wilf to serve him, calling him loudly 'old chap'. 'If music be the food of love,' he quoted inanely to Diana's hearty amusement.

There was no response from Wilf – though, by now, I was at my door, on tenterhooks – only the sultry mix of cinnamon and tobacco. It was Diana who spoke next, shrilly, 'Wilf! What on earth are you doing? You'll set us all on fire.'

The commotion was enough to bring me to the bottom of the stairs in time to see Wilf lift the heavy drawbridge of the bar and walk quite calmly towards the fireplace, placing his manuscript – all thirty pages of typing – on to the burning logs, a baby to a cradle. There was a great flare of heat.

'What on earth did you do that for?' Diana demanded. The whole room was silent. She took the poker to the fire in an effort to control the flames, thin grey wafers rising and disintegrating in the chimney.

The next morning Diana apologized stonily for the bother I'd been put to. 'All your effort,' she said. 'I don't know what got into him.'

But I was strangely uplifted by the breach I saw between them, relishing the prospect of typing the poems all over again. Wilf said nothing. His head was down. A day or two later I was impatient for some sign from him. I followed him outside, where he was polishing the lamps on the car. I said, 'I'm sorry about your poems.'

He shrugged as if it were of no consequence.

'I'd be pleased to type them up for you again,' I said.

He stared for a moment into his bucket. 'Not necessary,' he said, 'thank you.'

'I don't mind a bit,' I said.

'It's of no interest to me,' he answered, rubbing with the grubby yellow leather. 'I can't say it ever was.' He looked straight at me then. The pale frost of his eyes. And in a second I was annihilated, the creamy blossoms scorched brown, rotted on the bough.

# 16

## *Broderick's, January 1962*

*Poorly*, Auntie said, looking reproachfully at the leg of goose, the pile of sprouts, that on Christmas Day I couldn't bring myself to eat. It had been a lesson to me, long overdue: how extraordinarily effective an infatuation can be. Six whole months had passed since I'd arrived in Devon and I'd deluded myself that I had grown up. Wilf McManus had helped me consign the Upcotts to what I had decided was the fairy tale of my early life, and I quite resigned myself to the fact that my involvement with them was over. Not that I was unaware of them — but their presence was felt mostly by their absence from village life. The only time they appeared was for church and then it was only Robert and Frances, who would sit stiffly at one end of the old Upcott pew, leaving, when the time came, briskly and with hardly a word to anyone. When I asked after Tom, whom I hadn't seen at all since I'd been back, Joyce said there'd been incidents involving drink and rowdiness and that Tom – ever since his siblings banned him from the pub – had refused point blank to come with them to church.

I have come to think that bumping into Frances Upcott the very day I set off into Buckleigh – a determined effort to rid myself of Wilf – was no coincidence. It must have been the first market day of the year and I had done my rounds, my two baskets stuffed full. Armed with a shopping list from Joyce, I had one last call to make. Broderick's was the big shop at the bottom of the high street, on the corner from where I'd catch the bus home.

As soon as the door swung and the bell jangled I knew I'd interrupted something. It was extremely unusual for Mr Broderick to be out on the shop floor, but there he was, with his shiny scalp, his wire spectacles. He looked up from across the counter as I came in, made an impatient gesture for me to close the door, and resumed his position: an attitude of pained attention, one ear trained towards a customer who was holding out a scrap of paper.

Mrs Broderick was standing on her box at his elbow and resumed tetchily, 'I've explained, we have to sell 'em in pairs. That's right, isn't it? Wouldn't make sense else.'

Apart from the slant of light through the top window, which made a beacon of Mr Broderick's head, the shop was cluttered and gloomy. There was limited space for me to put myself: metal buckets to my left, a couple of paraffin heaters to my right and at head height, a dozen hurricane lamps, hanging from a shelf that in turn was laden with enamel-ware in every conceivable shape and size.

Mr Broderick drew a sharp breath. 'Now then,' he said.

'Let's see I've got this straight. You want us to take one shoe-lace from the pair?'

The woman, in her nip-waisted coat, had her back to me.

'Do you see our problem, Miss Upcott?' Mr Broderick continued – the name sending a jolt through my veins – 'They're bound together. There's no call for them singly. Do you see?'

'How many people break both shoelaces at once? she asked calmly.

'But can you see our problem?' he persisted, his voice rising, 'We can't afford to set a precedent.'

He coughed because the last thing he wanted was to be made to look a fool of in public. His eyes darted towards me. No one said a word. Mrs Broderick had arms like rolling pins. He coughed again. Suddenly, as if he could bear the strain no more, he said, 'Yes, yes, all right, this once, but I'll not get into this again,' and before his wife could protest, he fled towards the sanctuary of his storeroom. When Mrs Broderick addressed the woman again, she did it with her eyes averted, leadenly polite. 'Will that be all?'

'Thank you,' Frances said, tucking the twist of paper into her basket and turning smartly, looking straight through me as she made her way to the door. It turned me inside-out. By the time I had found my voice she had already vanished, the bell jangling behind her.

Mrs Broderick huffed. 'Give an inch and they'll take a mile,' she said, and then raising her voice so her husband would be sure to hear, 'You got to stand up to them.'

There was no response. She turned to me, exasperated. 'She'll iron out the old wallpaper and stick it right back on, that one.'

I didn't dare to enter that conversation. 'I've come for Mrs Fairley's order,' I said, holding out my list: paraffin, wicks, parcel string, greaseproof paper, tea.

Mrs Broderick ticked them off one by one and handed me the packets in a cardboard box. By the end of the list, her equanimity appeared restored. 'You look after yourself,' she said, trundling out from behind the counter to open the door for me.


'I saw Frances Upcott in town,' I said to Auntie as soon as I got back, making an effort to raise my voice to her.

'Yes?' Auntie screwed up her face.

'She was having an argument,' I said.

'Ointment?'

'About a shoelace.'

'What, dear?'

'A shoe. Lace.'

Auntie's deafness came and went. It was particularly apparent after she'd eaten.

'Frances Upcott,' I tried again, 'in Broderick's.' All I wanted was to talk about Frances. But she wasn't listening any longer. Her eyelids had dropped, her lips invisible, sewn-up tight.

# 17

## *Accounts*

Frances Upcott, Joyce warned me, had a way of treating you like dirt. Didn't I remember? Ever since she was a little girl. It wasn't anything she said, but a look. As if you were a penny short. She'd got it from her mother, Joyce said, although she hesitated to speak ill of the dead.

After Tom was born, Mrs Upcott had been confined to her bed. It had been the middle of a bad winter and the doctor hadn't managed to get to the farm until it was all over. Joyce had only been with them just over a year — she'd started straight out of school. Although she knew about babies, she'd never delivered one, not on her own. It ought to have been quick, given that there were two already, and Robert, she knew for a fact, had been an exceptional size; but Mrs Upcott was older now (almost fifty) and she was weaker. She suffered with her chest. The moaning she made, from beginning to end, was a constant reproach. Joyce wished she'd had help. She felt the weight of responsibility like a yoke: climbing the stairs a hundred times with pans of water, hot and cold, with half a dozen flannels. At the eleventh hour, Mrs Upcott clung to her as if she were drowning, pinching her black and blue. She was making the sound of a ship breaking, a violent shudder as she arched and abandoned the bottom half of herself to the sea floor.

That would be her, one day, Joyce was thinking — she'd been secretly engaged to Alfred since they'd left school — except, she'd resolved then and there, she'd never make such a song and a dance of it. She had to shake Mrs Upcott off to peer round into the wreckage where at last she thought she could make out a little hand, a frond of coral. She reached with her fingertips to encircle the miniature wrist.

'I can see him,' she said, although she hardly believed it. She grabbed Mrs Upcott's arm and yanked so hard it might have broken off. 'Once more. One more time.'

Mrs Upcott groaned from the top of her shoulders like a thick blanket shaken. The crown of the baby's head was round as an eyeball, tight in its socket, but Joyce was there the moment it breached the muscle, popped out — as if for one terrible second it wasn't meant to — and behind it, a slimy rush of squid-like limbs. Joyce took him by the wrists, gave him a slap across his buttocks, harder than you'd think, but she knew instinctively it was the right thing to do, and she watched the colour blossom in him like a flower, from blue to pink, and out through his mouth in a mucus-filled bleat. Then she hugged him to her as tight as if he were her own, tears flowing to squeeze him all together.

By the time the doctor arrived, she'd cut the cord with the kitchen scissors, tied it off with a strip torn from an old sheet and she'd handed Mr Upcott the bowl with the afterbirth to feed to the pigs.

'Doctor said I'd done splendidly,' Joyce said, 'that he needn't have bothered to come out at all. He patched her up. Gave her something for the bleeding. And two weeks in bed, was what he said. But she never left the room, not for months. I'd go in of a morning, and it was like taking orders from a shrew-mouse. There she'd be, all bundled up – you could hardly see her face between the blankets and the quilts. But I never thought for a moment she was dying: she was tiny, but she'd the will of an ox. Mr Upcott woke up one day with her next to him, stiff and cold. It didn't do him no good neither, sharing half the night, he came to believe it, with a corpse.'

From that day, on the domestic front, Mr Upcott deferred to Frances. For her eleventh birthday, he gave her a marbled ladies' fountain pen which she wore around her neck on a chain. With Robert away to school, he started to refer to his daughter as 'Mother' and now he put her in charge of the long wooden cash box and the leather ledger. Frances set out to restore order, writing everything down in a fancy italic script.

*September 1:*    *dozen eggs + 1*
                    *Rabbits – 8 in traps – 2 to the dogs*
                    *4 ewes put to Hercules*
                    *Potatoes: 4 sacks King George,*
                          *3 sacks Great Scotts*
                    *Milk: 3 gallons, 1 quart*

                    *Paid out: Broderick's: nail boots size 5, 25/-*

It had been a peculiar humiliation to Joyce, a married woman by then, to have her shillings and pence distributed by a child, from a doll's purse.

# 18

## *Mavis Imelda Cleverdon*

It may be a terrible thing to admit but in my short experience thus far people dying had brought me little but relief. Perhaps I'd been inured to it by the war. We each of us carried our spoonful of grief to the point that it would have been an embarrassment to have been caught without it. Grief by then was a national disease, common as a cold, which plugged us in to the spirit of getting through, of not making a fuss. In the scheme of things, I had emerged from Mother's dying relatively unscathed. In fact an objective observer might have said it was the making of me. 'If she *hadn't* died': that was a life I occasionally conjectured for myself, a dreadful vision of us sitting like resinous stumps in the forest-papered walls of our old front room.

Winter brought its own harvest. Mr Bird, who still lived with his mother next to Auntie, and spent most of his time gardening out of the back, thought at first he must be mistaken. He saw the heap of clothes just above the line of the fence, arranged on the ground as if it were a body sleeping. It took him a minute or two to realize that something must be wrong. This time of year. The two speckled bantams were pecking away quite blithely; one had hopped up, turned a full circle, and hopped down again. He didn't want to upset his mother so he went to fetch Joyce.

Auntie had gone out the night before, intending to shut up the chickens. The door to the shed was swollen and stiff, she set her shoulder to it; her fingers were numb, she fumbled uselessly with the wooden catch.

Pain entered just behind her nose, red hot. It was marble-sized, molten, and seared a hole through the cartilage as if it were wax. She couldn't comprehend why the pain should feel so vengeful, as if she'd taken an animal in from the cold and it had bitten her hand. Though she called for him, Ernest was nowhere to be seen. His head had been sucked under in the dark water, his arms and his legs wheeling away from her. She sank to her knees. The ground settled momentarily to present a hen's eye view – potato peelings, crusts of bread, three dried peas – towards which, in a spasm resembling greed, she dived.

People I'd hardly spoken to made a point of coming up to tell me that it was surely the best way. They clasped my hands in theirs. 'She was a proper lady,' they said, a status confirmed by her dying and the discovery in the dresser drawer of two full sets of silver cutlery. I didn't feel equal to the sympathy. I tried to drum up the requisite sense of loss. Everyone seemed to feel it more than I did, bringing out their little anecdotes to show me, like bits of food wrapped in handkerchiefs.

But there was a much more troubling aspect to her passing.

I didn't imagine for a moment that Daddy would bother to turn up for the funeral. He had written to tell me as much: Patricia couldn't possibly leave the house. *Lady's troubles*, as he put it, which had been mitigated somewhat by the arrival, on her birthday (as I could imagine) of a Pomeranian pup. But he hadn't counted on the uncles, who were, after all, Auntie's siblings. Though, by her own account, they had treated her with nothing but disdain, they were afflicted, it appeared, by a sudden rash of fraternal remorse and insisted that Daddy, with or without Patricia, accompany them down.

I had to brace myself. I was far better at imagining people dead than I was at thinking of them living a life elsewhere. In fact it was lucky that I hadn't yet explicitly told anyone that Daddy had died. As it was, he turned up in a paddy, making a dreadful fuss about the car. There was a stench in there, he was muttering, as if an animal had been locked in. Lucien had leaked on to the upholstery; Gilbert had thrown up as soon as they arrived, avoiding the car, but not his shoes. Daddy looked at me when I answered the door as if it were my fault.

'Got a cloth, Mavis – help us out?' he said irritably from the garden gate. There was no ceremony, as if we'd seen one another only recently.

'Sorry, old boy,' Lucien kept saying. Their black suits were car-worn and creased. They dipped their heads into their bowler hats after they'd shaken my hand. There was nowhere else to take them but inside. I hadn't had a chance to clear up, I explained.

'Utter chaos,' Daddy pronounced, looking around.

It was worse with so many of us standing about. 'She wouldn't let me help her,' I said.

'Old bat,' Daddy said. 'I'm surprised the place isn't infested. What? Where's that old dog?' Daddy asked.

'In the garden,' I said, 'buried.'

'What? Buried the dog?'

'She loved her,' I said.

'Rum old bird.'

Gilbert, whose shoes were still smeary from where they'd been summarily rubbed, began to plonk the piano.

We were late arriving and the church was already packed. Joyce escorted us to the front pew, Daddy and the uncles, nodding to the left and the right as if the array of ducked heads and bended knees were in their honour. When the time came, up in the pulpit, Lucien was bemused by the sea of expectant faces. He began to speak as if he were gnawing a chunk of wood.

*Younger sister — Mavis Imelda — game old bird — always the quiet ones — eh? — took off! — like that! — not so much as a by-your-leave — strange sort of place to end up —but, obviously — grateful — all that — tickler, she was — nuff said.*

He struck his breast in a Nelson-like gesture, gamely waiting for the ship to go down; he might have stayed there all day if Joyce, during 'Abide With Me', had not tactfully led him back to his seat.

Whatever they said, the uncles patently weren't up to bearing her out. Daddy and Alf between them took the front end of the coffin. Six of them in all passed her at knee-height along the length of the nave like a canoe. She was surprisingly heavy for such an old stick, Daddy said afterwards.

The turf in the new corner of the graveyard was peeled back neatly and she was lowered on ropes, hand over fist, to her berth. *Man that is born of a woman hath but a short time to live, and is full of misery. He cometh up, and is cut down, like a flower; he fleeth as it were a shadow, and never continueth in one stay . . .*

I was touched to see Frances Upcott at the graveside, though there was no sign of her brothers. She was wearing neat black gloves, the fingers of which were soiled with red earth. She cast her handful after mine, *ashes to ashes, dust to dust,* and then she moved to one side. By the time we took the path back down to the old school, I had lost sight of her. Joyce insisted I stand in the entrance, receiving the mourners like St Peter, a long line of hands to squeeze, of solicitous smiles — but no further sign of Frances.

It was inside over scones and tea that the idea for a concert first arose. The occasion, given the invasion of my relations *and* the presence of Colonel Bentwood (for whom Auntie, it turned out, like almost everyone else in the village, had once worked), was more formal than such affairs usually were. There was a respectful silence as the company withdrew from the fireplace, where Daddy and the Colonel had positioned themselves, engaging in loud and animated discussion. The Colonel was relating the story of Auntie's brief sojourn as nanny at the house. She'd ridden out from the village on her bicycle fearlessly in the midst of thunder and lightning — '*bouffe*', the Colonel raised his sandwich, '*boom*'. Uncle Gilbert was weeping with laughter — he could see it, he could see the determined expression on his sister's face.

'Damn lot of use it was to me,' the Colonel was saying. 'So, I said, *Let 'em have it*. I thought — *why not?*' He was explaining the background to his handing over of the Old School. Joyce had been instrumental in the negotiations and in raising sufficient funds to buy the building from him. She was attempting in another corner to have her own conversation. 'What a lovely way,' she was saying, 'to mark our opening. And wouldn't it be such a fitting tribute to Mrs Cleverdon?'

Daddy was laughing heartily at something the Colonel had said.

'Perhaps we might form a sub-committee,' Joyce persevered.

'Mavis!' Daddy called. He beckoned me over and as I approached I could hear him confide, 'Squirrelled herself away down here – after her mother died. What can a father do? Mavis! I don't believe you've been properly introduced . . .'

The Colonel took my hand cursorily, cleared his throat. Daddy was saying, 'We said, didn't we, Mavis, couldn't see what on earth you were up to, burying yourself down here? But as Patricia – my good wife – pointed out, a bit of country air might be just what's needed, eh? That's what she said, Colonel. And I must say, couldn't agree more. Lucky fellah.'


Once Lucien and Gilbert were safely installed in the back of the car, Daddy was eager to get going.

'Must be off. Long old journey, as you know. Good to see you. Glad it's worked out.'

We were standing at the very gate I'd been able to swing back and forth on so many years before.

'Do you remember?' I asked him.

'Eh?' He was looking up at the bedroom window. He shook

his head. 'If she'd have been living anywhere half decent . . .' he said. (His mother, Auntie's elder sister, had ended up in a room at the top of Claridge's.)

'She liked living here,' I said.

'Wasn't going to admit she was wrong! Bit of a stubborn streak – eh, Mavis?' He nudged me as if the condition went along with the name, then pressed a note into my hand, five pounds. 'Must say though, good of the old girl to see you right,' he said. 'Get the place shipshape. We might even persuade Pat to come down one of these days.'

# 19

## *Paradise*

Of the several factors that kept me in Shipleigh (my father's visit not the least of them), Auntie's death was by far the most practical. It appeared that she had drawn up her will only a week before Christmas. She'd written it completely without my knowledge, in freehand, and had it witnessed by Frances Upcott and Alfred Fairley. For all I know she might have tried and failed to discuss it with me. That Christmas, my head had been so taken up with Wilf McManus, I would not have noticed. I felt a pang of remorse. Everything she owned was to be left to me, barring the pair of Staffordshire spaniels, which were destined for Joyce (who'd so often admired them) and the rosewood music cabinet – albums and loose leaf included – entailed to Frances, the only one, as she said, likely to make use of it.

It was at least a week after Auntie's interment before I took up residence. Every time I opened the front door, long after she was dead, I expected to find her there, in the blue chair.

Instead there was only a slight indentation of the cushion. When I had brought the last of my possessions over from the pub, I stood in my coat in the middle of the front room trying to comprehend that this was my home. Furniture loomed from the walls – the dresser, the piano, the sideboard. There was a silver veneer of damp over everything, even the fireplace, the coal scuttle. The heavy green curtains were half-closed; I drew them back and the room stirred. The crisp afternoon sun put a nimbus around the tops of the chairs, the china on the dresser, glinted from the bevelling of the octagonal mirror above the fireplace. There was a bundle of sewing things set aside on the table – a thimble, a darning mushroom, an old stocking – as if waiting for me to take them up.

I was in no hurry to unpack, but I brought out my two framed photographs (the wedding portrait and a tinted post-card Mother had given to Daddy before they were married) and set them at opposite ends of the mantelpiece. I coughed to hear my voice, and when I turned to take the rest of my things upstairs, I made more noise than was strictly necessary, aware of the rug under my feet, and the movement of my body towards the door as it negotiated the chair, the footstool, the table. Ernest was waiting in the oval photograph, at shoulder height, just to the right of the piano. His violin was upright on his lap, the scroll glancing his cheek. He looked at me with wounded eyes. 'Mavis,' he might have whispered, 'Mavis, my songbird.'

The light was grainy on the stairs. The treads creaked a tuneless scale under my feet. I hadn't been in Auntie's room since I was a child. I put my thumb to the latch and drew back the door. As I stepped in, the temperature dropped. She'd moved the bed from where it had been, away from the window, out of the draught. I recognized the curtains, their blue and yellow sprigs, and the chest of drawers I'd once been forbidden to open, in case they unbalanced and tipped forwards on top of me. There was the pink china set I'd always coveted on its embroidered cloth, the two matching candlesticks, the monogrammed ivory hairbrush with several coils of her hair woven through it.

The smell of wild garlic I put down to the unaired chill of the room. I pushed open the window. It was the tart smell, I thought, of living on one's own. The bed was neatly made, the myriad hexagons of its quilt. If there had been a wardrobe, I would have looked in it, or a curtain to check behind. Only the bed presented a suitable hiding place. I crouched down and peered. There was nothing but the chamber pot, pushed back, its blousy transfer of roses. I stretched my arm to draw it out, covered my mouth. The pot was a third full: a resin-coloured liquid whose surface was the purple-yellow of a bruise. I held my breath, balancing the handle and the far edge of the pot between my hands at arm's length, and then, breathing through my teeth, I walked it carefully down the stairs.

Out in the yard, Auntie's two chickens immediately laid siege to my legs, hopping and clucking. I waded between them towards the back fence and tipped the contents of the pot into the brambles, expecting the leaves to blister and shrivel, while the chickens stupidly necked the loops of the wire fence.

I was shy about making any changes inside the cottage,

but outside it was a different matter. Over the last year or so, Auntie had let the front garden go to seed. Although I was not a gardener, we used to chat about my plans. Sweet William and columbine, they were Ernest's favourites. She had been quite willing for me to take it in hand and I determined, in the first instance that I would at least sort out the short cobbled path between the gate and the porch, before the weeds took permanent hold.

It was a consuming and satisfying job. At teatime, I was still outside, kneeling on an old hearthrug, trowel in hand, a growing pile of tubers and roots by my side. I was so absorbed in my task that I didn't notice the footsteps approaching until they stopped, almost under my nose.

The boots were burnished, the toes slightly humped. The hem of a brown coat, with a black fur muff that for a moment I took to be alive swinging alongside. I looked up, got to my feet, rackety from crouching for so long. The blood rushed to my head. It was Frances. She held out a gloved hand.

I turned over my filthy hands to apologize.

'I've been hoping to catch you,' she said.

We both stared at the mess on the path as if it might prove an impediment to entering the house. Clumsily I bent down and lifted the hearthrug, shook it.

'Come in,' I said, still unused to the idea that it was within my gift to ask her.

'I didn't have a chance to say at the funeral how sorry I was,' she said, sitting straight-backed. 'I was very fond of your aunt, you know.'

I hadn't realized that Auntie had preserved a relationship

with Frances. She had kept it to herself. But I said now, 'You'll want the cabinet.'

'No rush,' she said. 'It was kind of her to think of me.'

I had brought out the best teacups, the china so refined that tinkling it betrayed how ridiculously my hands trembled.

'Things must have changed a bit, since you were last here?' she asked politely. A minute or two later, it was just our cups: ting, ting.

'I remember your playing,' I said. 'I can hear it sometimes in the room.'

'She was a good teacher. She didn't want me to give up.'

'She didn't want me to start,' I said. 'It hurt her ears.'

Frances smiled. 'She was a *kindred spirit*, a rare thing in these parts.'

The way she said it, for a moment it was as if all three of us were ghosts.

'I came to see you once with my father,' I said shyly.

'In the war. I remember. Perhaps you'll visit us again when you're settled?'

I flushed. She was friendly, quite the opposite of the cold fish I'd been led to expect from village gossip. I couldn't help but be flattered, accepting it as an acknowledgement of a certain status: that I was my father's daughter and that she recognized it. Kindred spirits.

When I showed her to the front door, she slid her gloved hand out of the muff and took mine. There were flecks of hazel in her eyes. 'It feels as if she's still with us,' she said, 'don't you think? I'm so glad that you've decided to stay on.'

When she'd gone, I took myself off into the kitchen, making myself wash and clear away more assiduously than usual.

I folded the linen, set the kitchen chairs straight, polished the cutlery, all the while trying to keep a lid on a mounting sense of excitement. I half-expected to hear Auntie at the piano, tapping out a tune. I wished I could tell her that I was glad I'd come back. That I was sure, now, it was the right thing, if I hadn't felt so before.

# PART V
## *The Bird Preserver*

# 20

## *Comfortable Words*

Perhaps it was just that Frances never lost the habit of calling at Paradise Cottage? In the end, it suited me to slip into Auntie's shoes – a Mavis into a Mavis, the transition was virtually seamless. Frances would accompany me back sometimes after church. *Hear what comfortable words our Saviour has taught us.* We fell quite easily into discussing the sermon: that word 'comfortable', we agreed, a much finer word, for instance, than 'love'. Through such felicities – a shared liking for certain hymns and saints (Francis of Assisi, Joan of Arc) – our friendship began to blossom. We would chat together in the little sitting room, much as I gathered she and Auntie used to do. But I couldn't help wondering, after a while, if they had covered as we did such a wide range of topics – from varieties of spring cabbage to the most durable brands of hosiery. We left few stones unturned: little observations about the village, the uncouth habits of certain families; about the seasons, the hedgerows; about her own brothers.

Outwardly little had altered: I read, I knitted, I performed small services up at the pub, took in piecework from the solicitor in Buckleigh (I typed the articles and memorandum of the new Village Hall, for instance); but underneath there'd been a sea-change, a different pull to my universe entirely.

It helped, no doubt, that there was some history to our acquaintance, which we spent those first weeks carefully annotating. Things other than Auntie that we had in common – like the year or two at school we'd overlapped. It was a joy to me to be able to compare notes on the time, for instance, she had had Robert cut off all her hair; the time Tom blacked his face; the many times Tom ran away to the river and had to be fetched back.

'I found him there, sometimes,' I said. I was always pleased to be able to surprise her. 'Where the rivers meet,' I said. 'We had a camp.'

My prior knowledge gave her confidence. She began to treat me as if I were party to certain private family information.

'He's not changed,' she said. 'He brought in a dead badger the other day, laid it out on the kitchen table like a sack of coal.' She shuddered. 'It drives Robert mad. "What's the use in that?" he says. Do you remember when he was young, he used to sell his moleskins to the furrier? I doubt there was a mole left from the farm to the village at one time.'

Every story from her childhood involved her brothers one way or another.

'I wish I'd had a brother,' I said once.

'I can't imagine *not*,' she said. 'Not now.' Then she laughed.

'Though when Tom was born, I thought the world had ended . . .'

I must have looked surprised. She shrugged, 'Who knows how children torture themselves? It was the end of Mother, of course . . .' She drew herself up. 'But you're right. Without them, both of them in their different ways, I wouldn't begin to know who I was.'

# 21

## *An Evening of Celebration,*
## *27 April 1962*

From the handful of volunteers who'd put themselves forward to help with the concert, Joyce had been politic and settled on Miss Upcott and Mrs McManus.

'Perhaps you'd like to take the minutes for us, Mavis?' she asked.

I agreed on the spot.

We met in the snug. It occurred to me that I had never seen Frances in close company before; she had no reason to set foot in the pub. Diana brought out three glasses of hot port and lemon.

'Take the chill off,' she said.

Frances took one and politely sipped at it.

Joyce was businesslike. 'Well, I've had a lot of interest from those that'd like to take part,' she said. 'I must say there's a deal of talent, isn't there, for such a small village? Mavis, perhaps you could make a note . . .'

I had written 'Concert' at the top of a piece of foolscap, heavily embellished. I sat to attention, my nib raised.

'There's present company first off: Frances, Diana,' she said, nodding to each. 'I hope I'm right in assuming you'll each give us the benefit?' She continued, 'There's Mr Bird—'

'Mr Bird?' Frances interrupted. 'Does he play anything?'

'No, no. He's down for a recital. Devon dialect. He's ever so good.'

'But I thought it was to be a musical evening?' Frances said. 'Isn't that the point?'

I stopped writing. Joyce said, 'I think that people should be allowed to contribute in whatever ways they see fit. Don't you?'

There was a pause. 'I'm not sure I do,' Frances said coolly.

'When all's said and done,' Joyce said, eyeing Diana for support, 'it's a celebration – isn't that what we're about? From those who knew Mrs Cleverdon best.'

Diana was quick to chip in: 'Absolutely! We can't afford to be fussy – it wouldn't be fair, and so on. Not everyone has had professional *training*. One can't expect that, surely?'

Frances took a deep breath, pushed aside her glass. 'In that case, if you don't mind, I think I'll leave you to the detail. I'm sure you'll make a good job of it.'

She got to her feet; I was dismayed.

Joyce said, 'We can discuss it, Frances, by all means . . .'

'Too many cooks,' Frances said categorically. 'Though I've committed to my own performance. I shall honour that.'

As soon as the door closed on her, I felt I had betrayed her. Joyce and Diana began stoking each other up.

215

'Honestly! Goodness sakes,' Joyce said.

'Up on her high horse,' Diana said. 'Miss Pomp and Circ.'

For at least a week beforehand there was a frisson of excitement in the village. Diana and Joyce were busy in the kitchen and I put myself at their disposal, fetching and carrying. There were two shelves reserved at the bottom of the huge refrigerator where I deposited the fruit loaves, Victoria sponges and ninety-six sausage rolls.

On Wednesday they handed me the programme to type up and take to the printer. I chose an ivy leaf border. On the day itself, to cheer up the school, Joyce produced three bundles of coloured paper-chain links, which she had me frantically pasting together. An hour before anyone arrived I was standing on a chair, festooning in turn the frame of the clock, the women in the Garden of Gethsemane and a map of the Commonwealth of Nations.

By six o'clock everything was in place and Joyce opened the doors; there was a steady stream over the threshold, the hum of conversation. As the place filled up there was a general unbuttoning of jackets, a folding-up of cardigans and a considerate removal of hats. Additional wooden chairs had been brought in from the church and we'd agreed beforehand that, if necessary, the younger ones might sit on the floor at the front.

There had been a last-minute fuss over who was to host. Joyce did not like public speaking. All things being equal, it should have been Frances, but Joyce was blowed if she was going to ask her. On the other hand, she turned a deaf ear to the suggestion that it might be Diana, nervous of her ceding more sway than was absolutely necessary. Her only possible option was Alf, who, despite feeble protestations, knew he had no option but to do as he was told.

If he hadn't had to open his mouth, Alf, in his best double-breasted suit and his hair slicked back, would have been quite the part. But as soon as he moved or spoke, he betrayed his nerves. Once the hall was full and the door secured he put his hand up timidly as if he were in the classroom again and wished to be excused.

'Ladies. Gentlemen,' he began, reading from the script in his hand. There was a call for hush.

'We're gathered here. This evening. To pay. Tribute. To our. Late-departed. To Mrs Cleverdon, that was.'

'Hear, hear.' A general fluttering of papers.

'Now then,' Alf continued, squinting at his text. 'Us've put together this. Tribute. And — what is more — to raise the roof on the new — village hall.' Alf looked significantly to the plaster ceiling rose, to which all eyes followed, as if, any moment, it might burst into bloom.

'So. Without more ado' — he raised his hand a second time, gratified to discover how effective a tool it could be — 'may I present. Miss Upcott' — he nodded over to her — 'who'll be setting us off with, I believe, one of Mrs Cleverdon's very favourite tunes: "Wedding Day. At." Er—'

'*Troldhaugen*,' Frances supplied for him. 'Composed by Edvard Grieg.' She spoke quietly, rising to her feet with the gold-embossed music album in her hands.

She had removed her jacket, having taken the handkerchief from its pocket. She had a bad cold; the skin around her nostrils was pink and scuffed. She dabbed her nose and placed the handkerchief on the ledge at the far end of the keyboard, tugged back each of her silk sleeves, settling herself on the piano stool with a small winding adjustment to the knobs, and sat like a pillar of salt to wait for the audience's rustling to subside. Then she rolled back her head and lifted her left hand. There was a vacuum of hush into which her fingers dropped.

*Pom-pom-pom. Pam-pam-pam. Pom-pom-pom. Pam-pam-pam.*

Nothing could have prepared me. Even before her right hand swooped to begin its twiddly tune, I regretted having agreed to such an exposed position, sitting as I was at a right-angle to the front row so that I could monitor the children. I eased myself very slightly against the back of my chair.

The course of the music was so well ingrained in me that even now – almost twenty years later – I could anticipate every twist and every turn. Frances crossed her left hand high over her right and plucked the note from the keys like a hawk.

Instantly, I began to recall Auntie's voice, her rapt running commentary: *See how beautiful the bride is, hurrying up the hill in her billowing dress, racing to get to the little white church.* And I could picture Auntie running, that stamp of determination on her face.

*Here is the band, in the sunshine, cymbals crashing. Imagine the bower of hands through which the couple process, bowing their heads. She is his true love as well she knows. Can you hear it – that radiance?*

Frances's head was quivering, stray wisps of hair working loose at her neck, her arms plunging up and down the keys, hand over fist, unwinding to a final defiant blast, both hands plunged into the keyboard.

I'd never heard a roomful of people so silent. Her hands lifted as if someone worked them from above. She let them drop to her sides. The applause was like gunfire. Frances grabbed her handkerchief and attempted privately to wipe her nose; I could see the commotion had taken her by surprise. She turned in her seat and met my eyes full on. She flushed.

'Hurrah,' I heard myself saying, my throat tight. 'Hurrah,' pushing away my tears. She rose, blinking.

Alf got to his feet; he was in a muddle with his notes. Frances returned quietly to her place and sat poised and distinct. Alf still trying to sort himself out, muttering, 'Proper, that. Thank you. Miss Upcott. Now. What have us here?'

My mind suspended itself. A shy girl with a small harp plinked through two or three identical lyrics; Mr Bird recited the whole of 'Jan's Cricket Match', his lower jaw grinding itself into such peculiar shapes that an over-excited child in the front had to be taken out and given a talking-to.

Alf had become adept at bringing the room to order. 'Now, then,' he tapped the paper, 'us have here,' he read, 'a *particular* treat. All the way from the London Music Hall. A big hand for—' He looked anxiously towards the door, where, in the corner, Joyce had positioned herself to give the next performers their cue. She raised her hand.

'—for "Mister and Missus",' he said, managing a showman's inflection that was new to him. A discernible gasp went around the hall as Diana and Wilf MacManus took to the stage. Each wore a costume divided starkly down the middle: one half showed a trilby, a black moustache and a dark flannel suit; the other, a straw hat, a flouncy dress, one tan stocking.

219

Diana was immaculately straight-faced. 'Mister and Missus,' she announced in her wireless voice. Then she stretched her hands wide as if she were drawing out an accordion.

> *When Mister and Missus went out on the town,*
> *Says Mister to Missus, 'You're wearing my gown!'*

She took a step back and nudged Wilf, who stepped forward and recited deadpan,

> *'What a turn,' he declared, 'what an absolute mess,*
> *You in a suit and me in a dress!'*

Diana gave him a playful push.

> *'No, me in a dress and you in a suit.'*

Wilf delivered his line to the floor,

> *'A rooty, a-rooty, a-rooty toot toot!'*

A titter rippled along the back row. Victor began to hoot energetically and Joyce grabbed his arm to restrain him. Diana continued undeterred, supplying actions to her words, lifting and wiggling first her left foot then her right. Wilf looked aged and broken. My heart raced. It staggered me to think that only a few months before, I'd entertained even the slightest romantic notions about him.

There was a certain contingent present who'd never taken to the McManuses: she was stuck up; he was a dour old Scot.

While Diana took her curtsey, long and low, the applause carried a knowing, half-hearted ring. Wilf lost no time in taking his bow and exiting swiftly from the room.

It was late, and the children were getting fractious, the audience flagging. But Alf had one more item on his list, a last-minute addition. 'And, to bring us to a close, we're lucky enough to have Miss Manning, I believe, with a song to round us off.'

Beatrice Manning was eighteen years old. She moved with enviable confidence. She was wearing an emerald velvet dress she'd made herself, the three-quarter sleeves revealing the perfect bevel of her forearms. She'd been sent away to school. I had only ever seen her in the holidays at church, where she was always ceded prime position in the choir stalls. 'There is a Green Hill Far Away' and 'Once in Royal David's City', her voice carried easily, properly trained on arias by Handel and Purcell. When she found her spot, Beatrice took stock of her audience, drew a breath that filled her torso and appeared to lift her a little from the ground. Her pure, sharpened voice cut ribbons in the air like the tip of a foil. There was a murmur of admiration, a collective scrutiny of her throat, her bosom, her adamant shoe. *I know where I'm going*, she sang, *my dear knows who I'll marry,* and she sang it far above our heads, her eyes fixed to a tiny pinprick of light beyond the window, out in the sky, as far from this place as it was possible to be.

The row of Young Farmers at the back were straining for a better view, Tom Upcott among them. I watched his face. He was ablaze. It made me look at Beatrice again. I wondered if she was aware of the effect she had? The way she held herself, like the figurehead of a ship. She finished her song with a curtsey and a little bow. Someone shouted, 'Bravo, bravo – encore!' It was only as Beatrice edged past Frances to reclaim her seat that I noticed, alone among the audience, how determinedly unmoved Frances was.

In the general hubbub that followed (a clasping of hands and an impromptu performance in the back rows of 'Auld Lang Syne') Alf's final thanks were drowned out. The audience emptied through the door in a well-worn procession heading to the Seven Stars for refreshments. Four of us remained dotted about the hall, contemplating the chairs that had come askew, papers abandoned face down and scuffed underfoot. Alf, dazed, sat mopping his brow. Joyce bent down to retrieve a programme. Frances was gathering up her bits and pieces in the corner. I stood, uncertain, in the middle of the debris. In an effort of goodwill, Joyce made her way over to Frances. 'I had no idea you could play so well. It was a highlight. Most definitely. A real highlight.'

'Thank you,' Frances said. She had gathered herself together, sniffing. Her nose was running and she dived into her pocket. 'Oh,' she said, 'I'm like a leaking tap.'

'And it was ever so good of you to go on, with that nasty cold,' Joyce said.

'She would have loved it,' I said. I could hardly trust myself to speak.

We were all of us exhausted and at cross-purposes.


Meanwhile, across the Green, Wilf McManus had slipped unnoticed from the party and was all alone in his woodshed. He had packed himself a haversack before the concert and hidden it in there. Fumbling in the dark, he managed to extract from the bag his fisherman's sweater, a pair of trousers and a jacket. It took him a while to get changed out of the costume Diana had put him in, with its ridiculous ties and buttons. He left it like a skin, bundled in a heap on the floor of the shed. It was the last trace of him anyone ever found.

# 22
## *Passaford, 1962*

Frances had had a cough, in one form or another, for as long as I'd known her. Since the concert, it had become more pronounced, like a little lapdog wherever she went, yap, yap, yap, and distinctive in the spring sunshine because it was so clearly the wrong season for it. On Holy Thursday, queuing up for Communion that morning, Frances became so doubled up with coughing that she had to leave the church. I hurried out afterwards, finding her perched in the usual place at the family plot at the top of the churchyard.

John Edward Upcott, 1887–1951, beloved husband of Henrietta. *In life, in death, O Lord, abide with me.*

'I like to think of them together,' she said, crouched down, clutching the front of her jacket. 'He never got used to her being gone. It made him bad tempered.'

She extended her hand for me to help her to her feet, then steadied herself on my arm, light as a broom, looking around her at the sprawl of gravestones. 'I'll have to come up properly soon,' she said. 'Do some tidying.'

The cough was on her chest. Eventually she agreed to see the doctor, who was firm: he prescribed penicillin and bed rest, and said that if she ignored his advice he wouldn't answer for the consequences. It was from May that year that I began to make regular journeys down to the farm. Although I had shown little aptitude for looking after anyone in the past, I was the only person from the village whom Frances would brook having about the house. I became used to letting myself in, calling up the stairs so as not to alarm her.

The kitchen was six times the size of mine at Paradise, with a fire at one end and the Rayburn at the other, both of which, throughout the year, were kept ticking over. Even a pot of tea seemed an absurdly long-winded business – finding the right teapot, the wooden caddy where the tea was kept, a teaspoon for measuring – but before long I had mastered the awkward fit of the kettle lid and other such quirks: the cupboard where the mops were kept, the peculiar scrawls on the seed-merchant's almanac to indicate where Tom or Robert were most likely to be found; a pail of milk, I discovered, kept on a slate shelf in the scullery, which I'd sniff and sip as Mrs Connor used to do; and of the two tea services kept on the dresser – the gold-flecked and the rose – I knew to avoid the three cups that had been repaired with rivets.

Arriving, as I usually did, mid-morning, I rarely set eyes on either brother, though there was evidence of them everywhere. Tentatively I set about making things spick and span, clearing up the mess they had left behind them, sweeping crumbs from the table, gathering crockery to wash and dry, wiping down the sink and the draining board, polishing the square lids of the Rayburn until I could see my face in them.

Frances's preference for my company didn't go without comment. 'She's a farmer's daughter, no more, no less,' this was the constant refrain from the village. I was used as a conduit for stiff little messages of goodwill, for a posy of dried flowers, a pot of orange and lemon marmalade. One day, Joyce – who was the only one as far as I could tell with any possible grounds for grievance – insisted on sending me off with three chicken carcasses saved up from Sunday lunch. I was not used to cooking, my efforts by most standards perfunctory, but I was good at taking instruction – onions, carrots, turnip, thyme – and it pleased me, as long as I wasn't being watched, to have something purposeful to do about the Upcott house. I was never happier in a task than I was then, in the resplendent quietness of that kitchen, peeling and chopping vegetables into bite-sized pieces. I paced up and down the long room, collecting water, setting the iron pot on the hook at the back of the fire.

The more I saw myself as an exception to the other women in the village, the more grateful I was. The Upcotts had land and they had history, a combination that ensured that however straitened their circumstances, they would never be slaves to anyone but themselves. As Daddy would have put it, they were 'a cut above'.

My soup simmered on through the morning until the kitchen windows dripped with the condensation. When I took up my offering to Frances, she was propped anxiously above the bedclothes wearing a faded yellow cape that looked as if it might have been her mother's. She levered herself up from

226

the bed, which had been her parents' bed, swinging its loose change. I gave her a chance to settle before approaching.

'You've been cooking?' she said.

'No trouble,' I said, nudging the corner of the tray on to the table, pushing aside an empty glass and a copy of Paley's *Evidences*. The soup in its flat porcelain dish glistened and steamed.

'It may be too hot,' I said in my nurse–mother voice. She coughed painfully, holding the corners of the tray in bud-like fists to get her balance. She was still only in her thirties, but she looked older. Her rheumy eyes had the look of oysters. She took the spoon and paddled it, collected a small circle of the liquid, which she raised to her mouth, extending her neck to blow across it. I sat myself in the nursing chair, turning away from her as she ate, counting the row of brass shells which danced at the foot of the bed. How unaccountably elated I was to hear the tiny sucks of soup being drunk.

In practically every way my friendship with Frances provided all the sustenance I required; but I was almost twenty-seven and it would be futile to deny that the question of settling down had not begun to enter my head, or the fact that neither of Frances's brothers were yet spoken for. At first I hardly dared to think it: the idea of her and me as sisters, properly, was so overwhelming . . . But it wasn't long before I found myself wondering about Robert, my heart quickening at the prospect of seeing him, only to tie myself in knots trying to work out whether he was making a concerted effort to avoid me? I knew of course that farming was a busy and absorbing

227

life, but I had not realized quite how full. There was always something. He was at market, or hedge-laying, harrowing, ploughing, treating worms, milking cows. Sometimes, when I went to the coop to collect the eggs, I caught a glimpse of him trudging out on the hillside; once I saw him dive into the stable across the yard. For all I knew he lay in there, waiting until I was safely out of the way.

As soon as she was well enough, Frances ventured downstairs, wrapped in a shawl, taking tentative steps. She was grateful for my help, she said, which was encouragement enough. I was already used to the kitchen and it was no great leap to involve myself in the domestic running of the house, assisting her now with whatever there was that needed to be done – washing, baking, feeding the pigs and hens. Although I wasn't out there every day, I made the journey to Passaford at least two or three times a week.

When she'd been ill, I'd picked Frances flowers. She had been so appreciative that I continued to collect them from the hedgerows on my way over – foxgloves, stitchwort, buttercups – bunches of whatever came to hand. One morning, though, I noticed she was less receptive. Rather than putting the flowers in the jug on the kitchen table as usual to admire them, she let them steep in the sink. Later on, she tried to explain that Robert thought we were being silly: flowers were meant to be outside. Inside, they were nothing more than a quite unnecessary mess.

I could see his point, I said, eager to improve myself. If I had not understood it fully before, I discovered now that – even when he wasn't around – Robert could be an imposing presence. Frances deferred to him in even the smallest matters, as if he were constantly hitched to every decision she made; as if, without him, the whole enterprise, inside and out, would judder to a halt.

Between Robert and Tom there was a constant bristle. Robert was determined that Tom never pulled his weight and he was as rough with him as I imagine older brothers generally were with their younger siblings. Occasionally, even when I was around, Robert would stand out in the yard and bellow for him. Frances and I would jump to attention and break off whatever we were doing. If Tom happened to be with us, he would outright refuse to be hurried. He teased us that we were like two old maids. Frances encouraged me to treat Tom as she did, indulgently, as a wayward child. And I was happy enough to oblige, if it put me in the same bracket as Frances. An easiness developed between the three of us which, for the present time, kept Tom from seeming any kind of prospect.

Tom moreover had a reputation – harmless or otherwise, depending on who was telling it – for drinking and for chasing pretty girls. Although Frances had no patience for the alcohol, which she took to be a vice, she would turn a blind eye to the odd broken heart. It was never serious, she maintained. She had been used to mothering him since he was born, and although, in matters of the farm, she would always take Robert's side, she babied Tom, teasing him with stories from their childhood that kept him fundamentally hers.

'It was me who had to take him up to the school looking like that,' she said. 'Remind Rose Curtis of *that*, next time you see her . . .You were *Nigger-boy* for how long after that? I was never so embarrassed. I thought then,' she said, 'you'd never know when to stop.'

229

'Nothing's changed there,' he said.

She flapped at him with her cloth.

'I got to know the bottom of that trough well enough,' he said, raising his head. 'As good as my own reflection.'

I didn't understand him, but Frances did, of course. She looked at me, 'Don't listen to him,' she said, turning to Tom, 'You gave him cause, that's all I'll say: you answered back. Father couldn't abide that.'

'All right for you,' Tom said, 'you had him round your finger.'

'It's not true,' she said. 'And anyway, you were a savage half the time; you know you were.'

'You were his golden girl, till the Yanks come . . .'

'Don't listen to him,' Frances said to me.

'Bit different then, wasn't it?'

It surprised me how flustered Frances became.

'A certain Yank?' he said, needling her.

'Shut up, Tom,' she said sharply. 'Don't.'

'If he'd have known about that . . .'

Frances set her mouth. She glared at him.

He had been ready to tease her, but at that look, he erupted from his chair, his voice harsh. 'It's all right for you, is it? That's a *different* carrying on, no doubt. That's not the same thing at all.' He tore out of the room as if he'd no intention of ever coming back.

I was mortified. Frances on the other hand dismissed him after only a moment or two, collecting herself. 'You can see what he's like. It drove Father wild. He just doesn't know when to stop,' she repeated. 'Father did his best, I know that, whatever anyone says.'

230

It surprised me how quickly Frances recovered her composure. There was no need for me to go, she said, though I didn't usually stay so long. She urged me to come and sit with her by the fire, unpacking her darning, passing me her pattern book to look through. I did as she asked, not wanting to upset her further, but I found it impossible to ignore the reverberations in the room and, although I went through the motions of flicking through the pages of *Knitting for All*, my mind wouldn't settle.

'It's all right, isn't it, my visiting so often?' I asked eventually, not able to let it lie.

Frances looked up distractedly.

The odd time when Robert appeared at the back door to fetch his lunch, barely a word would pass between them. It made me yearn for the day when my silences could be as exclusive and as comfortable as theirs.

I said, 'I wonder, sometimes: whether your brothers mind me being here?'

'Why should it be anything to them?'

I turned a page or so of the book, read the heading EVERYDAY UNDERWEAR. SMART – WARM – SENSIBLE. Frances remained poised, the darning needle half-drawn. She said, 'If you mean Robert, he's not particularly good with people – never has been.'

'I didn't mean—'

'I expect most farmers are like it,' she said. 'They're better with animals. He's got a responsibility, you know. It's hard for him. They wouldn't understand that in the village. There's a great weight on his shoulders.'

I knew at once that I shouldn't have said anything. I had

spun out of orbit, a hundred miles from her. I watched her needle fussing in and out like a wasp in fruit. Then she tied the end and bit it off.

At that moment the front door scraped across the flags in the hallway. A second later, Robert strode in looking for Tom. 'Where's he to?' he said, his head lowered against the beams. He spoke unguardedly, three rabbits over his shoulder, elongated, dangling like one of Mother's old stoles, and he bent down and shrugged them off on to the tabletop.

'I won't be answerable . . .' As he turned to face Frances, he saw me there and stopped short, his face bulging with irritation. Immediately he scooped up the limp bodies, their stunned, grape-like eyes, and strode out of the room muttering something about hooks in the pantry. Frances didn't even look in my direction; hastily she dropped her sewing and scurried out after him.

It was hardly the greatest discourtesy and yet I felt devastated by it. One more push and I knew I'd dissolve. I wasn't going to wait for them to come back. I didn't want them to find me like this. Quickly, I gathered my things together and let myself out. In the yard, the air was dank, the light leaden. Each step was an unaccountable effort. By the time I reached the lane to the village my chest was raw and inflamed. I passed three buzzards, supercilious, high up on the new telegraph poles. *Nothing has happened*, I said to myself, *nothing*. But I was shaking when I arrived on Joyce's doorstep and probably told her more than I should have done, translating disappointment into complaint. Joyce sat me down by the stove. She put a blanket around me as if I were an invalid. She said that Robert was *ill-mannered*, which was the politest word she could find for it. Victor had borne the brunt of Robert's temper ever since he'd gone to work for them. As she'd said before, he was a perfectly good herdsman: the Upcotts got more than their money's worth out of him; he was strong as two men. She was pleased to have the opportunity to let off steam, the amount of time she'd had to pick up the pieces.

'T'isn't right,' she said. 'Not poor Victor, it makes him nervous. It's same as shouting at a horse. Don't do any good.'

The trouble, in Joyce's considered opinion, was the same as with all such farming families. 'You've only got to look at Cain and Abel, Jacob and Esau. You take two brothers, throw in a parcel of land, there'll be fireworks. I've known those boys since they were small. I brung Tom into the world,' she said. 'They weren't ever going to get along. The number of times Victor's come home: curse this, curse that. He's not used to it; he knows enough to know it i'nt right. If they was younger, they'd have their mouths washed out. I'd do it for 'em.'

I let her rattle on. The sound of her voice was the treadle of a machine: it soothed me like nothing else. I remembered Tom's blackened face that time. Joyce couldn't paint the Upcotts blacker than they painted themselves. I was cheered up. It was so warm in her small kitchen. The sharper the picture she drew, the more determined I was to hold on.


I didn't go to Passaford the next day, or the one after. But by the end of the week it was clear that I was punishing no one but myself. And as if to reward my prevailing good sense,

233

when I turned up in the yard that Friday, I found Frances outside waiting for me. My trouble, I decided in a flush of thankfulness, was that I had so little faith in how robust a friendship could be.

'There you are,' she said, smiling as if she had met me after a long journey, leading me into the house.

Fridays were washdays and no further mention of my absence during the week was made. I fell in with the routine in the scullery where the tub and dolly had been duly pulled out from the wall. The linens were already done: the sheets, the pillowcases and the tablecloths had been out all morning on the double line and were almost dry. We had a way of folding the big sheets between us, taking two corners and returning with the ends raised like country dancers. When we'd done, Frances laid them on the kitchen table and I brought the hot irons from the fire for her, replacing one for the other when they lost their heat.

We carried the finished basket, all folded, up to the bedroom. It was airier up there, the breeze billowing the curtains out under the open window frame high above the garden. I was aware of the privilege of being upstairs with her: this was the room where she'd been confined to bed, the room she and Robert shared. I never told a soul that fact – it would only have been misinterpreted. Frances trusted me enough not to have to explain herself. In any case, it was the largest and most handsome of the rooms upstairs: it had been their parents' before, and the bed into which they had each entered the world.

Frances dragged the nursing chair over to the tallboy and climbed up on to it. I stood below her and handed up the linen parcels for her to stack on the top shelf. Fixed to the back of the cupboard door, the same height as my nose, there was a bundle of dried lavender, a heady, musty sweetness. As Frances lifted the last of the sheets from my arms, my head began to swim; I heard myself muttering. In a moment, Frances was down beside me. She led me over to sit on the edge of the bed, her face looming next to mine. 'You'll feel better,' she said as she poured a glass of water from the carafe on the bedside table. 'Drink this.'

We sat for a moment side by side. Then she said, 'Wait. I'll show you something.' The bed tipped as she got up and went over to her dressing table. I noticed for the first time a small black lacquered cabinet sitting to one side. She drew back its shutters to reveal half a dozen elaborately decorated oxblood drawers, opened one and lifted something out.

'Shut your eyes,' she said, with her arms behind her back.

I waited until an object light as a pebble was placed in my hand.

'Open,' she said.

It was a heart-shaped, maroon leather box.

'Look inside.'

I pressed the tiny gold-pin button and lifted the lid. There was a mossy swatch of velvet, a flower-head of deep red jewels arranged around a single diamond.

Frances picked out the ring and put it over the top of her thumb. 'Mother was tiny, but she had big hands,' she said. The gold was rosy and warm.

'You try,' she said, and she held it out between her finger and thumb.

I offered her the spread of my fingers. I couldn't speak.

235

She chose the third deliberately and lowered the ring, twisting it gently over the knuckle.

'There,' she said leaning back, her eyes gleaming. 'What about that?'

In a sudden impulse I began to twist it off; I thought she must mean it as a trick, to flush me out. I was sure in any case that it would be bad luck.

She smiled at me. 'I've not said a word,' she said and she took the ring back, tucked it into its box and returned it to the cabinet.

# 23

## *Turdus Philomelos*

On my own I replayed that scene meticulously a hundred times, unpicking every detail. Whichever way I looked at it, it seemed to me that a line had been crossed, that one way or another – in spite of all my more sensible efforts to convince myself of the contrary – it was not so foolish to think the unthinkable: that one day we would be sisters, that Passaford might become my permanent home. Nothing more was said on the subject.

It was a week or so after that Tom burst into the kitchen, holding something in the cup of his outstretched hands. He brought it over to me. 'Must have coshed itself against the glass,' he said. He'd discovered the creature flat on its back just outside the scullery window. He laid it on the table, the two threads of its legs pathetically thin and straight.

Frances was stirring a pot on the stove. 'What are you doing with that?' she said, agitated. 'Not in here . . .'

He was craning his face close to the bird, put his finger to it, tracing the contour of its breast.

'Not where we're working, Tom,' she said. 'Not dead things. Go on.'

'It's a dirsh,' he said, smiling at me. 'A little songthrush. Look.' And I knew he must have remembered about my name.

'Not in here,' Frances said again. 'Doesn't Robert need you? You can do that later.'

'I want to sort him out before he stiffens up. Mavis doesn't mind, do you?'

The way he included me, my heart swelled. Frances untied her apron and stretched it out on the rail in front of the Rayburn. Then, glancing from one to the other of us as if she were above such things, she said, 'I'll leave you to it, then. I've got plenty to get on with upstairs.'

'Keep the cats out,' Tom said to me, 'while I fetch my things.'

I sat guard over the bird. It was like a child's toy brought in from the rain. Bedraggled. *Mavis*. My name.

Tom came back into the kitchen with a pile of newspapers and a wooden toolbox. He sat down and scooped the bird towards him. Then he put his thumbs under its armpits and prised open the wings, looking up to check that I was watching.

'See?' he said. 'It's stiffening up already.'

Gently he parted a line with a fingernail, between the downy feathers, from under its throat and down the middle of its stomach. He reached for the silver scalpel from the several odd tools he'd arrayed in front of him and pointed with the tip of its blade.

'Here. The skin's thin. A hairline, that's all: there,' he was teasing with the blade until there was room to insert his thumbnail.

'If you can pinch it here, it peels away. Look.'

The skin was fine as a peach; he rolled it back from pink marble flesh. There was hardly a mess, just a smeariness to the newsprint where it lay. He had a box of plaster of Paris; he dipped his fingers into the packet and dusted, a fine icing sugar. He moved so quickly, prodding, pressing, that it was hard to see what was going on. When he next lifted his hands, there were two connected parts: the bald purple-grey body and then, attached at the neck, a skin of feathers blown upwards over its head like an inside-out umbrella.

As I sat next to him and he shifted in his seat, I could smell him — a meaty, fecund smell. I wondered for a moment if it was something to do with the bird. Tom took up his penknife and with his teeth pulled out the blade. He cut through the cord that linked the parts together; then through the shoulder bone, the hip. Each cut registered in my head as if the sinews were intimately related to my own; and as he began to shave the fat from the bone using the very edge of the blade, I was aware for the first time of the multiple layers of my own skin. He took monumental care. Every last bit of yellowy wax he wiped from his knife on to the edge of a saucer.

'This bit, see?' He pointed to the base of the tail, lifting a membrane of stringy material. 'Gut,' he said. 'And there, see that little nick at the end? The *cloaca*.' He paused to take special care at a crucial point in the operation. 'It means sewer.' He raised his eyebrows at me, caught me looking at the fluff of hair on the back of his neck.

He cleaned the blade of the knife on the edge of the saucer where he'd amassed a pile of the innards and then, without warning, scraped back his chair, carried the dish to the scullery door. The two cats fell into the room as if they'd been eavesdropping, yowling, tails stretched to the ceiling. He wove between them out of sight. I heard the judder of the back door and then the clink of the saucer on the stone step.

When he returned he had a teaspoon in his hand. He lifted the bird and, holding its skull between his finger and thumb, began to scoop out the grey, jellied contents as if it were a boiled egg, neatly tapping them on to the newspaper.

'Lobotomy,' he said.

He reached for the tweezers and began to dig about. He plucked out a gloop of darker jelly. I couldn't look. When I turned back, he was tearing off a strip from a piece of wadding, twisting it to little plugs, which he poked into the eye sockets, two dark-rimmed slits, neat as button holes. Then he lifted the skull, gripping it at the base of the neck so that its beak opened like a snapdragon, and on the end of the tweezers he was able to draw out a pink sliver of muscle, holding it out to me to inspect.

'He's not telling,' he said. I bit the tip of my tongue. Then he gathered up the cloak of feathers and handed it to me, saying, 'Wash it for me?' nodding backwards to the sink.

It was a test of my squeamishness. I took the limp thing between my finger and thumb and walked it over to the window. There was a bar of Lifebuoy in a dish on the windowsill, slippery and too big for the task, but I began to rub gingerly into the mess of feathers.

He rattled out instructions without looking round. 'Hold him under. He's tougher than you think.'

I turned the tap and water came out in a cloudy rod. I held the feathery skin there, until it stretched long and stringy over my fingers like a pelt.

'Squeeze him,' he said, fumbling inside his box. 'Use a cloth. Wrap him up. Go on, squeeze.'

I did everything he asked and brought the bundle back to him.

Tom was fiddling with two blue pill bottles. He unscrewed the lids and tipped them, tapping on the sides to encourage the white powder out. I didn't question him. I was his acolyte, so attentive to him that the room shrank around the circle of us, heightening each tiny star of crystal he was pressing and embedding into the bird's skin. It was salt and it was snow, a glimpse deep into the laboratory. Concentrating so hard that his knee began to shudder very slightly: 'Argh,' he said, to restrain himself. He plucked a handful of fine dried grass from his box and moulded it between the palms of his hands. From a reel of black cotton, he broke off a thread and began to bind the body, stuffing stray tufts into the fold, adding here and there, prodding and poking with a long darning needle. His whole body appeared to vibrate, the air humming around him. He chewed his lips. From a coil of wire he cut five long lengths, straightened them out. He formed a loop at the end of one and skewered the body with the tip, straight up through the stomach, out through the cap of the skull. No compunction, feeding another wire through the hollow of a leg, out of the heel, between the toes; another, through the top of the wing, along the upper arm and out at the tip of the feathers.

He sucked his tongue as he lifted the cape of skin over the packed skull and stretched it around the cavities of the eyes. Then he brought the two flaps of skin around the body, pulled them together like the coat of a child being sent off to school. With a needle and a length of brown cotton he began to stitch in a hand delicate as any girl's, over and under, right up to the throat.

'Get the bear,' he said, nodding at the box.

There was a sandy-coloured teddy bear, which I brought out by its arm. It had paws of crushed velvet. Tom had the scalpel poised in his hand. The look on my face amused him. He snorted and took the bear from me, lifting the blade to its milky blue eyes – the taut give of a thread one side, then the other.

'You can look round now,' he said. He had the two buttons of glass in the centre of his palm. He took one up with the tweezers and pushed it into the eye cavity.

'Perfect fit,' he said. 'See the rim of brown around the blue?'

The bear lay awkwardly on its side, two worm-like threads that were its eyes. I resisted the impulse to take it up, because I knew from the way Tom had laughed that it had been another test. To put away childish things.

He was watching me as he set the bird along the length of his hand. Very gently he held it out towards the fire, rolling it in the heat, fluffing the feathers between his fingers. The hair pricked all over my scalp, partly because I believed, as he seemed to, that any moment the bird would burst into flight.

I struggled to be patient. It might have been a month since Frances had shown me that ring up in the bedroom and,

242

though she appeared to have forgotten all about it, I could think of little else. In between my visits to the farm, it became more important than ever to keep busy. I set my typewriter up on the kitchen table by the stove. I typed. If I had nothing formal to type, I typed for myself, page after page. It was my version of playing the piano, practising certain phrases, certain runs of letters. It helped to bring me to myself, tacking my feet with every *tap, tap, tap* to solid ground.

On market days I took the bus into town, not so much to stock up on provisions as to remind myself of the throng and how possible it was to be in it. Every Tuesday from three separate directions there was an influx of traffic that convened on the flattened fields behind the main market hangars. Trucks and pick-ups, tractors and trailers, horses and carts, bleating, lowing, clucking: the dust never had a chance to settle. There was the quick-fire rap of auctioneers everywhere – cattle and sheep in one pit, horses in another, poultry piled high in their wooden crates at the back of the coaching inn. I had evolved a circuit and a momentum that meant I could weave in and out of the huddles of men and the women creaking their chattels, without getting too caught up.

More often than not, I'd end up outside Heap's Auctions, on the high corner of the market square. It was the accounting office of the auction rooms, with a large window display of the smaller bits and bobs that hadn't been picked up in previous weeks' sales. I could never resist taking a look: an ornate Japanese vase, a pair of duelling pistols ('faulty'), a baby's silver and ivory teething ring, three large leather-bound volumes entitled *History of the World*. And then, quite unremarkable, I spotted the dome: a small, empty glass case.

243

I pushed the door impulsively. Mrs Heap looked up from her ledgers over the top of half-rimmed spectacles. My blood was pumping.

'What's that, dear?'

'The glass case.'

She got up from her chair and eased herself and her bulky astrakhan around the desk, stepping over a brass fender. 'Good condition, that one,' she said, pulling at the cream-painted panelling. A door opened into the void of the display. She leaned in and lifted the dome out carefully, as if it were a wedding cake, and set it down on a corner of the desk.

'Needs a spit and polish,' she said, blowing and brushing the top with her fingers, 'but it's *sound*.'

Mildew had formed a ring inside the glass. Mrs Heap put her hands to its sides and lifted. The glass came away neatly from its circular guttering.

'Good for precious bits,' she said.

I was sure it would be perfect.

The next day, I set out with the string shopping bag over my shoulder, and the dome carefully repacked and stuffed with its original balls of newspaper. The bag patted softly against my back in a quiet rhythm that encouraged me to keep count of my steps – three hundred and sixty one, three hundred and sixty-two. The breakable cargo made the going seem unusually precipitous. Six hundred and three, four, five, six. Every time my foot turned over on a stone, disaster was averted. As I drew near the farmhouse, I had to refrain from running, possessed by an overwhelming desire to unburden myself before it was too late.

Robert was out in the yard. He grunted at me, leading the

black horse by the reins, steadied it by the granite trough and then swung himself up into the saddle. I stood back as he thumped his heels into the creature's sides and took off, *like the devil*, I might have said.

I let myself in and went straight through to the kitchen. Frances and Tom were both there, standing in the shadows of the big fireplace.

'I've just seen Robert,' I said, ignoring the crackle in the air. I laid my bag on the kitchen table and began to unpack, pulling out the scrunched-up balls of paper and setting them in a clumsy pile to one side.

Tom moved towards me; he couldn't help himself. He was wearing an old brown suit of his father's. He was so close, I could see the filings of hair along his jaw, reddish as copper wire. I peeled the final layer of paper from the dome, all washed and polished, and set it down into its circular frame.

I could hear myself breathing. 'It's for the bird,' I said, my voice breaking with excitement. Tom lifted the lamp and for a moment the walls were liquid gold. It was better than I could have dreamed. It reminded me suddenly of the post-card Daddy had bought me years ago of a painting we'd seen in the National Gallery. An *experiment* it was called. A white cockatoo caught in flight, like an angel in a glass cloud.

'Where'd you find it?' Tom asked.

'Heap's,' I said. 'It was in the window.'

'Clever you,' he said.

He went to retrieve the small package from the cupboard, brought it over to the light of the window and began unpicking the cotton threads with the point of his penknife. The wadding came away like the thick shell of an egg. Tom held

245

the bird between his hands, manipulating the wings to spread them out.

'You have to decide: do you want it landing, like this? Or landed?' He folded the wings shut again like a fan. Then he changed his mind. 'No,' he said. 'Second thoughts. Let it be a surprise.'

# PART VI

*Husbandry*

# *Pastourelle*

Here I am in a dress that Frances and I have concocted between us, forty-eight pin tucks — twenty-four each side from neck to waist. It is the finest cheese muslin we could find, hung out to air on the line, smelling of whey and giblets. She fusses with the train outside the church, which spreads in a circle from my feet like a puddle, then squeezes my arm — sisters!

Daddy has come down especially. In the stripy ribbons of his suit, he is all attention and smiles. He produces a milky white brooch from Venice, two pale hands clasped to make a dove — it was his mother's, then Patricia's. I can't help wondering if, in that case, Patricia might have died, but I don't ask. I pin the brooch to my collar.

How sweet! The children have made pictures out of white stones and shells: a white stag, a horseshoe, a daisy chain. Daddy is not interested. He is polishing the toes of his shoes on his trouser legs, performing a hopping dance. There is an emerald tiepin glinting in his cravat and for the first time I notice how green his eyes are.

The church creaks. A fussy woman who has poked her

head around the heavy oak door, is telling us anxiously that there is standing room only, as far back as the belfry. She points to the step, which sags from so many boots.

'But here is the bride,' Daddy protests.

She looks me up and down, 'Quickly, then. You'll have to jump.'

She is right, the congregation is packed so tight, they have to lift their arms and breathe in to let us through. Daddy and I dip under. I drag my bouquet behind me. Auntie has made it with a special flower that blooms only once every ten years – it has been sitting in her kitchen in its cardboard box like an open coffin. It is traditional, she says, as are the ferns which accompany it. They sweep down to the floor and as the fronds curl I see that they are not leaves at all, but feathers – a cloak of feathers attached to my wrist.

Daddy straightens himself up; he is shorter than I remember. I take his arm. I lay my hand over his cuff. The heavy Upcott veil with its hundreds of embroidered butterflies billows out behind us. Above his glistening head I make out the smudges of faces; many I don't recognize, but among them I find Joyce and Alf, Victor . . . Joyce is nodding towards the front row as if there's a big surprise. She's nodding and nodding as if I will never guess.

Mother?

But at that very moment – of all moments, why this? – I feel the prod of a sapling just above my left hip. I gasp. Only this morning I'd plucked out a great black switch, horribly painful, from my chin. Now I see that whoever is sitting there at the front of the nave is encouraging it. I watch the rook-feather in the hat bob and tilt towards her knees, from where the nozzle of a can tips a film of water on to the slate floor. My dress sops it up; I can feel the damp under my arms, the gauzy material clinging to my legs so that it is virtually impossible to walk. I draw level and she looks round, lit up with her green face and her green spectacles – Miss Minchin! I am tangled and sodden and my legs are in knots. I hold myself tight as an anchor, hearing the loose cry of my voice trying to say something but making the sound of a bird – ai – ai – ai.

# 24

## *Harvest*

I had been back in Shipleigh just over a year. It was my second harvest and, together, Frances and I pronounced it our favourite season, *We plough the fields and scatter*, our favourite hymn. For the first time since I'd come back, I was more actively involved outside – as indeed, every able-bodied man, woman and child appeared to be. Every day from the middle of August, Frances and I trooped out to the fields with a heavy basket of things for tea – pasties, apple cake, thermos, jugs of cider. We took the back way, which was more level, through the orchard, past the pigsty, over the stile into Peasmeadow, lugging the basket between us to whichever field was being worked, depositing it in a shady corner where the spare tools were propped.

By the third day it was routine. We'd each take up a hay-fork and work our way up the long line of stooks, lifting them from the ground and propping them like raggedy tents to dry out. In no time at all our lips were parched and our clothes were sandy with dust. It was back-breaking work, and my back had never been right since school, but I threw myself into it until my arms were ready to drop off, following the clatter and swish of the binder that paraded in the neighbouring field, determined to prove myself sufficient. And in spite of the blisters on my hands, the purple brand on the back of my neck, I was thinking this was how I wanted to live, for ever and ever. It was like a story from the Bible, plain and simple, and here I was in the middle of it, blessed, rewarded for my prodigal return.

It was only when Victor unhitched the horses and led them down the slope of the field to the bucket of water that we broke for tea. He tied them loosely, smoothing their necks, offering them handfuls of oats, and then came lolloping over. Robert was moving against the horizon like a dancing bear, and then Tom, keeping his distance, lighter on his feet, both of them making their way along the hedgerow towards us. One after the other, they pitched down, the three of them, ranged in a row under the hedge where Frances had spread an old blanket. They were all arms and legs, hunched over, too exhausted to speak. Frances handed round the pasties, tin beakers of cider, and they crammed their mouths. For a while, all that could be heard was the sound of them eating, more noisy than a threshing machine. Frances and I sat a little apart on an old shawl of hers. There were woodlice nosing out of the stubble, dazed and bleary as if in shock.

'Be done by Friday, won't it, if it stays like this?' Frances said, paddling at the midges above her head.

Robert's shirt was dark and drenched. It clung to him. Victor, who was bulkier than both of them put together, stinking of dog, smiled so broadly I thought his lip would burst.

'They give it rain,' Robert grunted, wiping his mouth with the back of his hand.

'Don't look like rain to me,' Tom said combatively, looking up at the sky, which was buoyant with tiny scudding clouds.

Robert didn't answer. Tom said, 'Well, I'm planning on celebrating Saturday whatever happens. There's a dance in the Hall. Fancy it?'

No one answered him. No one was likely to, except Victor who was busy slapping at his leg.

'Mavis'll come, won't you?' Tom said.

I was flummoxed. I looked at Frances who was brushing cake from her skirt.

'That's to say we get it done,' Robert said.

'One way or another,' Tom said.

'Rate we're going,' said Frances, trying to include them both.

Robert had started poking the ground with a stalk. 'Man takes a drink. . .' he was muttering. Tom got to his feet and stretched his arms to the sky. His shirt was untucked and gaped at the belly, revealing a fine fluff of hair, soft as seed.

If there was a moment, finally, categorically, when my allegiance between the brothers shifted, then that was it. Even Frances was eclipsed. As if a trap door had opened in the floor of me and I'd fallen through: I flushed.

'Good idea,' Tom said. 'We'll take a jar or two up with us, shall we, Victor? Oil the works.'

Robert twisted to one side and spat.

'Robert!' Frances said, though she was looking straight at

me. Then she began to gather the tin beakers, shaking the drops out, stacking them neatly back into the basket.


At St Cuthbert's I'd learned to waltz with female partners and been told that I had two left feet, which for a while I took to be a bona fide condition. Joyce was adamant that in the village it would be no hindrance. I could always sit and watch, as she did; and I had a dress, which Margaret had made for me from a cotton voile I'd chosen one time with Joyce. There'd been no occasion yet to wear it. Such a beautiful thing. I hung it from one of the beams in the bedroom, so delicate and thin the light shone right through. I was careful easing it over my head, smoothing it down over my petticoat, the three press-studs under the arm. It was a close fit. I'd made myself an orange flower from silk ribbon, which I fixed below the smocking on the shoulder.

It wasn't long ago I'd told myself I'd never go to a dance again, but by five o'clock I was ready. I had pinned and undone my hair, pinned it up again. I sat downstairs in the blue chair. I couldn't sew, I couldn't read. I sat as straight as I could, practising my posture for later. I had an old metal-beaded evening bag of Auntie's on my knee. At half past six, I had begun to lose heart; I thought with piercing premonition: *he's not coming*. I went through to the kitchen, put the kettle on, *don't be silly*, I was saying, *don't be silly*. Tom Upcott: he'd have his eye on much younger, prettier girls; he'd never been interested in me. But I didn't take the dress off. It was still light outside, *still daylight*, I was thinking. Plenty of time.

There was a rap at the door just after seven. When I

opened it I almost cried. Tom was shining, his broad face: he was a vision in his black suit, his dicky-bow tie, his hair a rust colour, oiled tightly to his head.

'I'll get my wrap,' I said, turning away into the house, trying to pull myself together.

He was still smiling as I reappeared. I pulled the door shut and jauntily he offered me his arm, which I took: hook and eye.

'All done?' I asked.

He looked up at the sky, which was beginning to fade at the edges. 'Lucky, we were,' he said.

'Good,' I said, which covered everything.

Already we could hear music reeling out from the open windows of the hall. As soon as we reached the door, we undid arms.

'You all right, now?' he said and in a flash I realized that he was going to abandon me.

'Yes, of course I am,' I said, my mouth dry. I clutched my bag. Joyce and Alf and Sandy and her new husband were sitting in a foursome at one of the tables. Joyce beckoned me over,

'Mavis,' she shouted, 'pull up a chair. What a job Margie's done with that dress. Come and sit down. What a picture you are.'

Sandy was still shy with me. She was large and freckly and she sat holding her young man's hand under the table. He had an oily fringe and very large lips, apparently too heavy to open.

In the far corner of the hall, around the piano, there was an accordion player and a fiddle, churning away at full pelt.

The noise was loud and rattly and I was sweating now with the pitch of it and with the loss of Tom, who'd gone to fetch himself a drink. If only I'd listened to myself!

'Victor's up somewhere,' Joyce shouted across the noise. 'Can you see him? He says corn's all in?'

Over on the other side of the dance floor there were two long trestles with four or five clear demijohns of cloudy cider and an assortment of beakers, glasses and cups. Tom was leaning into the ear of one of the Knight boys, who were standing like storks, a leg raised against the wall, each with a large beaker, knocking it back. Sitting below, studiously ignoring them, Rose Curtis and her sister Gladys, arranged in a triangle with Beatrice Manning, aloof and immaculate.

'She's finished school,' Joyce said, seeing me. 'And she likes a dance. Come back for good now she's done her exams. Or as good until she's off again.'

Even Joyce was a little cool about Beatrice. Being an only child, Mrs Manning had let her have too much the upper hand. And anyone who knew anything about rearing animals knew that no good ever came of that. From a young age, Beatrice had kept herself apart from her peers, walked around with her nose in the air as if there were always more pressing things to be doing. It had surprised me when Beatrice's name came up at the farm, how vitriolic Frances had been: 'I've known her since she was a child,' she said. 'Wouldn't trust her an inch.'

Rose Curtis was beetroot. She had turned her back on Tom. As the next dance was ready to begin, she made a snap decision, dragged Gladys to her feet to partner her. The music struck up and several other pairings took to the floor.

Not Tom. He made his way along the trestle table towards Beatrice, who was now seated conspicuously on her own. He stooped, bowed his head. They were talking; I couldn't hear what they were saying, but every now and again, Beatrice lifted her chin and laughed, closed her eyes. When the dance finished, the two of them turned to clap. A moment later he was holding out his hand, which she made a show of inspecting before she agreed to set her own upon it, shifting her weight, levering herself to her feet.

The accordion player was drawing his instrument wide and short like a tide. A slow waltz made the other young couples shy, but Beatrice placed her forearm on Tom's shoulder, he curled his arm to take her in, and together they shuffled forwards, sideways, backwards, one, two, three. Eventually, the Knight boys, full of cider, stumbled over to ask Rose and Gladys to join them on the floor. Poking each other, the girls agreed, though I could see Rose continually peering round to find Tom, her distraction making her falter. Alf had partnered Sandy, just as he'd done – he liked to remind her – on her wedding day. A farmer from up the road was grappling sedately with his cumbersome wife. Every now and then, in the melee, I caught the side of Beatrice's face, poised like a card then withdrawn, turning in strict time.

Then my view was blocked by Victor who stood before me, arms dangling. He was wheezing with happiness, his shirt unbuttoned at the collar. He held out his huge hand, ingrained with dirt, with every confidence I'd accept. Joyce was nodding persuasively at me.

'I'm a terrible dancer,' I said, taking his uppermost finger between mine, knowing that I couldn't refuse.

As soon as we were on the floor, we blundered about as if our prime purpose had been to throw a spanner in the works. I tried my best to steer Victor but the more I tried, the more the two of us were at odds and tripped or buckled. 'I'm sorry,' I was saying over and over above the music. Someone elbowed me in the ribs.

'Victor,' I hissed into his chest.

He was too giddy to take any notice of me, buoyed with an energy that spilled out from him like marbles. We careered into a couple of chairs. I laddered my stocking. My dress would get torn. I was hot and sticky with the shame of it. 'I'm going to sit down,' I said, pinching his finger, 'I've had enough.' I pulled him back with me and handed him over to Joyce.

'It's the sun. It's given me a headache,' I said. 'I can't seem to shake it off.'

As I took up my wrap I couldn't help catching a last sight of the two of them – Tom and Beatrice – as they made the most of the space Victor and I had cleared with a slow slide and shuffle that I would never in a million years be capable of – straight from a Hollywood film. And as I walked home and the song ended I could hear the enthusiastic clapping as if everyone had known it all along. I imagined the way the two of them took it as a compliment; and all I could smell was honeysuckle, sickly and sweet in my nostrils.

# 25

## *Fishing*

'Can we go to the river?' Archie asked yet again. He'd won an orange fishing net in the Harvest raffle and was keen to use it.

'You promised,' he said.

There was something touching about the way he associated me with the river, as if I were its keeper. Although I had been rash enough to make the suggestion in the first place, things had changed: I didn't necessarily want to be the person who broke it to them. In any case, I hadn't been down there myself in years.

'One day,' was my usual refrain and somehow I'd managed to avoid the question all summer – not in itself such a difficult task, given how much time Archie was spending with Owen Knight at the farm. Owen had got him a pint-sized blue boiler suit from Cornwall Farmers and a flat cap that had belonged to his grandfather.

'Proper job,' Owen told him, and Archie had begun, I noticed, to chew before he spoke, to swagger a little as he walked, and to speak like Owen did, with a definite Devon burr.

In September, he was cut down to size, back in his scrappy school uniform. Although he still slipped off to the farm whenever he could, whether by choice or at his mother's prompting he spent at least one evening a week doing his homework with me. Egyptian Mummies. The Tomb of Tutankhamun. I noticed the change in him; his allegiances more settled. Where before everything had seemed to be a trial and a matter of getting it done in the speediest possible way, now he was more curious, more willing to investigate.

'There are two birds in your name, Mavis,' he said. 'Did you know that?' He was writing hieroglyphics for everyone he knew. 'The A is a vulture,' he said. 'Look! Our names are nearly the same. And we've both got reeds.' He held out the paper with his drawing.

'What about your mother?' I asked.

'I've done her here.' He turned back a page. 'She's got a snake in hers,' he said, 'and Owen, he's a chick.'

He was smiling at me in anticipation. 'She can't eat him,' he said. 'Owen's got water in his, too. He can get away.'

At the end of the month it was still warm, balmy weather and Eve came to call one Saturday afternoon – she and Archie were off to the river, did I want to come too?

She must have seen my apprehension. 'If you're up to it?' she'd said. 'It was Archie's idea.'

'Wait,' I said. I didn't give myself time to think further. 'I'll fetch my jacket.'

It was one of those days with no history attached, the hedgerows preening as if they'd got new clothes. Archie ran along ahead of us, ticking the long grasses with his net, dislodging small white butterflies and daddy-longlegs. Eve was stooped under her haversack. 'I've brought his wetsuit and towels', she said, 'in case. Did you ever swim down there?' she asked.

'I don't,' I said.

'I might put my toe in . . . you never know,' she said.

I was reminded how much I preferred talking outside to being stuck in the house. There were so many other distractions; and a diffidence to the landscape that made conversation less loaded. Archie had scampered off, well out of earshot.

'How long were you married?' I asked.

She considered. 'Nearly seven years, all in all,' she said. 'Six years of which, at least, were hell.'

'Oh dear,' I said.

'It was a shotgun wedding, I told you, didn't I?' she said. 'I was pregnant . . . history repeating itself.'

She'd worn an A-line dress made of bamboo fabric. Pale blue, like being Mary in a school play. 'Mum wasn't going to come. She was at the end of her first load of chemo so she had the perfect excuse. I think she thought her not coming might just put me off, or at least think twice.' She humphed. 'It didn't, of course. And in the end she turned up anyway, looking grim.'

'Was it a big wedding?'

'God, no. Absolute minimum. Marco's mum and his sister, who'd come down anyway to see *Starlight Express*, Eric – my brother – with the girlfriend he was about to dump, and Mum and Chris. The place was horrible, it smelled of disinfectant like a hospital or a school, and it echoed because there weren't enough of us in there.'

'It sounds awful.'

'I didn't really care. I was huge by then, with Archie, and I think my brain had shut down.'

It was hot in the lane. Ahead of us you could see the haze rising from the tarmac as if everything around us was a hallucination.

'You were too sensible to get married?' she said.

'Never asked,' I said. 'Too sensible to be asked.'

'The signs were all there,' she said, 'if I could only have seen them. I remember watching Mum. Marco was gagging for a drink the moment it was finished, and not bothering to disguise it. I remember her closing her eyes, grabbing on to Chris. When it came to the speeches, I couldn't believe it when she got to her feet. I was thinking, *Oh God, please don't let her say something terrible* — like the spectre at the feast. It shows how blind I was: I wasn't thinking about her at all. She said something like, "I hope you'll take good care of my baby and my baby's baby." It must have killed her to say it.'

'She wasn't to know, was she, how it would turn out?'

'But she was right. Completely right, though I never told her a thing. I didn't want to make it worse, when it all started unravelling. It was easier for both of us to pretend everything was OK.'

It surprised me how quickly we'd arrived at the crossroads. Archie was waiting for us, hopping impatiently on one leg.

'Are we nearly there?' he said.

'Not long,' I said.

'How long?'

263

'Another fifteen minutes or so?'

'That's ages!'

'It's not ages,' Eve said; 'it's less time than the school bus.'

'Ages,' Archie said, spreading his arms with the pole of the net extended as far as it would go, so that he could almost bridge the gap. The banks were overflowing, every plant and leaf, extending its neck to the narrow ribbon of sky above us. There was hardly a track any longer, it was more like a gully, stony and uneven with tussocks of dandelion and nettles.

'I don't suppose it's anyone's responsibility to keep on top of it,' I said. 'It was one of the old monk paths. Quite a main road once. There was a ford in the river.'

'It does feel ancient,' Eve said, peering forwards. Then she asked me, 'Are you all right to go on?'

'Yes, yes,' I said. *Everything is new*, I was thinking. Newly grown. It's hardly the same place.

'Marco used to say I was *crazy* and just like my mother,' Eve said. 'Any time we went to see her, he'd come back saying she was "losing it". That was his answer to everything: "You're mad". He might have been right. I was by the end. But it's amazing what having a child does to you. I was quite prepared to martyr myself, but I wasn't going to have it for Archie. And when I no longer had to pretend – after Mum died – it happened before I knew it. Marco was living in the kitchen by then, chain-smoking, drinking, hardly moving from his chair. He was like a corpse. And I'd finally had enough; I threw him out.'

'It can't have been easy for you,' I said.

She smiled ruefully. 'It might have saved him too, in the end. Maybe it did. One of us had to decide.'

'It sounds as if you did the right thing.'

'It's not ideal, but I think it was right,' she said.

'He seems happy enough to me,' I said, watching Archie, zigzagging, dragging his net like a tail. Occasionally he twisted round to check that we were following.

'What happened to the farm?' she asked.

I was quite aware that she hadn't asked me anything about the Upcotts, not since that awkward conversation after Club Day. I imagined she'd found her answers elsewhere.

'I think they managed to sell the land,' I said, 'but not the house. No one wanted it. There's no mains water, no electricity. A couple of times, people have looked into it – Joyce would tell you that – but the cost of bringing in electric, gas, whatever *and* a mile of proper road was always more than the house was worth.'

Archie had reached the gatepost. He had found a wooden board propped up and rotting in the ditch. 'Look,' he said excitedly. 'NO ENTRY. PRIVATE.'

'Is that it?' Eve asked, extending her neck.

The huge old barn that had once hidden the farmhouse from view had been reduced to a skeleton, beams and skirtings; beyond it, quite visible, the gaping black windows of the house, the east wing no more than a pile of rubble with switches of ash growing lackadaisically all over it.

'It must have been a lovely place once,' Eve said.

'It's probably not safe to go in,' I said. I didn't tell her what a relief it was. I hardly recognized it.

'Let's find the river,' Eve said to Archie, who was tugging her, 'and test your rod.'

I took the lead, prodding the path ahead with my stick as

if at any point it might give way under us. Archie was easily diverted and quickly overtook me. He began to pound with renewed energy down the steep incline, his wellingtons puffing like a train.

There were leggy trees either side of us, straining to reach each other above our heads. All of a sudden I began to panic. I had said nothing about Tom. Eve had said nothing. We had passed the farmhouse. The burden of it was beginning to press on my chest.

'It's so quiet down here,' Eve said. 'No traffic, no tractors, nothing.'

I wasn't listening. I said abruptly, 'It was Tom's place down here, his bit of the river.'

Eve had broken off a long stalk of grass and was trailing it to the ground. Archie was way below. She turned and as I caught up with her she said, very quietly, 'You think it could be him, don't you?'

She said it so directly that I was unprepared. I stopped. A lump sat at the back of my throat and throbbed. We watched the end of her stalk as it found out a trickle of water, punctured the skin.

'It wasn't as if she had lots of boyfriends down here, was it?' Eve said, looking up.

'No,' I said. My legs were trembling.

'No she didn't? Or no, he wasn't my father?' she asked gently.

I met her eyes and the core of me shook. Although her features were fine, she had a wide open face, just like his. 'I think,' I said, faltering, 'I think it's possible that he *might* have been — from what you've told me, from what little I know . . .'

266

'Really? You do?' She reached out and took my arm to help me over the trickle of water. 'I've only seen that one picture, but there is something, don't you think? It reminds me of the way Archie is. Do you know what I mean? Or am I inventing it? Tell me, if you think I am . . .'

I felt I wanted to sit down, but I made myself keep going. We had reached the bottom of the track and Archie was already up on the gate. 'Can we go?' he asked. Eve came level to him and peered over. 'They're only bullocks,' she said. 'We'll be OK. If we keep to the edge and don't frighten them.'

She heaved the gate, which was tied at the hinge end with twine, and supported it for me to squeeze through.

'Over there, see?' I pointed for him. 'The little gate.'

Archie ran off. Eve said, 'I do understand, if you'd rather not talk about it. I know it must be upsetting.'

I didn't know how to tell her. *The truth is not a storybook*, I might have said, *it changes every minute.* I tried hard to keep my voice steady. 'I should tell you,' I said, without looking at her, 'I know I should. And I will. But it'll be in bits. It's been a long time.'

I didn't trust myself then to say anything more and she was tactful enough not to ask. Once we'd caught up with Archie, through the fence, through the shoulder-height reeds, he'd already taken off his shoes and socks. Eve let the haversack drop. She opened it up. 'Do you want your wetsuit?'

Archie took it from her and made off with it.

'He's self-conscious,' Eve said. 'He won't even let me see him in his pants any longer.'

The sun was glowing down on us again full force, scattering discs on the surface of the water. When Archie reappeared

267

he was black and rubbery, all apart from his extremities, which were reddish from the sun. He turned his back to his mother for her to zip him up.

'You're like a slow-worm,' I said.

'A baby hippo, more like,' Eve said.

Archie grabbed his net and took off into the water instantly, flailing about.

'You'll never catch anything like that,' Eve shouted, laughing at him. 'You have to be quiet, sneak up on them.'

In no time, he decided to jettison the rod, shooting it like a spear on to the bank.

'Show Mavis how you can swim, then,' Eve said. 'Impress us.'

He arched his back and flung himself belly down on to the surface of the water. He had his own way of swimming. It was nothing like Tom's. Archie kept his head raised and back as if he were carrying it on a tray, his eyes blinking furiously.

Eve waved at him. 'We can see you!' She picked up a pebble. 'They've been doing heroes and heroines at school,' she said. 'Florence Nightingale, Wayne Rooney, Firemen. Do you know, Archie chose to write a poem about his dad? He's a fighter-pilot, apparently. He's the best dad in the world.'

'It must be a thankless task, sometimes, being a mother,' I said.

She shook her head. 'It made me realize – what you said – I have to let him go, to see his dad.'

'That's brave,' I said. Then, catching her eye, 'I mean, generous.'

'He's going after Christmas, for New Year. He can take the plane from Exeter. It's direct. They look after them.'

She had begun to unbutton her shirt. She was wearing a blue nylon swimming costume underneath. She stood up and unzipped her jeans, pushed them down her legs, bending right down so that she was level with me, her neck flushed. She said, 'Can I ask you something?'

My heart contracted.

'About Owen?' she asked.

'Owen?' I repeated, relieved.

She stood up with her long pale legs exposed, leaned back.

'It's embarrassing. I'm not sure when the last time was I was *asked out;* but he has, he's asked me — all right, Archie? I'm coming.'

I was embarrassed on her behalf. I said, 'I don't know anything bad about him . . .'

'I didn't know what to say,' she said, 'I said. I wasn't sure. Because of Archie. Babysitters. But then I realized how silly that sounded. Archie's old enough.' She put her toe in the water. 'He's not a baby.'

'I'd have Archie, you know that — any time.'

'Thanks.' She handed me her wristwatch. 'Wish me luck.'

She was ankle deep in the river and her smile stretched to a grimace, 'Ah! Freezing!' She lifted her arms like wings above her head. 'I thought you said it was warm?' she said as Archie began flapping water at her. Eve waded forwards and then plunged in. 'Oh my God,' she yelled, scissoring her arms and legs. I watched the two of them, the river lit up with swatches of their limbs and the splashing. And from a different time entirely, all along the opposite bank, where the high winter water had cut into the earth, the ancient roots of trees poked through, bleached like bones, bewildered at being so disturbed.

Eve was the first out, her lips purple, her arms dangling, dripping. 'I feel like I've been electroplated,' she panted. 'I'm a statue. Frozen. My teeth!'

She yanked out a towel and unrolled it, hugged herself with it, hopping about.

As soon as she began to unpack the haversack, to pluck out the shiny bags of crisps, Archie materialized, the water sliding off his suit. He turned automatically to let his mother unzip and peel back the top half so that the black arms dangled beside his legs like two tentacles, and then he sat hunched over his crisp packet, systematically feeding his mouth, his eyes bright as ice, his lips the same blackberry-juice purple as Eve's.

I ought to have told her before. I hadn't been thinking. It was the wrong order. Here we were swimming in the *same* river. They were the *same* trees, the same bones. The water winked and sluiced over the same murky bed. Would she think that I had tricked her? I accepted a crisp or two from each of them but the splinters stuck in the back of my throat.

'It was freezing, but I feel great,' she said. 'Don't you, Archie? Doesn't it make you tingle all over?'

I had to show her, or someone else would, eventually, and then she'd wonder why I hadn't said anything. I felt unaccountably tired, but I couldn't stop now – it was up to me. I got to my feet and steadied myself on Eve's arm.

'If Archie'll beat the way for us, we can get out up there,' I said, nodding upstream. There was a wide gate further on, left open in the summer for the cattle.

'Here it is!' Archie shouted, his voice lifting from the undergrowth. 'Found it!'

270

It was more difficult for Eve and me to get through. The haversack hampered our progress. I caught my hair and had to unwind myself backwards. When we reached him, Archie was testing the cowpats with his wellies. The sun had made cobbles of them, firm enough to step our way along and out through the open gateway, back into the meadow.

'What's that?' Eve asked almost immediately. And Archie was already clambering up on to its one step. He had his arm around the stone cross as if it were a man. I couldn't speak. I let her read it for herself:

### Thomas Upcott, 1936–1963
#### Who so loved this place
*He shewed me a pure river of water of life Revelations 22:1*

# 26

## *Gossip*

Margaret, Joyce's sister, cleaned three days a week at the vicarage and, if she had anything to report, she'd pop into the kitchen to see Joyce on her way home. This time she'd come with a newspaper.

'It's in here,' she said, tapping it. 'Mrs Manning seen it.'

Joyce dried her hands and came and peered over her sister's shoulder.

'Here, look,' Margaret said, pointing, 'Rylands Seedmerchants, plaintif etc.'

'Robert Upcott, Esquire,' Joyce said, reading. 'It's a writ, isn' it? Goodness, it's in the papers.'

'A writ?' I said, and my blood ran cold.

'I thought things must be bad,' Joyce said. 'But not as bad as this. I don't know what we'll do with Victor.'

'You can imagine,' Margaret said, 'Mrs Manning's got herself in a state.'

'Why should it bother her?' Joyce snapped.

'Beatrice!' Margaret said.

'There's nothing in *that*, surely,' Joyce said.

'It was you who pointed it out,' Margaret said indignantly, 'way they've been this last month or so.'

'I very much doubt it's serious.'

'Serious enough for Mrs Manning to be worried.'

'Well there's more important things to worry about,' Joyce said, nodding towards the newspaper. 'If it comes to that, I don't know what we'll do.'

Margaret said, 'I've told you before, Victor can help Michael – he could do with the help. He means it.'

'But you'll be out of a job yourself, if they go?'

'There'll be another vicar, won't there? Mrs Manning's sure to give me a reference.'

I had stopped cutting the parsnips. Joyce came over, silently taking the knife from my hand, and began to cut them distractedly into smaller chunks. 'Beatrice must be off to the university, anyway, isn't she, any day now?' she said.

'Exactly,' Margaret said. 'She'd have more sense – I told her, Mrs Manning – everyone knows what Tom Upcott's like.'

'Well, I haven't seen her putting him off,' Joyce said defensively.

'Bad blood,' Margaret said promptly, 'will out.'

'Don't say that,' Joyce snapped. 'I brung him into the world.'

'Even you can't wave a magic wand.'


It was a rotten day to go out, the sky threatening to implode any second. Everything was low-lying, hunched to the

273

ground. I knew it was love because it felt like death, or at least, how I imagined death would feel – fiery and dull at the same time. But I was determined that if I could only hold my nerve, perhaps the crisis would pass. Beatrice Manning, after all, had gone; that weekend, she'd been driven all the way down to Durham. Her father wanted to take a look at the cathedral again and Mrs Manning was eager to see her daughter's digs, to check that her fellow roommates were nice girls.

There was no one about in the yard when I got to the farm, but I noticed that the big barn door, generally bolted, was swung open. I'd seen the two horses on my way in, grazing out in the paddock, and I wouldn't necessarily have given the door a second thought except that, as I passed, I heard an unfamiliar noise. Usually the dogs, if they were loose, would run out to meet me. I braced myself, expecting one or other of them at any moment, but there was no movement, just an odd whimpering as if something inside were hurt. I was torn between going to the house to fetch Frances and investigating myself. I had never managed to be completely at ease with the dogs and saw it as something of a failing. I cleared my throat. 'Hector,' I called, peering into the doorway. The noise stopped.

'Hector, good boy.' I used my brightest fear-defying voice and followed it inside into the gloom of the barn. There was still no sign of the dogs. I began to imagine that it must have been pigeons in the rafters. But then I heard a sob, unmistakable. It was coming from the far end, human in its expressiveness.

'Hello?' I said.

274

The air was thick with the stench of effluent. I kept to the line of grimy straw. In the very last stall I could see that some creature was lying down – there were four horizontal poles of leg, the ebony-carved hooves. But it wasn't until I rounded the partition that I saw Tom. He was sitting low down in the filth, propped against the wall with the cow's head nuzzled in his lap. He must have heard me; he looked up, a face of unchecked misery. The pouched throat of the animal was stretched back, its hairy padded lips. Tom hung his head. I picked my way past the grid of legs, held my breath and bent down to him. The carcass of the animal reared like a shipwreck. I put a hand to Tom's shoulder; a tremor shook through his body like a curtain. I took tiny shallow breaths, the stench was everywhere. Every now and then he shuddered, disturbing my balance and rocking the head in his lap as if it were a defunct piece of equipment. It was just him and me at the back end of the world. Bombed out. Survived. I swallowed. Even in that filthy place, at the trip of a switch, I might have taken him and pressed him to me.

'What is it?' I said softly.

He didn't say a word. His eyes were so dark, they seemed to bore straight through his head. Then he lowered the pale lids and shut me out. It was unbearable. I used his shoulder to lever myself upright. There was a lump in my throat. I shuffled away a little, but as I moved, suddenly, his hand darted out and caught my ankle. My heart stopped. He held on, pressed so tightly I almost cried out. His eyes were wild, his face glazed.

'Gone,' he said, or I thought he said, and I knew he was talking about Beatrice. But it could have been nothing more than a groan, a cow's low moan. Then the pressure round my ankle loosened. I had no courage, cut to the quick, a part of myself that had never seen the light, unmasked. I stumbled away from him, backwards, and then, having chosen my path, kept doggedly to it, because I had no idea how I was supposed to behave.

In the kitchen Frances was preoccupied, she had a washboard upright in the sink and was rubbing against it vigorously. I stood by the Rayburn, burned my hands against the lids.

After a while she twisted round.

'Have you seen Tom?' she asked.

I nodded.

'Has he said anything to you. . . ? I don't know what's got into him. Robert's blaming him. He blames Robert. I don't know any more.'

'He's in the barn,' I said.

She was scrubbing again as if her life depended on it. 'The vet's been out. It's got a name,' she was saying, preoccupied. '*Joan's*, it sounds like. In the guts. Once one has it, it runs straight through the lot of them, nothing to be done but separate them out. Tom's saying we should have called him earlier. But Robert won't have it. He's like Father was. He hates to do that.'

Suddenly she stopped what she was doing. 'What are they saying in the village?' she asked, peering sharply over her shoulder.

I was tongue-tied. I didn't dare mention the newspaper Margaret had brought in. 'Have you said anything?' she asked suspiciously. 'I don't doubt they ask.'

'Nothing,' I said.

'Well I hope you'll stick to that,' she said bluntly, turning back to the sink.

I didn't understand about animals, neither the cost nor the care of them, that they weren't easily replaceable, that they didn't grow on trees. I didn't understand about writs, or about families, or about that kind of shame. Better to assume that I didn't know anything about anything. No one would have dreamed how ignorant I was, or that there might be any need to better inform me.

'There's nothing to be done,' she said again.

'I'm sorry,' I said, moving numbly around the room. She seemed to have more than one thing on the go. There was a small bowl of yeast bubbling on the table. I was so used to helping her that I fell in automatically, fetching for her the big tin of flour from the pantry. I reached for an apron and rolled up my sleeves. She leaned over the large yellow mixing bowl, measuring butter; she poured water from the kettle. When the time came, I tipped the yeast into the bowl for her, and then the flour, bit by bit. She bound it as usual with quick, efficient movements. Soon she had a thick rope of dough, which she divided, as she always did, in two, handing me my part, which I removed to the opposite end of the table. For a good while, all that could be heard was the suck and pummel of dough. But then, without any warning, she looked up. 'By the way,' she said, 'you haven't seen that ring, have you?' She dipped her hand again into the tin of flour. 'Mother's ring. It's gone from the drawer.'

I was drained, and she said it so inconsequentially that it didn't dawn on me for a moment what she was saying. Then she added simply, 'No one else knew it was there.'

My hands pulsed. 'The ring?' I repeated, because even then, I couldn't believe that she intended anything by it.

She smiled, a curious out-of-reach smile, staring across the surface of the table and refusing to meet my eye. The stain of accusation bleared my vision. I waited for her to retract, but there was no sign of it. I began to peel the rubbery mixture from my fingers. I loosened the ties of my apron and lifted it over my neck. Still she hung her head, refusing to look in my direction.

I dropped the apron on to the chair. For the second time that day I was winded. I moved with no feeling in my limbs, waiting for her to call me back, to shake her head, to say *never mind*. But she said nothing. I left the room, took down my hat, my coat. My tongue was crackly as a leaf. Any moment she must say something that would snap me out of it. I was asleep. I was awake. But all the while she stood against the table and I could hear the two great oars of her arms rhythmically plunging.

Outside the air was impassive, escorting me silently from the premises. Three black hens appeared from the corner of the barn, hopping to catch up, convinced too that I had something in my pockets. At the gate I shooed them back, the feeble sound of my voice bringing me round to the injustice of it. Tears splashed against my spectacles. I looked back at the farmhouse with its thatch pulled firmly down. Except that I had done nothing wrong, I might have been Eve thrown out of the garden, Judas and his thirty pieces of silver.

# 27

## *Leaning on a Lamp Post*

Sisterhood, family, a land of milk and honey: every waking dream I'd ever had, vanished like thread from a needle's eye. I saw nothing of them from October until the middle of December that year. Although I had never told Joyce what happened, she knew of course that it had something to do with the Upcotts. It always did, and I clearly had more time on my hands now I'd stopped going down to the farm. Joyce was kind and brisk with me, and understood immediately that I needed to be set to work.

It wasn't only the ring, it was everything. My brain would not be still, tormenting me at every opportunity, reimagining the dark hollow of the barn: the exact tilt of Tom's head, the depth and fixity of his eyes, and then, that bracelet of iron around my ankle. *What did it mean?*

One Friday, Diana was with us in the kitchen. Halfway through the morning, Margaret called in bursting with something to say. She faltered in the doorway, clearly not expecting to find Diana there. Diana looked up. 'Don't let me stop you, Mrs Knight,' she said. 'I'm sure Joyce has got time to put a kettle on for us.'

Margaret was in two minds about whether or not she should stay. There was hardly room for an extra body. But she agreed to take a seat and once she'd sat down, she couldn't help herself, saying in a rush, 'Ever since Beatrice come back at the weekend, he's been up there. Every night, apparently, outside the house.'

'Who's that?' Diana asked.

Margaret was full of it. 'They ignored him the first time. But he weren't going nowhere, or doing nothing but face tipped up to the girl's bedroom window. It frightened Mrs Manning. It was dark out. The Reverend went and asked him what on earth he thought he was going to achieve.' Margaret looked around, her forehead shining. 'It was like talking to a lamp post – they couldn't get no answer out of him. Mrs Manning as you can imagine's beside herself. *The way he looked*, she said to me, *as if he'd been pulled back and forth through a hedge*. She's not slept a wink.'

'She's back, is she?' I asked. 'Beatrice?'

'Christmas holidays,' Margaret said. 'She's doing ever so well, they say. Of course, they were hoping to have moved to Exeter by now, is what Mrs Manning said, and none of this unfortunateness would have happened.'

Joyce had bustled round the table and knelt at her sister's feet to pull a great tray out of the oven. She lifted it to the table, four grey-speckled trout, tinfoil eyes, steaming. She began to prod and poke to see that they were done.

'What's got into him?' Joyce said. 'It's a bad to-do down there, from what little I can get out of Victor.'

'Mrs Manning's worried out of her mind. She's got more than enough to think about with the move, she says. *Yes*, Beatrice told her, she danced with him; *yes*, she liked him well enough and he liked her, *yes*, he'd walked her home once or twice, when it was late— '

'There we are, then,' Diana said as if that were the crux of it.

'But, *no*.' Margaret shook her head. 'Nothing happened. *Did you let him kiss you?* Her mother asked her right out. *No, I didn't*, she said. She was hardly out of school. For all the way she looks, she'd never had a boyfriend before now.'

'She's got a boyfriend?' Joyce asked.

'Some chap at university snapped her up. A nice boy, Mrs Manning says. Studying for the law.'

'Well *there* you are,' Joyce said.

'But it turns out Tom Upcott gave her a ring,' Margaret protested, a revelation that she appeared to have forgotten or chosen so far to withhold. I leaned against the table for support.

'Well, she can't deny it then, can she?' Diana said.

'Only now he's asking for it back. It's hardly surprising she wants nothing to do with him. T'isn't her fault how pretty she is. You can't judge her for that. And you can't tell me Tom Upcott's so innocent, not the way he behaves himself. He's years older than she is – he ought know better.'

'I don't suppose you know anything about it?' Joyce asked me. But I was no more capable of replying than the fish, wadded in pink flesh, aware of my spine right to the roof of my mouth.


To this day, if there is a knock at the door, I can convince myself it might be Frances. I have a picture of her in my head, that long brown coat of hers, that moleskin muff, those grey-green eyes. I steel myself.

'Beatrice?' I said, confused when I found her on the door-step. I hardly knew her to talk to.

'I'm sorry to bother you,' she said, her precious voice, her small face for the first time I'd ever seen it, pale and anxious.

I brought her into the front room, noticing even then how beautifully turned out she was. She was wearing a green worsted suit, carrying a small black handbag. It made her look more grown-up than she was.

'I hope you don't mind,' she said. 'I didn't know who else—'

'Sit down,' I said.

I wasn't used to the shape or play of her face. She sat in Auntie's chair, her skin like whey. Her handbag was propped in her lap. She lowered her head for a moment, then she glanced up at me and said, 'I don't want to put you in an awkward position, but there's no one else I can think of.'

She unclasped her bag and brought out a small maroon box. She held it out.

'Could you take this for me, please, and give it back?'

I might have pretended that I had no idea what it was. I looked at her.

'It's a ring. I had it from Tom Upcott,' she said.

'I'm not sure I understand,' I said.

She was on the verge of saying nothing, on the verge of buttoning her lip. She darted me a look; her eyes swam. 'It needs to go back.'

I didn't take it immediately from her hand and she set it

down on the edge of the table, collected herself. 'I know it's a hard thing to ask, but *you* know the Upcotts, don't you? You go down there. I don't want to have to go down there myself.' Her voice trembled.

'Are you all right?' I asked.

'Perfectly,' she said. She smiled a brittle smile. 'I'm away now. There's no reason for me ever to come back, not after Christmas time.'

'We'll be sorry to see your father go,' I said.

'Please don't tell my parents, will you? Please. I've upset them enough.' Her voice wavered. She re-clasped her bag.

'I hope everything's all right?' I said, though I was relieved. She was going for good.

Her eyes trembled. She stared hard at the little gold clasp on her bag. Then she said, 'I don't want anyone to know, if you don't mind. About the ring.'

'I can't promise I'll go down there straightaway,' I said, my head already filling with versions of the story I'd tell and to whom.

'As soon as you can, that's all,' she said. 'Thank you.'

'You're sure you're all right?'

'I'll be fine,' she said determinedly. 'As long as this gets back to him, I'll be just fine.' She was biting her bottom lip; there was no sign otherwise but that she meant what she said.

'You sang beautifully,' I said as she got to her feet, 'for my aunt that time. What a lovely voice you have.'

'Thank you,' she said, and the shot of gratitude across her face made me soften towards her.

We stood by the front door. 'Is there anything I should say,' I asked, 'when I give it back?'

She looked down at the doorstep, a tiny greenish vein on her forehead. She thought for a moment, swallowed. 'You could say, *sorry.*' Then hurriedly, she took my hand. 'That's all.'

When she'd gone, I pressed the catch and opened up the box. For a moment it felt as if Frances was right and I had stolen the ring: my blood rose, my mouth watered.

Frances reappeared the Sunday before Christmas, sitting alone, without her brothers, in her usual place in church. During the hymns, the higher notes brought tears to my eyes, the *as we forgive those*, but the sermon provided a decent spell in which to steady my nerves. After the service I left in a hurry but I wasn't far down the path when I heard her behind me.

'Mavis?' She so rarely used my name, there was an edge of panic to it.

I didn't turn. 'Please,' she said moving quickly to catch up. I didn't stop until I was at the garden gate. She was right beside me and I felt I had no choice but to let her in. While she showed herself into the front room, I broke off into the kitchen, went straight over to the sink, where I clung to the cold metal cross of the tap. When I reappeared at the door, she looked up anxiously.

'I should never have doubted you,' she said levelly.

I didn't take up my usual seat but sat at a remove from her on the piano stool.

'It was Tom took it,' Frances said.

I smiled dryly to let her know that I knew already.

'I had no idea,' Frances said.

'Everyone else seems to know,' I replied, because I wanted to hurt her.

She had taken her gloves off and was plaiting the fingers together. 'You know how worried I've been? I was lashing out. I wasn't thinking.'

I stared at the tips of her brown boots. She said plaintively, 'They're moving out apparently. The Mannings. You probably know already. They're off to Exeter. Let's hope that'll be the end of it.'

Her eyes were fixed to the space on her lap, stretching the fingers of one glove until it lay like a blank along her thigh.

'I can't tell you what it's been like,' she said. 'On top of everything else, I had no idea that this was in his head.' She gazed at me wide-eyed. 'I'm at my wits' end.'

There was a terrible power, I discovered, in saying, doing nothing. She shook her head, 'He was out all night – three or four nights in a row – in this! I daren't tell Robert.' She glanced at me. 'I wish I knew what to do.'

Her feet were tilted over one another seeking warmth.

'Did you know he was trying to leave?' she asked. 'Did he speak to you about it?' Her eyes darted away from me. 'How could he? I've said all along, the girl is poison. It was her doing; I'm sure of that. She wanted the ground sold from under our feet.'

I had nothing to say to her. I watched the hand of the clock that had never in my lifetime worked, its unvoiced tick suspended above us. She shifted in her seat, then suddenly she looked at me with controlled fury.

'He's not the only one, you know.' Her eyes were defiant.

'I could have gone,' she said, 'I never told you that. I had the chance. But I didn't.' She pulled a bitter smile, sniffed at me. 'You don't believe it? I've got letters asking, begging me. Tom's seen them. He never could stop himself digging around. So he knows quite well, I could have gone. I told him then just what I'm telling you: *I didn't. The difference between you and me*, I said, *I didn't*.' She spat the words and then glared into her hands.

I had never seen her like this. I tried to be adult about it, but I felt affronted, like a child. I didn't recognize her at all.

'You think I'm a dry old stick, don't you?' She looked directly at me. 'They think it in the village,' she said, 'I know they do.'

'They don't know you,' I mumbled. And then, because I didn't want to hear any more, because I wanted her to be just who she was, I said in a rush, 'I used to sit and listen when you had your piano lessons. I couldn't wait for those afternoons. I wanted to be just like you.'

I was digging the fingernails so fiercely into my own hand that I didn't realize she'd already embarked on her own story.

He'd come in uniform, with a friend. Lieutenant Frank Burns. They left the jeep halfway down the lane. There'd never been a car down the farm track before, and Tom had come running from across the field to tell her. They were after eggs and milk. Frances was seventeen; she didn't know what to do, so she gave them half a dozen eggs and a pail still warm from the milking.

They came back a second time to pay up, said they were the best eggs they'd ever tasted.

The third time, Frank came alone. He'd brought a bunch

286

of bananas for the house and chocolate for Tom. They had bears, he said, where he was from, and mountains. Frances said he was exactly like a film star, as if he'd stepped down from the screen. Like Clark Gable, without the moustache. He'd asked her to a dance in Buckleigh, in the square, but her father wouldn't let her go. She was to tell him that, if ever he called again.

The fourth time, it was a particularly hot, listless day. Her father was out, so she agreed to walk Frank back to the jeep. She took her wide-brimmed hat. He had the bluest eyes, little chips of mosaic, and cheeks that were their own kind of geometry, very distinct from the wide moon-faces she was used to. She wouldn't ever forget the sound his boots made, or the way the hedgerows appeared to flare from inside, the trees to worship their passing. They were an arm's length apart though both had noticed ahead of them the way their long shadows converged. When they reached the end of the farm track, instead of turning right towards the jeep, they turned in the other direction, towards the river, just past the old monk's cross and then, at an angle, up into a field that had been put to grass. Neither of them said a word. Frank opened the gate for her and she followed him through. Once they were out of sight he took off his jacket and laid it down for her. The grass splintered as she sat on one half, and then as he joined her, their backs almost against the hedge, side by side, arm to arm, leg to leg. She closed her eyes. She was aware of his hands moving independently, expertly like two trained birds. The thin material of her dress was plucked, the tiny buttons at the neck loosened. She could sense the weight of him next to her, his breathing, the weight of the hedge behind them. The heat had slowed everything to syrup. When she opened her eyes, the softness of his dark head was upon her, clinging to her breast like a bee. Tiny hexagons of light spangled the brow of the field, sifting through the ears of the tall grasses. It was a pure crystal distillation imprinted on her memory like frost. She shut her eyes again and in another moment ice liquefied, spreading like a shadow, into every dip, every hole, obliterating everything.

And then, out of the haze, unmistakable, unhurried, the clop, clop, clop of a horse. She pushed him from her and he turned, wounded, his mouth full of secrets. She clutched the front of her dress, fumbled and then raised herself somehow to her feet, brushed her skirts. Instantly Frank sprang to lift his jacket, shook it out and managed to shrug it on to his arms just as, tall as a giant, the dark outline of a man's upper body appeared over the hedge. The two of them stumbled back towards the gate to face the combined body of man and horse.

'Lovely day for a walk, sir.' Frank gave Mr Upcott a salute and then he raised his arm to Frances. 'So long,' he said.

She stood trembling as she watched her father follow him at a lazy distance along the lane, drawing Tinker under the beech trees as Frank climbed into the front of the jeep, and then, as the engine spurted to life, Tinker dancing on the spot. As soon as the dust had settled, her father banged his heels into the animal's flanks, drew up the reins and turned the horse tightly, riding straight back past her towards the yard without a look or a word.

When she arrived in the kitchen he was standing with his hands behind his back against the fireplace. Robert was at the table leering at her.

'Never again,' Mr Upcott said. 'Do you understand me, that's an end to it. See?'

'Yanks,' Robert said as if that were sufficient. And Tom came rushing in with chocolate all round his mouth. *So long, so long, so long, so long, so long.* That was the wallpaper of her dreams.

Frances was making circles in the arm of the chair, that strange, sour smile set on her face. 'He used to write,' she said, 'long letters. About what he was up to. After he was demobbed, at college. He was training to be a dentist. Your aunt offered to take the letters in for me – she was the only one I ever told. He wanted me to go out there. Said he'd pay my way.' She reached for her gloves and began to stuff them over her fingers, locking her hands to push them into place. 'He wrote when he got married . . . Less after that. He built a house with three bedrooms, a study, a utility room. Had two children.' She looked up. 'That was the last I heard.'

# PART VII

*A Psalm in Winter*

# 28

## *Christmas, 2006*

I have never been much good at cooking in spite of all the time I spent in the Upcotts' kitchen. Living as I always have done, on my own, it has been easy to get away with it. I've had little cause to improve, and perhaps I've been spoiled: there's Joyce, who still treats me as if I'm inept and will often have me over to 'feed me up'. Because Eve is so much younger, it's different: I feel responsible.

She and Archie weren't going away for Christmas as I had imagined they might, and I found myself inviting the two of them over for Christmas lunch – unless, I said, they got a better offer. 'I'm afraid it won't be anything fancy.'

That night, I hardly slept, but it wasn't excitement that kept me awake, it was worry. I got up at six and began to tidy the already tidied house. There was a small service at half past eight in St James's, only the stalwarts of us there and a Dunkirk spirit because of the thick fog. When I got back, I allowed myself plenty of cooking time. I'd got the turkey from the Christmas market. It was laid out ready, a bleached, ugly-looking creature, with blond quills poking out around its shoulders. By eleven o'clock I was peeling parsnips and potatoes, cutting a criss-cross in the sprouts.

I filled the pan with water and covered the vegetables. I allowed myself a little glass of dry sherry, took myself into the front room for a sit-down. Generally I tried to ignore Christmas. After Daddy left, Mother and I had never enjoyed it much together. It was more or less the anniversary of her death and that time of year, even if nothing else had happened, has a depressing effect on me. From the window, although I couldn't see them properly in the fog, I could hear children's voices. There were two of them, in and out. I recognized Archie by the outline of his new puffy coat and another boy – it might even have been the boy who'd been responsible for the bullying on the bus. 'Nee-naw, nee-naw.' They were fire engines or bombers, hard to tell which. When they ran into each other they yelped with laughter, scooted away again to regroup. It cheered me up to see how adept and slippery Archie had become. When they reappeared, each had a stick from the log pile outside the pub. They waved them like spears, then cocked them horizontally to take out a cat or a phantom bird.

I could have sat and watched them all day, but the turkey needed to go in, the cutlery would need polishing. The tall cranberry Christmas glasses. I wanted everything to be right. I'd decided that we'd eat in the front room and from under the stairs, fished out the missing leaf of the table and the pliers to work the mechanism. It took all my strength and will to inch my way round the head of that nut in order to insert the middle section. But even after a polish, the leaves of the table top refused to match, and there was a corner where I'd once absently placed a hot kettle and the veneer had buckled. I dug out the cherry-red tablecloth and threw it over, straightened it out. I huffed against the wine glasses, into the spirals of wheat and grape and polished them with the edge of my sleeve.

At five past two I heard them at the door, untied my apron and reached up to check my hair before I ushered them in.

'Merry Christmas,' I said.

'Happy Christmas,' they said together.

Eve thrust into my hand a bottle of Cava and a bunch of winter jasmine wrapped in white tissue paper. 'How beautiful! Thank you.' I dipped my head to the tiny yellow buds.

The sense of occasion had made us horribly formal and now my hands were full I wasn't sure what to do next. I darted into the kitchen with the bottle and fetched the blue vase for the flowers, carried the arrangement through to the front room before coming back to take their coats from them. I was quite breathless.

'Shall we have a drink?' I asked. 'Are you any good at opening bottles?' I went and fetched the bottle back for Eve.

As she eased out the cork, we all responded to the kick of the explosion and the tongue of steam rising from it. We gave Archie a thimbleful.

'Cheers,' we said, clinking our glasses carefully.

'Well,' I said, 'I think we might start.'

Archie had gone over to the window to look out for his friend.

'Archie,' I said, 'you come and sit here, between us.'

'Come on Archie, sit down,' Eve said. 'You've gone to such trouble,' she said to me, looking at the table, where I'd laid everything out. 'What a lovely tablecloth! And look, Archie, crackers!'

'No trouble,' I said.

The vegetables were all done and sitting covered in Auntie's two Wedgwood dishes. I'd tossed the potatoes in some flour, as Joyce had taught me to, and roasted them in the fat. I went to pull the turkey out of the oven; I'd forgotten to take off the foil. When I got it up on the kitchen table the plucked skin was a cold tea colour. I prodded at it with a wooden spoon.

'Eve?' I called out. 'Would you mind?'

A chair scraped, her face appeared at the door.

'Do you think it's done? I don't want to poison anyone.'

'Have you tried it with a knife?' Eve said, coming over.

The curved blade of the knife in my hand was too blunt. I was beginning to feel flustered and regretted having asked her. She was watching me closely. I fished in the table drawer and pulled out a little vegetable knife.

'It's living on your own. Not having to cook,' I said.

She took the knife from me gently and began to poke into the blond flesh like a dentist looking in.

'I think it should be fine,' she said. 'How long's it been in?'

'Oh, three hours or so . . .'

'I'm sure it'll be OK. Let's cut it up and see.'

What sort of a mother, what sort of a grandmother would I have made?

Archie would only eat breast. 'I'll cut it if you like?' Eve said, and she made incisions either side, neatly stacking the best bits on a plate for him.

'Not sprouts,' Archie said. I'd filled a spoon.

Eve said, 'He thinks he's allergic to them. It's his latest thing, I'm afraid.'

'Never mind,' I said. 'You must eat what you like. And there's ice cream for after,' I said. 'I thought you might like it better than Christmas pudding, Archie.'

'Not until he's cleaned his plate,' Eve said.

'Oh. Silly. How absolutely silly. You should have said!' I scrunched up my napkin and got to my feet. 'I've forgotten the gravy.'

In the kitchen I chastised myself. *Silly, silly, silly.* I'd even polished the silver gravy boat. I came back through. It was an awkward shape to carry by the handle, a little too long, and it wobbled like a genie's lamp.

'There,' I said, laying it down.

Archie didn't like gravy.

'This is delicious,' Eve said, nudging Archie, 'thank you.'

'Shall we have a cracker?' I asked and Archie sat bolt upright. The crackers were in gold and green paper and had been given to me, thoughtfully, by Joyce, who'd nipped home after church to fetch them. We wove the three batons under and over our arms. Eve did a count. *Three, two, one . . .* Only one of them went off. *Bang.* 'A rabbit just died,' I said and Archie laughed. We tussled between us with his. *Bang.* And then he and his mother. *Bang.* I put my hand to my chest. 'My rabbit heart!' There was gunpowder in the air.

'I won,' Archie said, amazed, waving a tube of cardboard in either hand.

'What did you get?'

He had a small blue pencil sharpener the shape of a whale

297

in one, and a plastic box with twistable noughts and crosses in the other.

'Lucky you,' Eve said. She showed him her co-joined metal hoops. 'I can't work it out,' she said and handed it over to him too.

'I won nothing,' I said, turning down my mouth. I fished out a purple tissue hat from the rubbish and set it on my head. Archie's face lit up. He began to demolish the casing of the other crackers and found an orange one for him, a green one for his mother. Dutifully she put it on. It covered her eyebrows. We looked at each other with our wonky crowns and laughed.

'Well,' I said, feeling exhilarated, 'what else did Father Christmas bring you?'

Archie had an order for it: 'Football strip,' he said. He lifted his sweater to show the green and white stripes over his stomach. 'Celtic. Off Dad.' He tucked himself in. 'Twenty pounds off my gran, a globe-light off Mum, and a Harry Potter game off my Uncle Eric.'

'A globe? That's a lovely present. I expect you found where we are on it?'

'We did, didn't we?' Eve said.

Archie knew exactly what to say. 'We're at the top, near heaven,' he said.

'I don't think heaven's on the map,' Eve said, gently, eyeing me.

'No, he's right, we're *in* Heaven,' I said, beaming at Archie, because I'd told him that. I poured us another glass, took a sip from mine. 'I've no voice,' I said, 'but it's a song I used to sing with my father. Wait a minute.' I coughed, took another swig, sat up straight. '*Devon, I'm in Devon, and my heart sings so that I can barely speak . . . and I seem to find the happiness I seek . . . when we're out together dancing cheek to cheek.*'

'I love that old song,' Eve said, clasping her hands.

'Your mother had a proper voice. I'd like to have heard her sing it . . .'

'Cheers!' Eve said again, and we raised our glasses to Archie. Perhaps it was just the warmth of alcohol, but looking at their faces, buoyant and smiling as if they were happy to be here, made me gulp.

'I should have done this before,' I said.

'Thank you,' Eve said, raising her glass again. 'Let's hope it's a Happy New Year.'

As soon as the ice cream was finished, Archie asked to get down.

'Wipe your face,' Eve said and then, looking at me, 'is that all right?'

'Of course you can.'

Archie slid from his chair and stood for a moment at his mother's elbow.

'What do you say?' Eve prodded.

'William's outside,' Archie said.

'No,' Eve said, nudging his arm.

'Thank you very much for the dinner,' he said.

'Well, I think we can let you go,' I said. 'You've been very good. Thank you for coming.'

'Come back if he's not there, won't you?' Eve shouted after him.

As soon as the door closed on him Eve slumped, visibly relaxed.

299

'Come and sit down,' I said, relieved that the eating was done with. 'Bring your drink.' I stood up and muddled over to my chair. 'That's better,' I said, pressing myself against the cushions.

'His flight's at seven in the morning,' she said. 'I'm dreading it. I think he's a bit nervous too.'

'He'll be all right,' I said, though I had never actually flown myself. 'Thank you for the lovely flowers,' I said, turning to the vase on the table. 'I ought to have got something for Archie . . . I'll get him a book token, or something.'

'He's plenty of things—'

'I'd like to.' Then I had an idea. I put my empty glass down and got to my feet. 'Now, you may think it's a ridiculous dusty old thing . . . But I just wonder . . . ?'

Eve sat up in her chair.

I was standing next to the dresser, exactly as I had done almost a year ago when I'd found Archie that time. I waited until I was quite steady on my feet. Then I reached up and lifted the bird down again.

'It needs a good dusting. I'd have done that, if I'd thought.'

I slid the wooden base along the table towards her. 'It's a songthrush. Tom Upcott made it for me, years ago. I wonder if you'd like to have it? We had a joke. *Mavis*: the name means songthrush, you see. But I'd rather you had it now, if you'd like it?'

'*He* made it?' she said, drinking it in, gulping.

# 29

## *28 December 2006*

Eve looked terrible. 'Can I come in?'

'What's wrong?' I asked. It was only half past eight in the morning and I was in my dressing gown. She had a long cream cardigan, the sleeves of which were wrapped around her like a straitjacket.

'I hope I haven't woken you up?' she said.

'No, no.' I shook my head and motioned her inside.

'I'd have been better off at work,' she said.

'Did he get off all right?' I asked.

'Yes. He did,' she said, looking crushed. 'You should have seen him. He had to put a plastic thing around his neck, like a refugee.'

She sat down in Auntie's chair, huddled forwards. 'I could tell he was nervous. But he's so brave. He didn't want me to think he was worried.' She was pulling at the cuffs, a tag of wool that had worked loose. 'They look after them on the plane – it's not like a train, where he could get off, or be taken off . . .' she said, as if she were rehearsing for her own benefit, 'and his grandmother's there – there's family around.'

'I'm sure they'll look after him,' I said. 'He's a big boy. And he gets on with them, doesn't he?'

She shrugged. 'Children don't question it, do they?' she said, looking like a child herself.

She'd delivered him at the airport and then come home. Because they were busy at the pub and she'd got out of Christmas, she'd agreed to take on the late shifts through the week. She wasn't getting home until one or two in the morning. The second night, she'd forced herself to strip the bed, where she usually slept with him, removed the crackly plastic guard that made her sweat and fetched out clean sheets.

She'd brushed her teeth, undressed, surprised by how used she was to his routine, how meaningless time was without him. She couldn't sleep. She got up, boiled a kettle to fill Archie's hot water bottle. 'It's a bear,' she said. 'The bottle fits in the stomach. It smells of him.'

Still she couldn't sleep. There were no curtains at the bedroom window because she'd wanted to hang her own and hadn't got round to it. There was a toenail of moon, a spatter of stars. She got up to go to the lavatory in its windowless cell, leaving the door ajar so as not to set off the whirr of the fan. Instead of going back to bed she sat in the living room, perched on the square wooden arm of the settee.

'There's still stuff everywhere. Boxes I haven't unpacked. Books. Pots. I should take advantage of him not being here to sort myself out.'

She'd left most of her furniture behind in London, in the flat she was renting out to her brother, Eric.

She'd not been frightened at night before, as if Archie could have protected her. Now she lay awake, listening to the creaking of the walls. Every morning since he'd gone, she'd woken up at five and sat up, waiting for the morning, with the lamp switched on.

Archie had hugged her only briefly, embarrassed in front of the airport security men and she'd allowed him to be led off by a breezy air hostess through the swing doors. He didn't turn back to wave, though she'd stayed in case he might.

'It's like being in mourning,' she said. 'I've been sorting through his clothes, his socks and his vests, his Spiderman pants. You'd have thought I'd be glad to wake up without a foot in my chest.'

When things had got really nasty between her and Marco, he had threatened to take photographs of the flat – the kitchen surfaces, the bath, Archie's bed – to prove what a terrible mother she was.

'I've been ringing him every morning,' she said. 'His mother answers the phone. She treats me as if I'm making a fuss. "He's in bed," she says. "I'd let him lie."'

'But you know he's safe,' I said.

'There's not one bit of acknowledgement for letting him go,' Eve said. 'Nothing. No thanks. Nothing.'

She looked at me now with her face crumpling. 'Why did I agree?' She had a paper hankie, which she'd shredded to snowflakes in her hands.

# 30

## *New Year's Day, 1963*

Initially I resolved that I wouldn't go at all. Then I decided that I wouldn't go unless I was asked, specifically. The weather in any case was terrible that Christmas: wind and blizzards. There was no sign of the Upcotts on Christmas Day.

By New Year's Eve, we were stuck fast in the village and no one was venturing out unless they absolutely had to. At eleven o'clock, there were only half a dozen of us in the public bar. We raised a glass and then decided to call it a night. At one or two in the morning, I'd woken up in bed with freezing feet. I had dreamed that the path to Passaford was littered with the dead and dying bodies of white rats, some of them skinned, some of them with their eyes gouged out – it was almost impossible to walk without treading on them, the dull crunch of bones. I realized with a pang of self-reproach that although the weather had provided a convenient excuse not to visit, it was exactly the reason I ought to have made the effort. When I got downstairs I found the taps had frozen solid, the electric was off. Outside, the silence was so deep, it was as if every mouth and every doorway had been sealed up. The wind had finally dropped. As soon as it was light enough to see, I trudged up to the pub. Alf had got into the habit of helping Diana out. I found him already at work, scattering cinders on the path, too wrapped up in scarves to hear me. Everywhere was insulated with snow. The open linney was chock-full of it, a cart handle stuck out like an arm in the Arctic, the car outside the pub, cemented into its own Morris-shaped bunker.

'Morning!' Diana said, out of habit, polishing behind the bar. 'There'll be nothing doing today,' she said, flicking her cloth. The chairs were like crowns, upended on the tabletops.

Joyce was in the back making a list of what food there was in the larder. She had breakfast to cook for a couple who'd been coming every Christmas since the war. They'd not been able to get away.

'Have you heard anything from Passaford?' I asked as soon as she came through to report to Diana.

'Not a peep,' she said. 'I 'spect they're having trouble getting out.'

'You know Tom's been ill?' I said. 'I thought perhaps I should go over there.'

'You'll never get down. Not in this. I should leave it be a day or two. Stove's lit. Go and get yourself something hot to drink.'

Not long after that, we heard the convulsions of a tractor engine, which stopped abruptly right outside the door. Diana went to investigate. 'Michael' – her ringing tones – 'that's good of you to come.'

Michael Knight followed her inside; he was wearing a

305

thick balaclava, moving with a rocking motion, a bundle of logs in his arms, which he dropped like thunder to the side of the fire basket. He wiped the thaw from his whiskers. 'Happy New Year,' he said.

Diana flapped around him in gratitude. Joyce appeared with a spatula in her hand. 'How's little Owen doing?' she asked.

'He's a pair of lungs on him. But I expect you'll say that's a healthy sign?'

'Course it is, clever boy. We can't wait to see him, can we?' Joyce said. 'Little man.'

'Anything I can get you? I'm off to Buckleigh if I can get through.'

'Could I come?' I asked. 'Far as the Cross?'

'Come as far as you like, if you don't mind budging up,' he said.

While he unloaded the rest of the wood, I went back to the cottage quickly to fetch my basket. I grabbed a packet of Indian tea from the cupboard, a tin of peaches and a jar of greengage jam. I looked around the room. I took the holly table decoration, then I went over to the bookcase to find something for Tom. Another thought occurred to me as I scanned the shelf: I hadn't yet returned the ring. I wasn't going to go out of my way to do so, but in case the opportunity presented itself, I grabbed the box and pushed it deep down into my skirt pocket.

Diana and Joyce were out front to wave us off.

'If only he weren't so flaming cold,' Michael said as he climbed up on to the tractor, clapping his arms about his chest.

'You going to be warm enough?' Joyce asked me.

Michael leaned from his seat and stretched out his hand. I

set my foot on the iron stirrup and let him haul me up. I sat as delicately as I could on the rim of the metal seat, not realizing how closely pressed our trunks would have to be. The years flashed through me: I'd run around with Michael when we were children. Yellow gingham knickers. As the engine set up, phut-phut, its little perforated chimney spluttering smoke and water, I nearly shook right off the seat and I had to grab on to his belt.

It was impossible once we got going to talk above the noise and the blast of the icy air. In places we were higher than the hedgerows and able to see across the great bed-span widths of them. Beyond, in stiff peaks and folds, the whole world had become a laundry, bleached clean, stretched out to dry. I was half frost and half fire: all along my right hand side, I had the benefit of his animal warmth. But it wasn't long before we arrived at the crossroads and the tractor came to a stuttering halt.

'You'll be all right from here?' he shouted, the engine still turning over.

I twisted round to clamber down. He held my hand in his great paw, then passed me the basket from where he'd hung it behind us.

'Not being funny, like, but you watch yourself,' he said, and as the engine revved, shouted over his shoulder, 'They be giving more of it.'

It was as if a whole layer of clothing had been stripped from me, icy air insinuating itself into the slightest opening. I wrapped Auntie's shawl more thoroughly around my head, covering my mouth and nose, and set off along the track. My progress was slow. By the time I arrived at the farm gate, the wool across my mouth was stiff as cardboard. The farmyard looked like a plaster cast of itself, the buildings fat with their render of snow, almost indistinguishable from one another. There wasn't a creature in sight. The heavy front door was caked in. I knocked three times. Eventually I heard a scrabbling from behind and an effort to pull it back. Frances's face appeared, sharp and pinched. She seemed surprised to see me, then pitifully pleased. She made a great fuss, grasping my hand, taking the shawl from my shoulders, shaking it out and rushing through to the kitchen to hang it above the fire. I removed my heavy coat and boots and followed her in though I could barely feel my feet – a train of wet prints across the flags. I stood while Frances stoked the fire.

'You must be perishing,' she said.

If I turned my head just a fraction, I could see the ghost of my breath. All along the row of windows, lit by the unnatural brightness outside, the frost was exposed in every feathery detail. The rest of the room was a cave.

Frances had tucked a shawl around her in an 'X', a big belt to hold it in place.

'I'm sorry,' I said, handing her the basket, 'it isn't much. I should have thought.'

'Thank you,' she said, her voice unsteady. 'It's very kind of you to think of us at all.'

She took it over to the table and began to take things out. 'Thank you,' she said again, arriving lastly at the table decoration, a half-spent candle, which looked suddenly tiny and mean-spirited on the great boards of the table.

'The book is for Tom,' I said.

She was looking at me. 'You're frozen,' she said, 'you're shivering, I can see you are. Go and sit down by the fire.'

She took the kettle from where it simmered on the stove and filled the enamel bowl, brought it over, billowing, setting it down on the floor.

'Take your stockings off – they're sodden, look at them.'

She was kneeling on the hearthrug with a linen towel across her lap. The parting of her hair was straight as a die. I dipped my feet, holding them under the water until I could feel the outline of them again. I reached out for the cloth. But she insisted, taking one foot and then the other between her hands, rubbing and patting them until they throbbed.

'Have you been out at all?' I asked, awkward at her show of penitence. 'It would be beautiful, wouldn't it,' I said, trying to think of things to say, 'if it wasn't so cold?'

'It's good of you to come,' she said, still holding my foot, 'good to see your face.'

She went out of the room and upstairs to fetch me some dry stockings. When she came back into the room I asked, 'How's Tom?'

Her eyes moved to the beams above our heads. 'Still in bed. The doctor came out before the weather turned. He thinks it might be pneumonia. But he won't get out again until after the snow lets up.'

'Pneumonia?' I said. The word alarmed me. 'My mother had pneumonia,' I said, 'you should have come and fetched me.'

She moved away, got up from her knees and backed herself into the chair opposite. She wrapped and rewrapped the towel around her fist.

'It's a worry, I can't say it isn't. He's not eating. He's thin as a rake. He's asked for a bottle up there, so he doesn't even have to get out of his bed.'

Her eyes darted in the fire like a cat that has been caught with something in its mouth and won't give it up.

'Could I go up and see him?' I asked. 'I could take up that book,' I said, rising to my feet.

'Mm?' She was in a trance. 'I'm sorry,' she said. She shook her head. 'I've not been sleeping. Yes, yes, by all means.'

I was aware climbing the stairs that at any moment Frances might change her mind and call me back. Above the diagonal line of the wooden dado, the wallpaper, where it was still intact, bore an elaborate pattern of deer and huntsmen, a pelt of hounds, a horn. At the top of the stairs it became blue baskets of fruit, all the way along the corridor, around the L-shape to Tom's room.

I stood before the panel door and tapped gently, then took the large ball handle in my hand. There was an indeterminate moan from inside.

I'd been in Tom's room only once before, the Yellow Room, the ceiling sagging inwards like a tent. High above the bed, under the dado rail, a stag's head poked glumly through the wall, its antlers dangling trails of cobweb. Beneath it, there was a mound of grey blanket, a floral eiderdown, and then the mattress sagging like a hernia.

'Tom?'

I waited. A great chimney breast rose through the floor like an iceberg. In the far corner, a chest of drawers, the ball of a leg missing, the top drawer hung open.

'Are you awake?'

There was a small, low-lying window. My eyes were adjusting to the dimness of the room. Beside the chest of drawers, there was the old scullery table, and on top of it, I made out the shape of the dome.

310

'Did you finish the bird?' I asked, stepping forwards over the heaps of sacking and old clothes, the piles of newspaper. I stood next to the table. Now I could see that the thrush had been fixed through its toes to a forked branch, globs of moss and lichen stuck around and under it to disguise the wires. The wings were pinned behind its back, beak lifted, chest out. Its schoolmarmish appearance was heightened, I realized, by the addition around its eyes of a pair of handmade wire spectacle frames.

There was a colossal shuddering from the bed, and Tom's head and shoulders emerged like a skeleton from a grave. His skin was imprinted with the lines of the bedclothes, mealy and pitted. He lifted his chin: 'Recognize it, do you?' he croaked.

I couldn't help smiling. 'Is it supposed to be me?'

'Can't imagine why,' he said, and I smiled.

'It's a perfect fit.'

'Waiting for her prince to come, something like that,' he said. And it was as if he'd poked that part of me that had already sustained its wound. He grunted. 'Have it. It's yours.'

I moved closer to the glass. 'It's lovely,' I said. 'I can almost hear it sing.'

'Cat got its tongue,' he said, 'if you remember.'

'I brought you a book,' I said, moving towards him. 'Maybe you've already read it? I used to, whenever I was ill in bed.'

I handed him my copy of *The Water Babies*, but he barely looked at it. Then I reached impulsively into my pocket, remembering what was there. 'Something else,' I said.

I waited for him to stretch out his hand before I dropped the ring box into it.

'I'm sorry,' I said, though I'd thought I'd be glad to be the one to return it.

His hand began to shake, perhaps even the small weight of the box enough to tip the scales. 'Did *she* give you it?'

'She wanted me to give it back to you.'

'When did you see her?'

'In the village. They're leaving, after Christmas,' she said.

'How was she?' he asked grimly. 'She didn't say anything, then?'

I didn't want to make it any better for Beatrice. I said, 'No, she didn't. Just to give it back.'

His hand fell to one side. 'She's flown,' he said. 'I always knew she would.'

I pursed my lips. The ring lay between us. I couldn't help wondering if it was too late for me. If I could be content with knowing that I wasn't ever going to be as beautiful or as clever as she was.

Suddenly with a spurt of energy, he snatched the box under the bedclothes. There was a creak on the stairs. Tom turned his head away from me; there were footsteps along the corridor. Frances appeared in the doorway.

She looked at me coldly as if I were an intruder. Tom shut his eyes. She bustled over to the bed and began tugging at the sheets, pulling them straight. He swung away from her, upheaving the whole lot, the mound of his back in its grey flannel shirt.


'He needs rest,' she said. 'That's what the doctor says.'

'It's so cold,' I said when we got downstairs.

'Freezing everywhere.'

'Couldn't I help?' I asked her. 'I could help clean up.'

'Don't you think I've tried?' she said, and then she smiled weakly, trying not to sound cross. She was so thin, her cheeks had hollowed out.

'He won't let me touch a thing up there,' she said; and then, as if to dismiss all talk of him, 'Come and tell me what's been happening.'

She went to the cupboard and, as if it were one of our usual days, brought out the basket of darning. I accepted a sock from her and a darning needle and thread. *Isn't this exactly what I wanted?* I was thinking, pushing the mushroom into the toe. After a while, we felt no compulsion to speak at all, the light from the two hurricane lamps and from the fire, dodging about us like moths.

Every now and again as she tied off a heel or a toe, Frances looked up to check on me. At one point she lifted the basket from her lap. 'Looks as if it might be setting in again,' she said, sitting tall, peering towards the window. She got to her feet to inspect, leaned out against the sink, so that her reflection appeared in the black glass like a hoary ghost.

'Robert's out in that. Look at it! You'll never get back in this, not on your own.'

I came and stood next to her. She was right, it was impossible to see anything but thick tufts of snow gathering and disbanding.

'You'd better stay until it clears. I can let you have a nightdress. Stay until morning. Robert'll go back with you then. You can have the brown room. Upstairs.'

313

# 31

## *The Brown Room*

By the time Robert came in, it was dark. Frances was boiling kettles to fill the two stone bottles they used to warm the beds. I wasn't sure if he'd seen me. He flung himself straight down by the fire and let Frances unwind his muffler, unlace his boots. I could tell that she didn't want to disturb him with details. We padded around and she indicated that I should follow her up. We carried a bottle each, wrapped in a thin linen towel, and Frances held the tall candlestick for us.

The brown room was at the opposite end to Tom's. Frances opened the door and led the way in. The shadows flared raggedly about us. She set the candle down on the deep window ledge and closed the curtains, stuffed the hot bottle down between the sheets, stretching her arm as far in as it would go.

'Shall I take Tom his?' I said. My ribs and forearms were searing from the heat of it.

'We'll both go,' she said. 'You'll need the light.'

We retraced our steps to the other end of the corridor and Frances knocked.

There was a jangling from the bed.

'You go in,' she said. 'Here, I'll let you have the candle – you can see yourself back. I'd better see to Robert. He's tired out.'

The candlestick immediately dripped wax on to my fingers. I held the hot bottle under my arm like a goose. She pushed the door open for me and I walked in nervously.

I wondered if he'd be pleased to see me. I laid the small furnace beside him on the bed. 'I came to say goodnight,' I said. 'It's snowing again. I'm staying. I'm in the brown room.' His back was to me and before he turned round, I half-imagined the pleasure on his face. But when he peered back over his shoulder, his eyes in the guttering candle were dull and weary. I had to check myself, remember that he was unwell.

'Take the bird away with you when you go, won't you?' His voice, thick with phlegm. 'I'm sick of looking at it.'


It was almost dawn when Frances came in and drew the curtains. To my surprise I had slept. I must have been tired, I told her. I must have dropped straight off. She had the edge of the curtain lifted in her hand and was peering out at the sky.

'I wonder if it's clearing?' she said.

She'd brought me a cup of tea, and stood waiting for me to prop myself up. There was no hurry, she said. She reminded me of the time I had looked after her; it was good, she said, to be able to return the favour.

When she left the room it was soft with the grey outlines of things, the washstand, the pink wicker chair and her black

315

lacquered sewing machine like a funerary pedestal for a
beloved dog, tucked in the corner. The teacup at my shoulder smoked. There were forests of ice on the windowpane. I
drew myself together under the bedclothes, listening to the
slow whirrs of activity downstairs: the front door launched,
feet stamping, a shovel dug into the snow. It wasn't the best
of times, I knew that, but at least I had been accepted back.
Suddenly I was filled with the optimism of a New Year: Tom's
illness was not a hindrance, it was a gift. I would help to nurse
him back to health, slowly and patiently, and there was every
chance, wasn't there, that in the end he would come to love
me for it? I was drowsy with content; lay back, closed my eyes
and must have drifted off again.

When I woke, it was with such a start that for a moment I
wasn't sure if the voice wasn't from inside a dream. It was
bright and sharp in the room: the pink chair, laden with yesterday's clothes. It took a moment for me to untangle what
was being said.

'How long have you been keeping this *filth*?'

'You've no right,' Frances said.

The voice was Robert's: 'I've a right in this house, under
this roof.'

'They're nothing but old letters,' she said.

'No wonder babby-boy thought it rich: one rule for him,
another for you . . .'

There was a fluttering sound as if a bird had got in. Frances
appeared to have no answer. She was on her knees, retrieving
with sweeps of her hand.

'When did he tell you?' she asked indignantly.

'Why's it matter *when*?'

'How long have you—?'

'Known? Your little secret? I suppose you counted on him?'

'Robert,' she said incredulously. 'It's nothing. It's an old box, you can see that.'

'Why hide them', he said, 'if there was so little to 'em, tell me that?'

She said weakly, 'Because they are mine, because they were sent to me.'

I imagined Robert in the shape of a sower, a dark silhouette, broadcasting, *flutter, flutter,* the elevation of his arm. *We plough the fields and scatter.*

There was a violent clatter, a hollow din on the flags as the empty tin skimmed towards her.

She stopped what she was doing. She said flatly, 'I don't know why I kept them. I had no reason.'

'I daresay you liked to read them?' Robert said, and then, tapping a paper in his hand, he began reading out: '*My Dearest Frankie, My Dear Girl.* Where'd he learn to speak like that?' he said. '*You remain as ever in my thoughts.*'

'Stop it. I never saw him again,' Frances said, 'you know that. When would I have? I didn't see him again, not after the war.'

'And why wasn't he writing to you direct then? If you had so little to hide? What's all this business with the address?'

She had no answer.

'So half the village knows your dirty secret?'

'He wasn't even in the country!'

'What difference does it make? You lied. That's what matters here. You lied.'

317

'I am not a liar. Don't use that word.'

'You lied to Father that time; I saw you do it. I was there, remember? He told you, *never*! You've been lying all this time to me.'

I was rigid under the sheets. It was as if Robert had only just discovered his voice, it ruptured from him like dirty water from a pipe.

'It turns my stomach to think of it, you, in our own mother's bed, breathing so easy with whatever was going on in your head How ignorant was I not to have seen it?' He was pacing the room, his voice like a shuttle, back and forth. 'When did you think to take him up on it? Spring? Or were you waiting till the bailiffs come? No wonder you were so quick to jump on Tom – he couldn't be off, could he? Not before you got yourself sorted. That'd snarl up your plans. No wonder you've been pampering him.'

'It's a mountain out of a molehill, Robert. You know it is. You're tired out, that's what the matter is. There's bigger things to worry about than this. Nothing but a few old letters. Years old if you care to look.'

'And *kept. Delighted* in. I'm right! I see it in your face. Don't tell me you've not encouraged it? Why would the boy keep writing, if he'd had no encouragement? You wouldn't have dared, not if Father'd been alive. He'd have locked you up.'

For a while there was no sound but the desultory hushing of things being swept up. Then she said gently, as if she were coaxing him round, 'I know things are bad. I know they are. It's impossible to think straight. But we'll be all right. Of course we will.'

'Don't tell me what to think!'

318

'I was silly to keep them, that's all. They don't mean a thing.'

'*Silly?*'

'I put them in a box,' she said in a voice that had finally cracked. 'I put them away in a box. Tom should never have gone looking through my things. I don't know what he was doing.'

'And all the time he was sickening about the place like a useless piece of dirt, you've been at it too. I thought you were on my side! The two of you, every time I'm out. Till my back breaks. Till the place rots in hell.' I could hear the gut-strings of his throat.

A noise had sounded on the landing, a thud. I froze — it would remind them I was up here. My heart contracted like a sponge.

Frances came out into the hall. 'Tom?' she called, taking charge of her voice. 'Tom, go back to bed. I'll be up in a minute.'

It sounded as if he were already at the top of the stairs, inching his way forwards.

'It's a pigsty in here,' Robert was muttering, striding about the place. 'You live like pigs.'

'Don't,' she said.

I could hear movement from the kitchen to the parlour, from the hall to the parlour, a roll of things bulkily deposited from one place to another.

Robert said, 'I've had enough.' As he moved heavily from door to door, there was an accompaniment on the stairs of shuffle and thud.

'What's he think he's doing?' Robert asked suddenly.

'Tom,' Frances said, 'please. Go back to bed.'

It was as if a cargo were being rearranged, taken from one

part of the hold to another. Frances sank down and abandoned herself to piteous sniffling.

A door slammed. A minute or two later, Frances appeared to collect herself, cajoling him again. 'Robert, what are you doing? Let me in, please, Robert. Let me in.'

'Burn in hell.'

'Why did you have to do it?' she said, turning her voice sharply up the stairs. 'See what you've done?'

'Ask him where *he* gets to after market,' Tom said. 'Ask him the knicker price in South Street, if he's so right and proper.'

'Let me sort it out,' she snapped at him. Then, with supreme effort, 'Please, Tom. Just go back to bed. Please.'

Suddenly the parlour door burst open. 'If he's well enough to be up, he's well enough to work. Get him out. Those horses need feeding. Get him off his lazy stumps.'

'He's not dressed,' Frances said, panicking.

They were all three hugger-mugger at the foot of the stairs and for a moment I imagined the knot of their bodies writhing. Like lifting a piece of rotten wood on a nest of worms. Out of the fray, the heavy front door was heaved open – there was an exchange of bodies – and then it was banged shut. Frances was crying. 'You can't put him out there. Robert? It's freezing. Don't blame him. He's not well. I'll go. Let me go and feed them. Robert?'

The parlour door slammed flimsily and the bones of the house shook. I could hear her weeping at the bottom of the stairs; but though I envisaged myself creeping down, leading her by the elbow back to her room, the weight of her against me, getting her to sit down on the scalloped bed, stroking back the damp hair from her temples, I couldn't move. I knew that I had heard too much. Robert would likely kill me, I thought, for being a witness. And though I kept thinking, *this is my chance to rescue her*, I couldn't risk the repercussions.

'Robert? Please open the door,' Frances started up again. 'Please. Let me in. There's nothing to it. I promise you.'

'I'm burning every one of them. As you should have done,' he yelled at her.

She was whimpering. She had begun to climb the stairs, pulling on the banister. She must have been halfway up when in a spasm of pent-up fury she turned and wailed down at him, two separate words: 'You. Beast!'

Below her, the parlour door swooped open. Silence. Then she gave a yelp, and lunged for the landing, along the corridor and fumbled frantically at the bedroom door, which – as he leapt after her, two steps at a time – she managed to open, slammed fast behind her, turned the key in the lock.

I was terrified that any moment she'd call for help. I could hear Robert's breathing outside like a pair of bellows. If I moved, the bed would squeak; one peep and he'd discover me. He began to pound the door for her.

I needed to hide. I hardly drew breath, pulling the sheets and the blankets loose bit by bit. Then I lifted my feet over the side of the mattress, planted them along the floorboards, step, step, step, until I reached the long panelled wall. The door to the cupboard was buried in the panelling, tall as my shoulder. I eased it open. The space inside ran the length of the room, a void between the brown room and theirs. It was piled on either side with redundant furniture – chairs that needed seats, clock cases. In front of me there was a platform, thigh deep, with curtains, blankets, an old bolster. As quickly as I could, I tried to make room for myself, pushing the pile in towards the back of the cupboard. A chaff-coloured moth flitted into the air, another crawled from a crease. I pressed down with all my weight and climbed up, curling in my head, reaching out with my little finger, just small enough to get a purchase in the loop of the keyhole, pulled it towards me, my finger in the tiny hole like a dam.

But it was worse than anything: as if I'd put a great bell over my head. Clang, clang, clang of the pounding on the door; it was as if I were in the same room as she was.

In a frenzy of rage he was shrieking, 'How can I do it? How can I believe anything you say?'

It was only between his attempts to batter down the door that I became aware of a noise in a totally different register, quietly persistent like an insect in wood. Then Frances saying shakily, 'Stay away. I mean it, if you come near me, if you don't stop this now, I swear, I'll jump. I will, Robert, I'll jump.' With a final kick he'd split the bedroom door from its hinges and her voice rose like a flag for a race. It was the yoke of her shoulders, tearing upwards to prise open the window frame, the splinters eating into the back of her neck. He roared at her, but only to see her vanish, disappearing like Joan of Arc, out of the window. There was a dull thump. Within seconds Robert had reached the sill. He moaned like an animal. Then he stumbled back into the room, then blundered out on to the landing, where he bellowed her name as he thud, thud, thudded down the stairs.

I had bitten through my lip, I could taste the soil of my blood. My arm had turned to iron, the hook of my finger braced against the opening of the door. My legs from the knee down were dead. The back of my waist ached as if a stake had been driven through it. Only my eyes moved. The cupboard door swung away from me. I dropped woodenly from my shelf, expecting to find chaos. The bedclothes were as I'd left them, the sewing machine, prim on its iron stand, a trail of cotton threaded through the needle, the pink chair.

I was barefoot, shaking; I patted across the floor and peered from the window. My reflection revealed the shock of my hair. But through and beyond it I saw the black of his jacket below. He was crouched beside where she was slumped, face down – beside the granite of the gate post, over the low garden wall – his arm hovering at her shoulder, pitiful, begging her to look at him, to say something.

She'd loved the snow, she had told me. Not once did she do anything to dissuade him or shake him off. He lowered his head further until it touched hers and then he lay across her, pressing himself so completely to her that she vanished altogether.

I sat down where I was and hugged my knees, looked up. The sky buffeted the windowpanes, pearly grey. I watched as the icy tips of the feathers began to dissolve. After a while, the house itself seemed to relax, prone as an empty glove, as if nothing untoward had happened. As if I'd invented it all. Perhaps she'd be there when I went down, mopping the table, stoking the fire, blowing wisps of hair back from her face?

When the shot came ricocheting from the orchard, I was grateful and relieved. There was an upshot of crows scattering gunpowder into the sky. As if the world had started up again. I pulled myself to my feet and stood at the window, looked down to where Frances was lying alone, uncovered, showing no interest at all.

# 32

## *2 January 2007*

Eve's got a red Fiesta, which I doubt has ever been washed. She apologized for the mess.

'Archie treats it like a skip,' she said. There were bottles of water and cans of drink rolling about under my feet, twists of sweet wrapper. She made a move to lean across and tidy up, but then she smiled and said, 'You're used to our mess,' which I took to be a compliment.

I'm not usually a nervous passenger, but I found that Eve had a way of turning her head to me when she spoke with complete disregard for the road. I'd meet her eye briefly and then turn resolutely forwards, willing her to pay a little more attention.

'I don't know how you survive without a car out here,' she was saying. 'It's hopeless. Public transport is a joke.'

'I never learned to drive,' I said briskly.

'Really?' Even a short word like that, she was able to spin out.

We'd been driving for over an hour when at last we began to see signs for the airport. The roads were getting faster and wider and my mouth was dry as we wove among the juddering lorries, the little sports cars so close you could see a driver at the wheel picking something from his ear.

We were flying on a wide ribbon alongside Exeter, passing the blinking metal and glass of the city and out the other side, turning off after a mile or so of grinding road at an unpromising enclave of mini-roundabouts, a clutch of temporary-looking buildings. Eve had slowed down and was hunched forward over the wheel, straining to follow the signs.

We parked in the long stay. I was so shaken by the journey that I could hardly open the door, pushing at it as if I were emerging from a crash. It took me a while to straighten up and find my legs.

Eve was incredulous when I told her I'd never flown. She had become purposeful again. She marched me through the sliding doors of the concourse and over the light grey linoleum as if she flew every day of her life. The place was deserted. There was a line of desks against the far wall, separated from us by an area strung at waist height with a maze of blue plastic tape.

Eve knew exactly where to go and was standing below a high-mounted TV screen with a chequered orange list that kept printing and deleting itself.

'Glasgow.' She said. '15.15.' She looked at her watch. 'Half an hour. Let's grab a coffee?'

She led me over to a windowless area in the far corner. Two children were goading each other, climbing over and under the beige seating. I sat down at an empty table and let Eve go up to queue behind a large man at the counter.

From where I was sitting, the lino spun off into the distance like the still surface of a lake; there was a depth of reflection as if we were floating in some sort of strange holding station. On the walls, there were three identical blown-up photographs of a girl, her lion's smile gleaming over a stadium sized cup of cappuccino. Two women had stationed themselves below, turned resolutely away from each other, keeping an eye on three enormous suitcases.

'Give it a rest!' the younger woman snapped at the children, sucking hard as if she were dragging on a cigarette. The fat man moved off from the counter towards them, balancing the stacked packages and beakers of his tray as if it were a game of skill, edging it on to the table. The older woman began to dismantle it, keeping back the packets of crisps, which she held to her chest as the two children bounced around her: *promise to be good, keep quiet for your nan.*

I wondered whether it might occur to them that we were family, Eve and I.

'Oi!' the little girl shrieked as a packet was snatched from under her nose, spilling luminous shavings to the ground. She threw herself under the table.

'I hate airports,' Eve said, as she came and sat down. She handed me a wooden stirrer and rolled her eyes towards the girl who was using her arm as a dredger to gather up the crumbs. 'Sometimes I'm glad Archie's an only child.'

The little boy had begun to wail, clamping a hand to the place where his mother had grabbed his arm.

We sat politely averting our eyes. Eve was scraping the

milky froth from the bottom of the cup, spooning it into her mouth.

'I forgot to ask if you'd seen Owen again,' I said.

'Oh,' she looked embarrassed. 'No. Not properly. Not yet – next week, sometime, I think.' She gave me a taut smile, and put the spoon down precisely. 'Speaking of which, perhaps we'd better think about moving. Archie'll be here any minute.'

Eve led me outside again into the cold and then into the blast of heat in the building next door, arrivals. There were half a dozen people propped against the walls where we stood, an unmanned information desk, a drink dispenser.

'That's where the bags'll come out,' Eve said rather loudly, pointing to a snake-like arrangement at the far end. A small balding man had turned around irritably as if we were in a library. Eve lowered her voice: 'Archie'll come through there.' She nodded to a discreet door tucked away in the corner.

'I'm excited now,' she whispered, hugging herself and inching forward. 'It's almost unbearable, this last bit.'

There was a mechanical judder, which made us both jump. The horizontal flaps of the luggage track began to move, a clunking noise, and after a minute or two, with little hiccups, a motley collection of suitcases and rucksacks emerged from behind heavy strips of plastic.

'Here we go!' Eve could hardly contain herself.

By now an older woman with a ruddy garden face had placed herself in prime position, her hand weighted outwards as if carrying a set of secateurs.

At last the door swung and a scrawny man shot through

in a suit with a small case; then a woman with two carrier bags and fat knees; a young skinny girl, who stood startled, until, with a yip of recognition she ran past me, into the arms of a young man in red trousers, who was running from the opposite direction and lifted her off her feet. They drew a circle as they spun and kissed. From the corner of my eye I continued to watch them, the immoderately long, drawn-out kiss, while the door in the corner continued to flicker open and shut like a cartoon.

'Where is he?' Eve was hopping. 'He always lags behind!' She was still beaming.

Gradually the flow of bodies began to dry up.

'Where is he?' Her face was fragile with expectation.

'Perhaps they save the children until last?' I suggested.

A petite, official-looking young woman came through with a small boxy vanity case. She was wearing a cap and a blue nylon jacket and skirt, efficient court shoes.

'Excuse me,' Eve said, approaching her, 'I'm waiting for my son.'

The girl's green eye-shadow flashed when she spoke. 'Was he on this flight, madam?'

'He was supposed to be. Yes.'

'Will you let me have his name and I'll go and check for you?'

'Archie. Archie Manning. No, sorry. Maretta — Maretta's his father's name. That's the name on his passport.'

She had a Scottish accent, 'Archie Mar-e-tt-a? I'll go and check a minute. If you'll wait here.'

As the girl clacked off to the information desk, Eve looked at me and said through gritted teeth, 'I can't believe it.' She began to look around wildly. 'I'm going to ring. Will you wait – in case he comes out?'

She marched past the desk where the girl was on the phone herself and signalled to Eve that she was waiting for someone to get back to her.

I watched Eve through the glass. She looked small, her head bobbing against the mobile phone in her hand. I couldn't hear a word, but suddenly, she thrust the phone away from her. Her face was raised to the sky like a woman grieving under the cross. She clicked the phone shut, stuffed it into her bag.

She strode in through the automatic doors, a trajectory that gathered me towards her so that we arrived in front of the girl at the desk together.

'It's all right,' she was saying to the girl. 'I don't believe it. Shit. I don't believe it. He's missed the plane.'

The girl and I exchanged glances. Neither of us knew what to say.

Then she said, 'I'm sorry, madam.'

Eve was dissolving. I thought she was going to sink to the floor. 'Let's sit down,' I said, taking her elbow, leading her towards a row of linked chairs.

'He's putting him on the flight tomorrow.'

'I'm sorry.'

'It's such a nightmare. I was so looking forward—'

'I know.'

'I can't believe it,' she said. 'And *you've* come all this way too . . .'

I was holding her wrist. I had never seen her cry before, childish hot tears bouncing from her cheeks.

'I want to kill him. Bastard. I would. I'd kill him for this. I can't bear to go all that way back,' she said. 'I'd rather camp out.'

Then she looked at me, catching herself mournfully, 'It's all right. I'll be all right in a moment.' She grabbed me as if the thought had only just occurred to her, 'All that drinking. It's Hogmanay up there. They go mad, don't they? He wouldn't get drunk with Archie there, would he?'

# 33

## *Cockcrow, 2 January 1963*

Under my feet the carpet fed all the way down the fanfolds of the stairs. There wasn't a sound on the landing, but I could smell burning. At the foot of the stairs the parlour door hung open. The room, the one room in the house that was usually so immaculate, was unrecognizable. I was drawn in; I clambered over a drift of newspapers, a coil of fraying rope. There was sacking, chairs from the kitchen that had been wrenched of arms and legs arranged in a great heap, and scattered everywhere there were small envelopes, some with blue and red bunting around the edges, others with airmail stickers, or 'airmail' handwritten. The address was the same on each, written in the same neat hand, Auntie's address, mine: c/o Paradise Cottage, Shipleigh, Devonshire, England. At the foot of the piano there was a large empty tin, the hinges yanked and broken, the lid showing an embossed reproduction of blue roses.

It was a tiny thing, but distinct from the letters, under

the piano stool, I noticed a small white square. I picked it up. Someone had written a date in pencil, 3 February 1959, and the legend, 'The New House!' I turned it over. It was a photograph: a man in a pale-sleeved shirt, a child at his trouser leg, another child on a tricycle, nearer the camera, blurred. The house had large fishtank windows – it could have been the suburb of any city, but I knew that it was America and that it must have been him, Frank Burns. And yet he wasn't shrinking from the camera. There was no longing, no desire for anything different, not for the life not lived, or the road not taken.

The newspapers were thick with damp, like everything else in the house. Flames had bitten at the edge of things in brown crescents but had fizzled out without taking hold. Robert hadn't had the patience to sit and wait. Out in the hallway, the huge front door was very slightly ajar, whistling to itself. I pulled the iron bolt towards me in an arc. The glare was like a glacier, but as my eyes adjusted I could make out signs of working: boots, dog-prints, the drunken line of a wheelbarrow. It was a quarry of snow, excavated and packed like china clay. I followed a solitary trail of footprints, unquestioningly, as if I were in a fairy tale, past the hay barn, its sugared stacks, round towards the orchard. Everything was static and bluish: apples, pears, pomegranates, figs.

From the corner of my eye I saw a robin hop, blink, guarded. It stood on duty next to a mound, earth-coloured. I moved in tiny steps not to frighten it. The mound was steaming like dung, the curious sun turning it over. As I approached I saw a boot stretched out, another kicked off, its tongue hanging freely; then the zip of a winter fly investigating; another, touching and taking off, touching and looping the loop.

I knew it was Robert. As if he'd been tripped running away, the suitcase of himself spilled out on the ground before him, the silken liquid of petticoats, such a beautiful deep crimson, blaring out of the snow like a cockerel crowing. The shotgun from the kitchen had kicked out sideways; there was a bootlace carelessly strung around the mechanism. My first thought was to run and find Frances. She would know what to do. I retrod my steps back towards the house, into the blinding silence of the yard. She was out in the garden, I reminded myself, pegging out washing . . . I walked around the side of the house and through the gate towards where she was resting. I crouched down and pressed her shoulder. 'Frances?' I said. There was a stain in the snow under her head, her skin was blue and yellow. I sank down to be as like her as I could, the soft snow all around us ringing.


It was Victor's first day back after Christmas. He was later than usual; the roads were impassable on his bicycle, so he'd decided to walk, to show willing. The dazzle of light took the edge off the cold; the sky, which for a fortnight had been indistinguishable from the ground, was now restored to its full height. These were the deep lanes of Heaven, jewelled with prisms of green, violet and orange, exhaling rainbows. Victor scooped the whiteness in his hands, soft as feathers. He wondered how many sheep he would have to dig out, whether Frances would have remembered to put aside his piece of Christmas cake.

333

It was unusual when he got to the yard for the dogs not to run out to meet him. He thought perhaps the snow had thrown them off the scent. But then he heard them scrabbling at the base of the cattle barn, where they'd been shut in, whining penitently.

He lifted the latch and pushed. The dogs bolted out and then began pattering around the yard in circles. The horses were there, snorting and bumping against their stalls; to the right, the cattle pens were empty, swept and sluiced down to the stone, just as he'd left them. Victor came out, puzzled. The farmhouse door was wide open. The dogs had taken off towards the orchard; he followed them. But he stopped just short of where they stopped, pawing, whining, chasing off a cluster of fat flies. Victor stumbled backwards, sideways, his stomach ready to tip its barrel of worms.

When he found me I was kneeling into the snow, asleep, face down. He shook my shoulders, rubbed my hands in his: *Ache up. Ache up. Ache up.* He lifted me and staggered to his feet, carrying me into the house. He elbowed open the kitchen door and set me down in Mr Upcott's chair, tore the cloth from the table and wrapped it around me. The fire had gone out in the kitchen. He lit another. I had woken up; I didn't want to wake to this, the house, shackled around us. When he came to look at me, he was breathing sewer into my face. He smelled of the old world. I couldn't speak. Something had snapped in my throat. He brought Robert's heavy coat and laid it around me and he pressed me to the seat saying, *shush, shush, shush*, showing the palm of his hand to keep me there, backing out of the door, before running, three miles solid, the snow like glue, his footfalls in the distance, felted hooves.

And Tom. It was typical of Tom, Robert would have said. He'd ignored everything that needed doing, only to please himself. After Robert had thrown him out, he wasn't going to go back into the house. Over his nightshirt he had pulled on the dirty orange waders, right up to his chest, the old elastic braces holding them up. He'd taken Robert's hunting jacket from where it was hung up with the other tack. It was big in the arms but did the job. He put the tin of flies in a pocket, took down his rod and the poaching bag for his catch. His legs were jelly from being in bed so long; he stumbled along the track with the weight of what he carried. Before he had got halfway down, he decided to abandon the bag, the reel of black thread, the fishing rod, the tin of flies. Nothing extraneous. When he got to the river, he crashed his way along the bank, brittle with hollow reeds poking through the crusty snow for air. Even the pebbles had a dusting of it. He stooped and brushed one off, then lobbed it into the deep water, to see how it disappeared, how it pulled itself down by the back of its head, closing its mouth tight as a purse. He began now to scrabble about, collecting a pile of stones into a small cairn. Then, one by one, he posted them into the waders, feeling the press over the bridge of each foot, around his ankles, his calves, like concrete girders. When he was satisfied, he walked as if he were in battle armour, clanking, articulated steps, clearing the margin of ice, which buckled and complained as he passed, out into the brown drag of the river. The fast-running water rushed to embrace him and he to shore it up. Deeper and deeper until he was up to his waist. A tentacle slipped over the rim of his trousers, an eel's long arm, and gradually he grew fatter and fatter on it. He attempted to sit but the river insisted, pressing him to his feet, leaning him like a tower at an angle, and then pebble for pebble, it rose up to his face, it force-fed him, a feast of solid water, glug, glug, glug, until he lay back, sated with it, resting on his laurels, nothing between him and the wide open sky.

# 34

## *Arrivals*

Eve had been awake most of the night, she said; the skin around her eyes was bruised and puffy and I didn't think she should go on her own. I told her, I wanted to go back with her.

'It's easier not to argue,' I said.

And apart from the disappointment of Archie not being there, I had rather enjoyed the outing. 'It's good for me,' I said, 'to lift my eyes.'

She apologized again for the mess in the car.

She shuddered. 'I hate airports! There are no secret places any more. It's impossible to go anywhere without Duty Free. They'll have it on the moon when we get there.'

She was concentrating in the narrow lanes, craning her neck round when she was forced to back up by an approaching car. It wasn't until we'd reached the dual carriageway that she began to talk again.

'Were *you* close . . . to *your* father?'

I sniffed. 'When I was small, I was. I didn't see him much after they divorced and then I moved down here. I didn't see him at all. He was married again. I hardly knew who he was any more. I suppose, too, that I was part of the life he was keen to forget.'

'Men can be like that,' she said. 'Bastards.' She had become more intimate, less careful around me.

'He was weak,' I said. 'I think they must have tried to have children of their own. Maybe I was a reminder of that.'

*I used to get the same postcard from him every year from the villa in Majorca. You could see the swimming pool like a piece of sky cut out with scissors. It didn't take much for me to imagine the scene: him skittle-shaped, bobbing and ridiculous, floating with mechanical flipper arms; Patricia in her heavy-boned, tasselled bathing suit, her pastry legs and arms. Still woozy, finding it hard to stand, wafting a book at one of the boy cooks from her sunbed to get him to see what Daddy wanted with all that splashing. Then, Fletch! a cry that echoed from the walls like a tennis ball, and then fury. Help! can't you see he needs help;* atiende! *Get him out!*

*She'd clawed the dark glasses from her face and screwed her eyes up in the light, not quite believing that he wasn't fooling around. She shrieked again.*

*They'd been drinking pink gin and frisking in the way they occasionally did after a few shots in the lethal holiday sunlight. Daddy had plopped into the pool for a float on his back.*

*The grief came in a torrent with the trouble of importing him home. So troublesome, so much paperwork that it was beyond her to give any notice for the funeral, which, she explained to me afterwards, was tiny. There'd be a memorial service, she wrote, for which, gratifyingly, she said, there was something of a clamour.*

'There was a big memorial service,' I told Eve. 'In that church on the Strand. I went up to London for the day.'

'He must have been important.'

'He sold the business in the eighties when he retired. They were rich. But he'd done something in the war that Patricia thought he never got enough credit for. *Their dirty work*, she said. If only he'd have lived a little longer, she said, he'd have got a knighthood. It peeved her more than anything. She said, "he'd have got it any minute *if only he'd hung on*."'

'What did he do?'

'I never really knew. Foreign Office something. Special editions for the troops ... Courtier. She was his most successful, M. E. Courtier – the first writer he took on. In fact I met her, at that memorial service. Her name was Mavis too. She introduced herself. You could tell she'd been beautiful once, thin as a rake, silver-white hair. She said how pleased she was to meet me.'

*When Mavis Courtier was introduced she took my fingers in hers and shivered, 'Oh, you're cold!'*

*'Bad circulation,' I said. 'I got it from Daddy.'*

*Patricia had sniffed, 'Little reminder, then.'*

'Is that why you're Mavis?' Eve asked.

I made the sort of noise that Mother would have made, through my nose.

'Father always told my mother that M. E. Courtier was a man. But Mother wasn't stupid. I don't think she ever really took to me, not with that name. It was typical of Father's luck that he had an aunt called Mavis (it wasn't the most common name, even then). It's why he brought us to Devon in the first place – to prove a point. However wrong he was, he had to be right.'

'You think he was having an affair?' She looked round too

eagerly and I nodded towards the road ahead to keep her on track. 'My mother thought so; and he was never able to convince her otherwise. A leopard doesn't change its spots.'

'Mhum!' she agreed ruefully. I sat back. Suddenly I was less anxious about the hurtling landscape and the hurtling pace of it. As we neared the airport, I hardly questioned the fact that a plane rose over the road in front of us, its underbelly flashing like a river trout. It passed over us and away. 'Sometimes I feel as if I must be from a different age,' I said. 'When the world was flat, when there were dragons and angels.'

'Better not to question it,' she said.

There was a queue for the car park, which was noticeably fuller than it had been the day before. We attached ourselves to a caravan of people dragging large, wheelie suitcases, and followed them through the sliding doors once again on to the main concourse.

I followed Eve to the lavatories. The cubicles were tiny and it was awkward to get myself in with my bag, to deal with the bulk of my coat, my skirt and tights, and to sit down. It reminded me of Auntie, how unhelpful I'd been, how horrid Daddy always was about the smell of old people. The chain flushed in the cubicle next to mine, the lock unclicked, a tap outside began to gush.

When I emerged, Eve was peering at herself in the mirror. Above us, the soft, greeny light of an aquarium. Generally, if I caught sight of myself in a mirror, I had only one expression by which to recognize myself. The photographer from the *Western Morning News* had lain in wait outside the council offices after the inquest. 'Miss Mavis Gaunt', the caption had read: 'devastated'.

I shook water from my hands. Eve jutted her chin towards the mirror. 'God, I look dead,' she said.

'Wait till you're my age,' I replied, letting my hands rest on the sink. In the mirror we were a portrait, the pair of us. Her eyes met mine and mine hers, and it set us off, that odd picture, the two of us smirking as if we'd shared a wicked secret.

Eve ordered coffees and I shuffled off to claim the one free table, piled with crisp packets and empty cans of drink. I began to clear up.

When she brought over the cups, she sat down and shrugged off her jacket, saying, 'It feels as if we're stuck in a loop, don't you think? What's the betting we'll be back here tomorrow, and the day after and the day after that?'

'*Tomorrow, and tomorrow, and tomorrow* . . . Let's hope not,' I said, although the idea was not as appalling to me as perhaps it should have been.

She was twitchy, but making an effort to chat. 'It's busier today. There's a flight to Majorca in an hour. I can't believe you've never been abroad. Not even France?'

'Mother gave up going when she married my father. I think she thought that if she went back to France, it would be the end. She never really accepted he had left us.'

'Archie had a phase like that,' she said. '"Can't Daddy come with us?"' She emptied a paper straw of sugar into her coffee and stirred vigorously.

When the time came to go through to arrivals, Eve held back. She said, 'I can hardly bear to look.' But we didn't have long to wait. Archie was one of the first off, with his very own minder, who went through the motions of checking Eve's driving licence before she handed him over.

Archie was smiling shyly, as if his mother was a stranger; he spoke very little. He'd grown, Eve said, in just a week.

'You're taller, you definitely are,' she exclaimed, stroking his head, pulling him towards her chest. Yes, he'd had a good time. Yes, the flying was OK. He was wearing a new T-shirt over his sweater. It was red with a large black crab holding between its pincers the letters, *Don't Be Crabby*.

'Aimed at me, no doubt,' Eve said stoically. 'Well,' she turned him to face her. 'Tell me. What've you been up to? Oh – come here!'

Archie let himself be hugged again. His face around her shoulder looked uncertain.

'But you've enjoyed yourself?' she said, setting him straight.

'Yes.'

'How's your grandmother?'

'Fine.'

'Did she say anything about me?'

'No.'

Eve clutched his hand to her chest and squeezed so that he winced.

'Hello, Archie,' I said.

'Come on, what do you say?' Eve said.

'I expect you're tired,' I said.

'Let's go, shall we?' Eve said. 'Let's get out of this awful place.' She took Archie's rucksack from his shoulder. Through the doors, we collided with an anxious-looking family, hurrying, dragging their cases like grumbling beasts. We reached the crossing.

'Wait,' Eve snapped, putting her arm out as a barrier that included both Archie and me, looking right and left. A white catering van crawled past, a blue car.

I didn't register what happened until we were safely on the other side. It was small and it was quick, but the moment we stepped off the kerb, Archie reached out and took my hand.

## Envoi

That postcard of the bird, do you remember? I looked it out: 'An Experiment on a Bird in the Air Pump'. The painter's name is Wright of Derby. The National Gallery was around the corner from Daddy's office at Seven Dials, a place that once or twice, in the days when he took me out, we visited. I was perhaps seven or eight, the same age as the girl in the painting. I remember admiring her pink dress, but not understanding why she should be so frightened – her daddy was *there*. It is only now I look again that I can see the horror of the experiment. The man in the red dressing gown with the silver hair is slowly pumping out the oxygen. The bird's beautiful wing is extended in a paroxysm of suffocation.

I never questioned what was wrong with Mother; as long as I'd known her, it was just how she was. But I can see her now in the cage of the hospital bed, her eye, as black and desperate as the eye of that bird. 'Love' in our household wasn't a word that was ever used – not as it is nowadays, at the drop of a hat – so it was only after she died that I realized it was life and all to Mother; that when Daddy stopped paying her attention, she had no other reserve.

Dear Eve, I don't mean to rattle on, but if you have read this far, you will know everything that it is within my capacity to tell you, including that last thing, love. If I'd had the chance, I'd have loved your father, you can see that. I never said it before but I would have loved him like the air.

Long ago I found out how indifferent Nature is: though it has its compensations – beauty being one. But you cannot live on beauty alone. Yet it wasn't until years after it all happened that I was able to discover this: that in the backs of kitchens and village halls, in choir stalls, at bus stops, there are places where scraps of love persist. After that, I couldn't dream there would be more. And yet there was.

I'm leaving you the cottage by way of thanks, not because I want you to stay, but because I want you to have a choice. You are young; the world is different to the way it was: I thought there was no way forward and no way back. I was wrong, you have shown me that.

Typing must be like riding a bicycle. Although my fingers are not what they were, I never lost the knack. I've written everything out for you as neatly as I can in the hope that, once you've read it, you might grant me this:

Commit the typescript with my body to the cremator's fire. Then carry the pot of mingled ashes down to the river. Take off the lid and scatter me, every word of me. I have pictured it often: as you cast me out, soft and flaky, how easy it will be to be reconciled, melting into the stream like snow.

345